THE COFFIN DANCER

"Engrossing, entertaining, and fizzing with energy"
Val McDermid

"Deaver is just as cunning and deceptive as his killer;
don't assume he's run out of tricks until you've run
out of pages" *Publishers Weekly*

"A terrific, high-paced thriller" *Wales on Sunday*

THE BONE COLLECTOR

"Sophisticated chiller . . . compulsive reading"
Guardian

"Another genuinely compulsive chiller from the best
psychological thriller writer around" *The Times*

About the author

Jeff Deaver was a lawyer before quitting work to become a full-time writer. He divides his time between Washington, DC and California.

Shallow Graves

Jeffery Deaver

CORONET BOOKS
Hodder & Stoughton

Copyright © 1992 by Jeffery Wilds Deaver

The right of Jeffery Wilds Deaver to be identified as the Author of the
Work has been asserted by him in accordance with the Copyright,
Designs and Patents Act 1988.

Originally published by Avon Books
Published in the United States of America by POCKET BOOKS,
A division of Simon & Schuster, Inc.
First published in Great Britain in 2001 by Hodder and Stoughton
First published in paperback in 2001 by Hodder and Stoughton
A division of Hodder Headline

A Coronet Paperback

1

British Library Cataloguing in Publication Data
A Catalogue record of this title is available from the
British Library

ISBN 978-1-444-71321-3

Typeset by Palimpsest Book Production Limited,
Polmont, Stirlingshire

Printed and bound in Great Britain
by Clays Ltd, St Ives plc

Hodder and Stoughton
A division of Hodder Headline
338 Euston Road
London NW1 3BH

"A man should keep his word."
         – James Stewart as Rupert Cadell
           in Alfred Hitchcock's *Rope*

SHALLOW GRAVES

1

"I heard this scary story about you one time," Marty said, "and I didn't know whether it was true or not."

Pellam didn't look over. He was driving the Winnebago Chieftain 43 back into town. They'd just found an old farmhouse a mile up the road and had offered the astonished owner thirteen hundred dollars to shoot two scenes on his front porch, provided he didn't mind if a combine replaced his rusting orange Nissan in the driveway for a couple of days. For that kind of money, the farmer said, he'd eat the car if that was what they wanted.

Pellam had told him that wouldn't be necessary.

"You used to do stunt work?" Marty asked. His voice was high and Midwest-inflected.

"Some stunts, yeah. Just for a year or so."

"About this film you did?"

"Uh." Pellam pulled off his black 1950s Hugh Hefner sunglasses. The autumn day had dawned bright as blue ice. A half hour ago it had turned dark and now the early afternoon seemed like a winter dusk.

"It was a Spielberg film," Marty said.

"Never worked for Spielberg."

Marty considered. "No? Well, I *heard* it was a Spielberg film. Anyway, there was this scene where the guy, the star, you know, was supposed to drive a motorcycle over this bridge and these bombs or something were blowing up behind him and he was driving like a son of a bitch, just ahead of these shells. Only then one hits under him and he goes flying through the air just as the bridge collapses . . . Okay? And they were supposed to rig a dummy because the stunt supervisor wouldn't let any of his guys do it but you just got on the bike and told the second unit director to roll the cameras. And you just, like, did it."

"Uh-huh."

Marty looked at Pellam. He waited. He laughed. "What do you mean, 'uh-huh'? Did you do it?"

"Yeah, I remember that one."

Marty rolled his eyes and looked out the window at a distant speck of bird. "He remembers it . . ." He looked back at Pellam. "And I heard that the thing was you didn't get blown clear but you had to hang on to this cable while the bridge collapsed."

"Uh-huh."

Marty kept waiting. It was no fun telling war stories to people who should be telling them to you. "Well?"

"That's pretty much what happened."

"Weren't you scared?"

"Sure was."

"Why'd you do it?"

Pellam reached down and picked up a Molson bottle wedged

between his scuffed brown Nokona boots. He glanced around the red and yellow autumn countryside for New York state troopers then lifted the bottle and drained it. "I don't know. I did crazy things then. Stupid of me. The unit director fired me."

"But they used the footage?"

"Had to. They'd run out of bridges."

Pellam floored the worn accelerator pedal to take a grade. The engine didn't respond well. They heard the tapping of whatever taps in an old engine when it struggles to push a heavy camper uphill.

Marty was twenty-nine, skinny, and had a small gold hoop in his left ear. His face was round and smooth and he had eyelids connected directly to his heart; they opened wide whenever his pulse picked up. Pellam was older. He was thin too, though more sinewy than skinny, and dark complected. He had a scrawny, salt-and-pepper beard that he'd started last week and he was already tired of. The lids over *his* gray-green eyes never lifted very far. Both men wore denim – blue jeans and jackets. Marty wore a black T-shirt. Pellam, a blue work shirt. In clothes like these, with his pointy-toed boots, Pellam looked a lot like a cowboy and if anyone – a woman anyway – would comment on it, he'd tell her that he was related to Wild Bill Hickok. This was true though it was true in some complicated way he'd distorted so often that he couldn't now remember exactly where the gunfighter had figured into his ancestry.

Marty said, "I'd like to do stunt work."

"I don't think so," Pellam told him.

"No, it'd be fun."

"No, it'd be painful."

After a few minutes Pellam said, "So we got a cemetery, we

got a town square, two barns and a farmhouse. We got a ton of roads. What else do we need?"

Marty flipped through a large notebook. "One big, big, big field, I'm talking sonuvabitch big, a funeral home, a Victorian house overlooking a yard big enough for a wedding, a hardware store, a mess of interiors . . . Goddamn, I ain't gonna get to Manhattan for two weeks. I'm tired of cows, Pellam. I'm so damned tired of cows."

Pellam asked, "You ever tip cows?"

"I'm from the Midwest. Everybody there tips cows."

"I've never done it. I'd like to, though."

"Pellam, you never tipped a cow?"

"Nope."

Marty shook his head with what seemed like genuine dismay. "Man : . ."

It had been three days since they'd pulled off the Interstate here in Cleary, New York. The Winnebago had clocked two hundred miles, roaming through knobby pine hills and tired farms and small, simple pastel cubes of houses decorated with pickups in the driveway, cars on blocks, and stiff laundry pinned and drying on long lines.

Three days, driving through mist and fog and yellow storms of September leaves and plenty of outright rain.

Marty looked out the window. He didn't speak for five minutes. Pellam, thinking: *Silence is platinum.*

Marty said, "Know what this reminds me of?"

The boy had a mind that ranged like a hungry crow; Pellam couldn't even guess.

"I was an assistant on *Echoes of War*," he continued.

This was a sixty-three-million-dollar Vietnam War movie that

Pellam had no desire to scout for, now had no desire to see in the theaters, and knew he wouldn't rent when it came to Tower Video in L.A.

Marty said, "For some reason they didn't shoot in Asia?"

"That's a question?"

"No. I'm telling you."

Pellam said, "It sounded like you were asking me."

"No. They decided not to shoot in Asia."

"Why not?"

"It's not important. They just didn't."

"Got it," Pellam said.

"They shot it in England, in Cornwall." Marty's head swung sideways, the grin spreading into his big, oval face. Pellam liked enthusiasm. But enthusiasm went with people that talked a lot. You can't have everything. "Man, did you know they have palm trees in England? I couldn't believe it. Palm trees . . . Anyway, the set designer made this totally incredible Army base, mortar holes and everything. And we'd get up at five a.m. to shoot and I'd get this weird feeling. I mean, I knew I was in England, and I knew it was just a movie. But all the actors were in costume – uniforms – sleeping in foxholes and eating rations. That's what the director wanted. I tell you, man, standing around, I felt totally . . . queasy." He considered if this was the right word. He decided it was and repeated it. "Queasy. That's what I feel like now."

He fell silent.

Pellam had worked on several war movies but at this moment, none of those came to mind. What he was thinking of now was rosettes of broken glass on the side window of the camper, a day after they'd arrived in the area here. Winnebago makes strong

windows and it had taken a real good throw to get the bottle
through the glass. The note inside had read: "*Goodbye*." The
camper'd been subjected to all kinds of creative destruction
over the years but nothing so ambiguously disturbing. Pellam
noticed the vandals had had the foresight not to pitch the
message through the windshield; they wanted to make sure
the Winnebago would have an unobstructed view when it drove
out of town.

He also noticed the missile had been a bottle, not a rock, and
could as easily have held gasoline as a carefully lettered note.

That's what John Pellam was thinking of now. Not stunts,
not war movies, not ominous dawns in tropical England.

"Getting cold," Marty said.

Pellam reached for the heater on the dash and turned it up
two notches. They smelled the wet, rubbery scent of the warm
air filling the cab.

On the floor Pellam's boot crunched several pieces of shat-
tered window glass. He kicked them aside.

Goodbye . . .

Downtown Cleary wasn't much.

Two laundromats, a Chase branch, a local bank. Two bars
outfitted by the same prop department. A dozen antique stores,
their windows crammed with tea tables, presidential cam-
paign buttons, sconces, trivets, tinware, scraps of faded rugs,
elegant Victorian tools. There were two real estate brokerage
storefronts, a music store specializing in marching-band instru-
ments, a hardware store. The tea shop – a little, hobbity place
– did a bang-up business selling muffins laced with fiber and
granola and honey.

An old wood-floored five-and-dime. A couple of drugstores, one with a lunch counter right out of the fifties, so authentic a set designer couldn't have done better. Several houses had been turned into small businesses. *Crystalmere – Original Jewelry Designs by Janine. Scotch Imports, Shetland Wool Our Speciality.*

Two teenage boys, large, with scrubbed faces and pick-a-fight grins, stood outside the hardware store, under an awning, shirts open over their beefy chests, acting like the brisk wind was nothing. One of them lifted his middle finger to the passing camper.

"Assholes," Marty said.

(The locals were friendlier in Mexico, where Marty and Pellam had been last month, though that may have had something to do with the exchange rate; U.S. currency makes for a great deal of international brotherhood and understanding.)

Pellam shrugged.

Marty's eyes remained outside the camper, looking at the sidewalks. He said, "They don't have many women in this town." He was frowning, as if he were disappointed he couldn't find any young ladies in store windows wearing *Sports Illustrated* swimsuits.

"Sent 'em all to the hills when they heard you were coming." Pellam looked for a place to park.

"I haven't seen a movie theater, either."

"You better hope they've got one of those, boy," Pellam told him. "You're gonna have more luck with a movie than with women."

Marty ignored this and asked, almost reverently, "Man, isn't it the best to make love to country girls in strange hotel rooms?"

"Instead of normal hotel rooms?" In fact, Pellam thought that it *was* good, though probably not the best, and he didn't call it making love. He also didn't get all adolescently lustful like Marty. Pellam had to keep an eye on the boy. He tended to lose control and flirt relentlessly with blondes in small-town cocktail lounges – women light-years tougher than the most steely-eyed sleek Manhattanite or Los Angelina.

They hit the middle of town just as the rain had congregated all it could in the thick clouds overhead and poured down, slashing streets and slapping leaves to the ground. Visibility dropped to zero and the camper swayed like a boat in a squall.

"Whoa," Marty said. "I'd say it's 'bout time for us to get drunk."

Pellam pulled into a parking place. In the torrent of rain he missed the curb and rode over it with a grind of metal. He couldn't remember if there were parking meters in downtown Cleary but if so there was one less now.

The rain fell and fell. It pounded like a dozen break-dancers, spinning and tromping and moonwalking across the roof of the Winnebago. It slid in thick sheets down the windshield and windows.

Pellam climbed out of his seat and looked at Marty. "On three."

"Oh, hell, Pellam, no, it's wet out there."

"You wanted a drink."

"Wait till it—"

Pellam opened the door. He jumped out. "Three."

"—lets up."

In the eight leaping steps it took them to find refuge they were completely drenched.

They swung through the door with a hollow ringing of cowbell. Marty stopped short. "This's the diner, Pellam."

"Close the door, boy!"

"It's the diner."

Pellam said, "Too early to drink. Besides, I feel like some cake."

"Cake, Pellam? Damn."

Marge's Cafe was all turquoise and plasticky and unhomey. The fluorescent was green – the light that took you right back to every high school corridor you'd ever walked down.

They sat at the counter and pulled napkins out of a metal holder to wipe their faces and arms.

Two scruffy men in their fifties, maybe grain elevator operators or farmers, stocky, with black grit seated in their pores, sat hunched over bulletproof white coffee mugs. They kept their conversation going, not missing a word, though their eyes followed Pellam and Marty like retrievers sighting birds.

"Yep, had his Massey near upside down."

"On the interstate? I'da paid to see that."

"Addled a whole mess of drivers . . . I ever tell you 'bout the time I took my Harvester over the crick?"

Marty said he'd love a beer and the country girl, pretty face, hugh hips, thirty-three-ish, said she'd love to serve him one but too bad they didn't have a license. "Too bad, too bad," she repeated, trying fiercely to think of something to add. She decided on: "What else kin I gitcha?" She asked the question adoringly. Marty shot a black glance at Pellam then smiled at the girl and settled for a bowl of chili and a Coke. Pellam ordered coffee and a piece of chocolate cake.

"That really homemade?" he asked.

"You'd call A&P a home then you bet."

She added some infatuation to the adoration and said to Marty, "Onions?"

"Yes'm."

"Nope," Pellam told her. It was a small camper.

Marty sighed. She looked at him and he shook his head no. She asked Pellam, "You be wanting that à la mode?"

"Alamo?"

She glanced around. "With ice cream, you know."

"Oh. No. Just the cake."

"That's an all-right camper you boys got yourself." She wasn't moving. "My daddy had us a Travel-All one time but he backed it up the wrong way – we was going to Lake Webster – and cracked the yoke."

Pellam said, "You've got to be careful."

"She never welded proper either."

"There you go."

After a moment she waddled into action. The spherical thighs swung as she stepped to a counter.

Marty was excited. "That five and dime, Pellam? Across the street?" He was looking out the window. "I was in there yesterday. It is a totally excellent place. I mean, they sell wigs there. A couple rows of them. What other store in the world can you walk into, pay nineteen ninety nine and walk out with a wig? I ask you? Can you do that on Rodeo Drive, can you do that on Michigan Avenue?"

"You *are* getting a bit thin on top."

The rain hit the large plate-glass window with a slap and there were several huge claps of thunder. As Pellam turned toward the noise he saw a woman running into the diner, the door flying open, the cowbell dinging. She pulled off a green cape. She was about his age, a year or two more maybe, wearing a faded purple dress, the waist high, just under her ample breasts. A granny dress, he remembered they were called. Her long hair – brown with a silver sheen to it – was parted in the center.

She scanned both Pellam and Marty. To Pellam she gave what could have been a smile then turned back to the counter, wiping the rain from her face.

Pellam and Marty turned back to the counter. They took the Polaroids out of their pockets, lined them up on the counter and started talking about camera angles.

The woman in the granny dress glanced over at them, casually. Then she looked back to the counter girl and ordered herbal tea and a bran muffin. She glanced again at the two men, then away.

The waitress set the coffee and Coke in front of the men and lifted a piece of frothy cake out of a cello-window carton. She disappeared into the back to collect the chili.

She delivered the food – adoringly in Marty's case. They ate. The granny-dress woman ignored them – even when Pellam said, "Hollywood," twice in one sentence.

"How's the cake?" Marty asked.

Pellam had three bites and couldn't take any more. He pushed the plate toward Marty, who dug into it with a spoon still containing a helping of greasy chili.

More thunder, shaking the windows. Huge detonations.

Pellam said, "What else is Lefkowitz doing now?"

Marty thought. "That European thing?"

Pellam shook his head.

Marty said, "Oh, I know. The Western?"

Pellam smiled. He stood and walked to the telephone. He called to Marty, "Look at this." He was genuinely surprised. "Still costs a dime to make a phone call." The granny-dress woman was looking at him now. Smiling. He smiled her way. She turned back to her tea.

Pellam punched in the number and was put on hold, the first of several times.

Finally, the assistant producer came on the line and said, "Johnny, my boy, where you been?"

Pellam knew he was a young man but he couldn't picture him. "Around."

"Ha, 'around,'" he said. "Ha."

"So," Pellam said lazily. "How's the weather in Tinsel Town? Damn hot out here. Close to a hundred."

"Johnny, how's it going?"

"It's going."

"I'm not kiddin' you, friend, the man's got a righteous hard-on for this project and we don't get the locations buttoned up soon all God's chilluns gonna be in serious trouble. Where the hell are you?"

"Think I've got just the spot for you."

"Oh, I love the sound of your voice. Marry me."

"It's perfect."

"Talk to me, Johnny, talk to me. We got pressure, hombre. I'm talking righteous pressure, dig?"

Pellam wondered where you learned producer-speak. Maybe it was at UCLA. He winked at Marty then said into the phone, "Lefkowitz's going to go hog wild. The dawn shots'll be so beautiful . . . Desert for miles around. I mean, you cannot *see* a goddamn tree, I mean, *see* one, unless you look west, then you'd need a telephoto, and—"

"Desert?"

"Then there's this little shack . . . You can't shoot inside—"

From the other end of the line: the silence of the universe's outer reaches. Then: "Shack?"

Pellam continued, "—but don't worry. There *is* a corral. Oh, and I thought you could move some of the interiors out there. The scene where—"

"You ragging me, John."

Pellam sounded hurt. "Ragging you? No, when I say it's perfect, it's perfect. I wouldn't—"

"You're ragging me."

Marty shouted, "Tell him about the arroyos."

"Oh, yeah, the arroyos. You know the scene where the Comanches are sneaking up on the cabin?"

"John, not funny."

Pellam said, "What do you mean?"

"It's not a Western."

"What do you mean it's not a Western?" There was a pause, while Pellam pretended to examine the script. "What do you call Arizona in 1876?"

"You'reinArizona?" The voice was a tenor car alarm. *"Theysentyouthewrongscript?"*

Pellam said, "Uh . . ."

He tried. But he couldn't keep it in a second longer. Marty, who'd heard the assistant producer's cry, had lowered his head to the counter and was shaking uncontrollably. Pellam joined him.

"You goddamn son of a bitch, Pellam," the A.P. muttered.

Pellam rocked against the side of the phone stall, immobilized with laughter, trying to catch his breath. "Sorry," he gasped.

"That . . . is . . . not . . . funny."

Though there was considerable evidence to the contrary. Pellam finally caught his breath then looked at Marty. He lost it again, quivering with laughter. After he'd calmed, Pellam managed to say, "We're in a place called Cleary. Upstate New York. It looks good. I think it'll be perfect. We've got 27 out of 51 setups but we did the principal-shoot first so it's mostly just background and establishing shots we've got left. We'll finish the snaps and get you the report in a couple days." He paused for a moment then said, "I've been looking at the script. Can I talk you into a few changes?"

"No way. It's carved in stone." Now the A.P. was laughing too, an indulgent chuckle, just to show he was a good sport and now it was time to put the joshing aside and give straight answers. "You mean it, John? It looks good?"

"It's—"

"We can't wait any longer. The big man's gonna have my balls for breakfast if we don't move fast. What were you going to say?"

"When?"

"Just now. I interrupted you."

"Just, it's a good town. It'll work." He recited slowly, "Chill out, man."

"Haw, haw."

Pellam said, "I'm gonna be serious for a minute."

"We're listening, dear."

"The script. You're not going to like this but I've been doing some doctoring, and—"

"I don't like, I don't dislike. I ignore."

"The story needs a little help."

"Forget about it. Lefty'll cut your balls off too, you even mention it."

Pellam remembered another Hollywoodism. "The thing is, it's a good property; it's not a great property."

"But it's *Lefkowitz's* property."

"Your loss," Pellam said.

"No, my ass."

"Okay. I tried . . . Oh, before I go I should mention . . ."

"What? Problem?"

"Not really a problem, I don't think. It's just finding the airfield's been tougher than we thought."

"The—"

"Marty and I are flying to London tomorrow. We'll be in Dover by five."

"Dover?"

"That's London time."

"What airfield?"

"You know, the paratrooper scene . . ."

"John, you're a prick, anybody ever tell you that?" He hung up.

He joined Marty and said, "No sense of humor."

Marty began working on the cake again.

A half hour later the rain had slowed to a fine mist and the thunderstorm had passed. The granny-dress woman, after a couple soulful glances at Pellam, was back at the salt mine – the way she phrased it to the waitress, who was herself hard at work adoring Marty.

"Let's roll," Pellam said. The men stood.

"Bye-ee," she called.

"See you later," Marty said. "Thanks for the fine service."

"Anytime," she said.

When the door closed behind them Pellam whispered, "Anytime, anyplace, any way you want it, lover doll."

"Pellam, it's not my fault I'm a stud."

"She wants you, boy. She wants you to be the father of her children. All twelve of them. Look at you, rosy cheeked, cute as a button. Oh, she'll be dreaming about you tonight."

"Hang it up, Pellam."

"Maybe," Pellam said seriously, "you should think about settling down here. Get yourself a NAPA franchise, wear a CAT hat to cover up that thinning hairline of yours, join the Elks . . ."

"You should talk, old man. That other lady checking you out in there reminded me a lot of my mother."

"They're the most experienced."

"They—"

Both Marty and Pellam stopped short, twenty feet in front of the camper.

"Jesus," Marty asked. "Wait. What is that?"

Pellam was surprised the boy couldn't figure it out but then he guessed it was like those optical illusions in science books, the ones that some people see right away and others you've got to explain it to them.

This one seemed pretty clear to Pellam. On the side of the camper, in black spray paint, were crude images of the mounds of two graves with crosses stuck in them. Scrawled beneath them was that word again. *Goodbye.*

"Oh," Marty whispered, getting it at last. "Damn."

They walked closer, then around the camper, expecting some more damage, but, no, there was none – just the artwork. They looked around the street. Deserted.

"Who was it, those kids we saw before?"

"Maybe," Pellam said.

They stood for a moment looking at the crude, feathery lines of the bad drawings. Pellam started up Main Street.

"Where're you going?" Marty asked.

"Buy us some turpentine and steel wool. Can't go driving around looking like an ad for a funeral home."

2

———•◦•◦•———

Pellam said to Janine, the granny-dress woman, "You'd think they'd come up with some more money for that. It's going to represent something, it ought to have a little class."

He was looking at the tiny, overpainted black cannon, donated to the town by the Veterans of Foreign Wars. It didn't seem capable of lobbing a shell more than ten feet. They sat in the town square, where he'd been sitting, marking Polaroids, when she walked past casually and sat on the bench next to his. He'd smelled minty tea – what she'd been drinking yesterday in Marge's diner – and when he'd looked up she'd smiled at him. He'd scooted over four feet of bumpy wood and they'd struck up a conversation.

"Maybe it's valuable," Janine now said. "Looks can be deceiving."

Pellam liked her outfit today better than what she'd worn yesterday: a long skirt, boots, a big bulky-knit sweater. Her hair – in the sun you could see some red – was still parted in the middle. She was an easy forty, looking older straight-on, though she probably wasn't. That happened to a lot of these poor flower children; maybe they're limber and they live a long time, but sun and fresh air can do harsh things to your skin.

"Where's your boyish partner, with the cute little tush, the one who's probably a year or two under my limit?"

"He rented a car and went out to the hinterland, checking out some parks. We've got a lot of scenes left, so we split the troops."

She asked, "What company you work for?"

"Called Big Mountain Studios."

"Didn't they do *Night Players*? And *Ganges* . . . Oh, that was a great film. Did you go to India for that one?"

Pellam shook his head.

"Wow, do you know William Hurt? You ever meet him?"

"Saw him once in a restaurant."

"How about Willem Dafoe? Glenn Close?"

"No and no." Pellam's eyes were scanning the downtown, which almost shimmered in the heat. It was eleven a.m. The temperature was up by twenty degrees over yesterday. Indian Summer.

"Tell me about the film you're working on now."

"We don't like to give too much away."

She socked him playfully on the arm. "Excuse me? I mean, excuse me? I'm a spy? Like I'm going to sell the story to MGM?"

Pellam said, "It's called *To Sleep in a Shallow Grave*."

"Wild. Love the title. Who's in it?"

"It's not cast yet." It wasn't for location scouts to give away too much.

She said, "Come on now. I don't believe you." She tilted her head coyly and her hair fell straight across her face, leaving only her eyes exposed – like a veiled Islamic woman. "Give me a clue."

"A few supporting actors you couldn't possibly know." He sipped his coffee.

They always liked details. Who in Hollywood was playing musical beds. Which actresses had had implants. Who hit their wives. Or their husbands. Who liked boys. Who had orgies in Beverly Hills.

Some people even wanted to know about the films themselves.

He said, "It's about a woman who comes back to her home town for her father's funeral. But she finds out that he might not have been her father after all and maybe he killed the man who was her real father. It takes place in the fifties, a small town called Bolt's Crossing."

He stood up. She watched him toss the coffee carton into a trash basket painted with tulips, and she scolded, "You drink too much of that. Caffeine. Yuck. Don't you have trouble sleeping?"

"Which way's the cemetery? I want to get some more 'Roids."

"Some? . . ."

"Polaroids."

"Follow me." They turned east. As they walked along the road, Janine said, "Tell me more about the film."

"That's it for now."

She gave him a pout with her full lips. "Maybe I won't be your guide if you're not nice to me."

"Aw, I need a guide. I may never get back to civilization without one."

She grimaced dramatically and waved her arm around downtown. "Bad news, Charlie. This *is* civilization. It don't get no better than this."

They walked for a half hour and found themselves in the cemetery.

His reaction to the place was the same as on the day they'd arrived in Cleary, the day Marty had spotted the cemetery from the highway; it was perfect for the film. Tall black trees bordering a small clearing in which battered tombstones tilted at exotic angles. No big monuments, no mausoleums. Just hunks of stone, spilling right out of the forest.

Pellam pulled the camera out of his pocket, took three or four pictures. The cemetery was filled with an odd, shadowy light, which seemed to come from the underbelly of the low wispy clouds. The light accentuated contrasts: bark was blacker than in bright sun, grass and milkweed stalks paler, stone more bleached; it was white like old bones. Many of the tombstones were badly eroded. Pellam and Janine wove through the grass, toward the woods. A rusty barbed-wire fence of taut strands separated the cemetery from the underbrush.

Wait . . . What was that? Pellam stopped suddenly, stared into the trees. He was sure someone was watching him, but as he stepped to one side, the voyeur, if it was anybody at all, vanished.

Janine said, "All I'll say is, if it has Redford or Newman in it and you don't tell me I'll never speak to you again."

"It doesn't."

"I saw *Butch Cassidy* twelve times. I only saw *Let It Be* eight.

"Were you at Woodstock?"

She smiled, surprised. "Yeah, were you?"

"No. But I wanted to go. Tell me about the cemetery."

"What's to tell? Dead people buried here."

"What sort of dead people? Rich, poor, smugglers, farmers?"

She couldn't quite get a handle on what he was asking. "You mean, like what does it say about the history of the town?"

Pellam was looking at a grave.

Adam Gottlieb
1846–1899
A sailor on your ocean, Lord.

He said, "Man missed the century. Bummer. Yeah, that's basically it. The history of the place, the atmosphere."

She danced over a grave, girlish. "Can you imagine what Cleary was like a hundred years ago? Probably only five, six hundred people here, if that."

He snapped several Polaroids.

Janine took his arm and hooked it through hers. He felt the heavy pressure of her breast against his elbow. He wondered what her chest looked like. Was it dotted with freckles? Pellam really liked freckles.

They walked for a few minutes. He said, "I don't see any recent tombstones."

"Is that bad?"

"No. I'm just curious."

Janine said, "There's a new cemetery outside of town. But that's not the answer. The answer is that nobody ever dies in Cleary. They're dead already."

She now grew serious and started playing with the top of her tea carton. "First, there's something I have to tell you. I'm sort of married." She looked up. "But we're separated. We still groove okay, my old man and me, but it's not like on a physical level, you know? He's living with a bimbo runs a motorcycle repair shop near Fishkill. Her husband split too. He comes back now and then but mostly he's split."

Pellam tried to sort it out. There were two husbands, was that it? One of them kept coming back? To who?

Janine said, "Just want the facts out, you know. Like, in case you heard something . . . Well, you know how it is." She was looking at him. He felt the weight of her eyes on him, as heavy as her breasts. A response was in order.

"Sure do," he said.

This seemed to satisfy her. She kicked at some leaves. Pellam hoped she didn't want to go for a leaf fight. There was nothing worse than somebody on the threshold of middle age going zany.

"Tell me about Hollywood. The parties are pretty wild, huh?"

"I don't go to Hollywood very often."

"Isn't that where the studio's at?"

"Century City."

"Where's that?"

"Now it's office buildings. It used to be the Twentieth Century Fox back lot."

"How 'bout that! Super."

They walked back to the town square. Pellam reloaded his camera. He looked up. From three different windows, faces were staring at him. They looked away quickly. One woman paraded her six-year-old daughter past. The woman pushed the girl forward. "This is Josey," she said. Pellam grinned at the girl and kept walking.

The word had spread into all the nooks of Cleary. Somebody was going to make a Movie. David Lynch, Lawrence Kasdan, Tom Cruise, Meryl Streep, Julia Roberts had all been sighted. It would have a cast of thousands. They needed extras. They needed stuntmen. There'd be tickets to Hollywood. Union contracts. Line up for your fifteen minutes of fame.

None of the hoverers had actually asked for a part yet but Pellam was getting a hell of a lot of silent auditions.

"What does everybody do for entertainment around here," he asked, "when they're not trying to get a role in a movie?"

"We all have great fun robbing tourists blind. You sticking around till Saturday?"

"Maybe."

"Wait till you see it then. It's leaf season. Hundreds of cars, everybody gawking at trees like they were mandalas. Totally far out. They spend an incredible amount of money. I had a tea shop for a few years before the jewelry thing took off. I'd charge two dollars for a scone. A granola muffin was two and a quarter . . . They paid without blinking."

"What do you all do when you're not ripping off the *turistas*?"

She paused to consider. "Socializing. Me and my friends usually get together and hang out. Trivial Pursuit or Monopoly. Rent movies a lot. There are carnivals, parades, Future Farmers of America. Down home, middle America. The workers – I tend to think of it in terms of class; I was a Marxist once – they go in for raising kids, Kiwanis, pancake breakfasts, turkey shoots, church in any one of a number of interchangeable Protestant denominations. But we're very tolerant – both Jewish families in town are well liked."

They walked for a few minutes more. Pellam glanced at her; she was preoccupied, thinking of something that would summarize. "It's a hard place to be single."

He let that sit for a thick moment then said, "The film's got a dark side to it, violence in a small town. Any of that?"

"Oh, yeah. A lot of domestic stuff. Last year a man took a shotgun and killed his family. They found him at home, watching *Wheel of Fortune* with the bodies all around him. Then the police found a couple guys from New York City murdered not far from downtown."

"What happened?"

"Nobody's sure. They were just businessmen. Looked like robbery but who knows? Then you have your assorted drownings, car wrecks, hunting accidents. A lot of those."

Pellam took more Polaroids. "Look, they call it Main Street. Great."

"Yeah, they do. I never thought about it. Outa sight."

He paused, looked across the street into the window of the Dutchess Realty Company. The morning light fell on the storefront glass and he thought somebody else was staring at him, a blond woman. But she wasn't like the other supplicants; there was something intense and troubling about the way she studied him.

Then he decided he was just being paranoid.

Goodbye . . .

He looked away, then back. The blond voyeur was no longer there. Just like the imagined spy in the forest overlooking the cemetery. *Maybe* imagined.

Janine said, "I've gotta open the store now but, you want, sometime I can show you the only building that survived the Great Fire of 1912."

"Love to see it."

"You mean that?"

"Sure do," Pellam said.

No, we'll split the worm . . .

Pellam was walking down a side street in Cleary. The red-covered script was in his hand. He made notations, he shot 'Roids.

No, John, really . . . I insist.

He was thinking about the assignment in Mexico last month.

He and Marty had found a great jungle outside of Puerto Vallarta and after the principal photography had started, the two men had hung around and drunk mescal with the crew and watched the director waste eighty thousand feet of film (shot through a Softar filter so the flick would have that smoky soft look of a Nike or IBM commercial). The story had something to do with forgers and Swiss businessmen and skinny dark-haired women who resembled Trudie, a woman Pellam occasionally dated in L.A. (Damn, he'd forgotten to call her. It had been five days. I've gotta call. I'm going to. Definitely.)

In Mexico, Marty had spent time looking over the director of photography's shoulder – the boy wanted to be a DP himself one day. Pellam had been on plenty of sets, too many, he'd decided years ago, and so he hung out mostly in the one bar in town, which was filled not with roustabouts, like the crew in the opening scenes of *The Treasure of the Sierra Madre*, but with urban Americans on seven-night, six-day packages. Pellam avoided them like the local water and spent his time with a senior gaffer, an old bearded guy, who had two intense loves – one was antique generators and the other was emaciated brunettes.

The latter Pellam shared with him – the love for, not the Gold's Gym'd bodies themselves, since he was among the caste of mere hirelings. Oh, a pert little assistant from wardrobe or makeup might make herself available to Pellam but any woman whose name was on a Screen Actors Guild contract was off limits to the likes of location scouts and electricians.

In two weeks, the men had polished off bottle after bottle of greasy liquor, in which agave worms floated like astronauts spacewalking. They shared the worms. The last one they cut in half with Pellam's buck knife and dropped into the last shot of the granular, smoky drink. The gaffer swore it had hallucinogenic effects and muttered some mumbo jumbo as he tossed back the shot.

Pellam told him he was crazy and didn't feel anything but extremely drunk.

The movie stank but Pellam'd had a good time. For Christsake, it was Mexico. How could you lose? The final scenes (*final* scenes? Hell, the whole movie) involved more explosives and machine guns than acting but Pellam was happy to watch the liquor in the bottles sink toward the fat worms and listen to the explosive charges, which were so much quieter in real life than in the final cut of a film itself, after the sound effects were added.

Whump whump whump.

After a while, things got boring in paradise and Pellam, who maybe didn't smile a whole lot and whose eyelids didn't grow as wide as Marty's but who loved pranks, came up with some good ones. On that Mexican trip, he got a lot of mileage out of stuffed Gila monsters and latex rattlesnakes. The best was when he talked a stunt man into hanging from boots bolted to the ceiling of the director's hotel room. When the director, stoned on some powerful ganja, walked into the room, the stunt man shouted, "Man, you're on the fucking ceiling! How do you *do* that?" The director stared at him in shock, frozen like James Arness in the big ice cube in the original version of *The Thing*. The stuntman began to pass out, both from laughter and blood to the brain. Pellam recorded it on videotape and planned to send the tape to selected friends as Christmas presents.

Pellam got away with a lot. Location scouting is to the film busines what Switzerland is to war. Whatever cataclysm, betrayals and victories occur in boardrooms and on sets and casting couches, nobody has much of an opinion about scouts. Producers are thieves, actors are brain damaged, cinematographers are *artistes*, the trades are gorillas. Everybody hates the writers.

But location scouts, they're cowboys.

They deliver then they're gone.

That, or they sat on the sidelines drinking mescal, picking up script girls and trying to pick up actresses, and *then* they're gone. Nobody thinks twice about them. Pellam had had other jobs in film, and no jobs other than in film, but scouting was the only one he'd kept at for more than a couple years.

Mexico last month. Georgia last week.

Now, Cleary, New York. With clear-cheeked blonde-bait

Marty. With a busty former hippie. With a hundred squares of slick Polaroid pictures. With a cemetery.

With some people who weren't too happy to have him in town.

Goodbye . . .

He paused on a small road that led to what looked like a town park. It might have been private property, though; the lots in Cleary were massive. He thought about his place on Beverly Glen, whose lot line you could measure in inches and not end up with an unwieldy number. Pellam stopped and gazed at the property, at the huge robin's-egg-blue colonial in the middle of the beautiful yard. So, it wasn't a park at all. It was a residence. And it was for sale. The sign was stuck in the front yard.

Pellam wondered what it was like to own a house this big in a town this small. He counted windows. The place must have six or seven bedrooms. He didn't *know* five people he'd want sleeping in his house. Not all at the same time.

He started across the road. What would a house like this cost?

What was the backyard like?

He never found out.

Pellam was halfway across the road when a small gray car crested the hill, hit a patch of leaves slick as spilled oil and skidded hard. He tried to dance out of its path but a part of the car – some piece of resonant sheet metal – caught him square on the thigh.

John Pellam saw:

A sea of leaves, mostly yellow, rising to the sky. A flare of sunlight on glass. A huge oak tree spinning, the blue house turning upside down, caught in a tornado. Then someone swung the curb at him, and everything disappeared in a burst of dirty light.

———◆◆◆———

3

"Where'd you get that scar?"

Pellam opened his eyes. Thinking only that he wanted to throw up.

He told this to the white-jacketed man standing above him, muscular, in his forties. And, as the doctor was telling him that it was normal, Pellam started to.

A bedpan appeared just in time and, while Pellam was busy with it, the doctor continued his calm monologue. "You wake up from a concussion, you always see regurgitation. I don't mean stunned but actually knocked unconscious. Yep, completely normal reaction."

He looked like a veterinarian Pellam had taken a dog to once. A standard poodle, he thought, but he couldn't remember for sure. He liked standard poodles but he didn't think he'd ever owned one. That bothered him, not remembering. Maybe he had amnesia. Or brain damage.

He groaned. After the completely normal regurgitation, he felt burning stomach muscles and a fiery throat join the agony that swelled inside his skull, a balloon that wouldn't stop expanding until the bone cracked and the pressure hissed out like steam from a burst pipe.

He took a mouthful of water, rinsed, and spit into the bedpan. There was no nurse and the doctor disappeared with the pan. He returned with a clean one and set it on the table next to Pellam.

No, it wasn't a poodle, it was a terrier. One of Trudie's he believed (Trudie, Trudie . . . had he called her?).

"That should be about it," the doctor said and didn't explain any further.

Pellam did a self-exam. He wore just his Jockey briefs under a blue cloth robe. He lifted the sheets and checked body parts in descending order of importance. The only sign of damage, apart from the bandage on his head, was a bruise on his thigh the color and shape of a mutant eggplant.

"I wouldn't drink anything for a while," the doctor said.

Pellam said he wouldn't. Then added, "I got hit by a car." He was disappointed that this was the most significant thing he could think of to say.

The doctor said, "Uh-huh." Mostly he seemed curious about the scar. It was a foot long, a gouge of glossy, indented skin across Pellam's right biceps and chest. It was a memento of the time an arms assistant got the charge instructions wrong during a car chase gag and used dynamite instead of smokeless powder in rigging the Oldsmobile Pellam was driving. When the car exploded, Pellam got an eighteen-inch auto part in the chest. The medic told him that if it'd been going straight it would've pinned him to the wall. "Lahk a stuck piyag, Pellam. You a lucky somvabitch."

"Used to do stunt work," he now said to the doctor.

"Oh, you're the movie man, huh?"

Pellam focused on him. He really looked like he should be treating fuzzy terriers and poodles and mending tipped cows.

"I'm the movie man."

"Don't do stunts anymore, I hope."

"Life's exciting enough."

"I hear you," the doctor said.

"How am I?"

The doctor said, "Nothing serious. Concussion but no cracks. You fell good – I guess because you're used to stunts. That scrape on your head is wide, it can get infected pretty easy, so keep an eye on it. I'll give you some Betadine."

"This a hospital?"

The doctor laughed. "It's got me, a mini lab, a podiatrist, an OB-GYN. If that's a hospital, this is Cleary General."

"Can I leave?"

"Nope. You'll have to stay here the night. You'll be pretty dizzy for a while. I wouldn't want you to fall. I've got plenty of magazines. *Reader's Digests.* Some *National Geographics.* Good things like that. A bible, if you're interested."

"I've got to get a message to somebody."

"There's a phone in the lobby. I can make a call for you. If you—"

"No, not a phone call. Somebody'll be waiting for me back at my camper. It's parked on Main Street." Pellam told him that Marty would be returning about six.

The doctor said, "I've got a son works at the IH plant. He's a manager. He can take some time off and leave a note on your camper door."

"Be obliged."

Pellam watched the doctor take a small chart from beside the bed and write on it.

"Who was it? Who hit me?"

The doctor kept writing.

Pellam wondered if it was a hit and run, wondered who the driver was – some hotshot, a kid, probably.

Wondered too if it *really was* an accident.

Thinking of the mural of crosses on the Winnebago.

Thinking: *Goodbye* . . .

Maybe he should call the sheriff. That'd be the smart thing to—

The doctor looked up. "She's outside."

"What?"

"She's here. She's been waiting to see you."

"Who?" Pellam asked. (Did he mean Trudie? Damn, I hope I called her.)

"The driver. The woman who hit you."

"Oh," Pellam said. "With a lawyer?"

"Just by herself."

He said, "Can I see her?"

"You want to see her?"

"I guess."

The doctor said, "Then you can see her."

Pellam's first reaction was that she was pretty but not sexy. Pert 'n' perky, he thought, discouraged. Not his type at all. A girl with a mile-wide smile.

She was maybe thirty-two, thirty-three, but looked older – something about the teased blond hair, the heavy pale makeup, the fleshy pantyhose made her seem matronly. Pellam could picture her as a Miss America contestant, with a baton, sending it sailing up into the height of the proscenium. Her face was blank when she entered the room but as soon as she was over the threshold, she grinned shy crevices around her mouth.

He was expecting: *Goshhowya'llfeelin'?*

But she didn't sound that way at all.

"Welcome to Cleary," she said in a low, sexy voice that almost made him ignore the mask of pancake makeup. She walked right up to the bed and stuck her hand out.

She saw the scar and it threw her. The facade cracked for a minute then the down-home smile returned. "Meg Torrens."

"John Pellam."

Her mouth went tight. "I don't know what to say."

Pellam knew what to *think*: Bummer. He'd done a fast inventory. A cocktail ring that wouldn't quit, wedding band, a fat rock of an engagement ring.

Pellam said to her, "Not a problem. These things happen."

(Pellam had a lawyer one time, a former flower child who'd done a pretty good job for him on a legal matter – at a time when he needed a lawyer to do a pretty good job. The ponytailed man'd been real concerned about what Pellam said in public and he'd drummed into his client's head that there were a lot of things you shouldn't say to people you might be involved with in court. It occurred to him now that he probably shouldn't have said, *Not a problem.*)

Her eyes were on his scar.

He said, "You're not responsible."

She blinked.

He touched his arm. "Not for that, I mean. I'd show you the

bruise that's got your name on it but I don't know you well enough yet."

She said, "That one looks pretty bad."

"Happened a long time ago."

"I don't think I want to know how."

"I was driving an Olds 88 and firing a machine gun out the window. Somebody shot the car with a rocket. I think it was a rocket. I'm not sure. It blew up."

She stared at him, waiting for the truth, then gave a burst of polite laugh, which faded fast. "A machine gun."

"An Uzi, I think." Pellam frowned and thought hard. "No, a MAC-10."

He nodded again. Right, a MAC-10. And a rocket. And a terrier that looked a little like a poodle. He didn't have amnesia. He looked at her. What was her name again?

"A MAC-10," he repeated.

She stared a moment more. She handed him a white plastic bag with handles on it. "Present," she said. Her cheeks were red and Pellam loved that. As much as he loved freckles he loved blushing women even more. He couldn't remember the last time he'd seen a pretty woman blushing. In L.A., all women were like Trudie; genetically incapable of it.

He opened the bag. The present wasn't wrapped but there was a bow on the box. A new Polaroid camera.

"What happened to the old one?" he asked.

"It got kind of mashed."

He laughed. "You didn't have to. The company'll pay for it."

She smiled cautiously, maybe not sure whether he meant her insurance company or his film company. What he'd meant was his company but then he figured it was all going on her tab anyway – camera, the veterinarian's bill and a little moolah for pain and suffering (the eggplant bruise would look great in court and now, thanks to her, he had a new toy to immortalize it with). He said, "Thanks."

He fiddled with the square, sleek camera, not sure what else to say. He loaded it then held the camera up suddenly and took a picture of her. She blinked and for an instant got a nervous look, as if she suspected him of gathering evidence. *Bzzzzt.* He loved that sound.

But he just looked at the picture as it developed – not quite in focus, tilted, washed out; her lids were half closed. He handed the picture to her.

"What?—"

Pellam shrugged. "A present. You can frame it."

She looked at the square. "It's awful." Then she put it into her purse and looked up at the wall, at an eye chart that must've been thirty or forty years old. She was squinting slightly and he wondered if she was giving herself an informal exam or whether she was appraising its value, picturing it in her tastefully paneled dining room she'd share with a husband rich enough to buy her the Hope Diamond's cousin for her petite finger.

She asked, "You're the man making movies?"

"Nope. I just look for locations that the studio decides they don't like."

"Just like me," she said. "I show houses to people who don't buy them."

So, not a housewife. A businesswoman person. Watch it, Pellam. Middle America ain't the same as when you left. Patronize at your own risk.

She said, "What kind of movie is it?"

"An artsy movie," he said.

"Big Mountain Studios. They're famous."

"Sort of famous," Pellam said. "How did you know the name?"

"You had this permit in the window of your trailer thing. Your Winnebago."

Pellam nodded. Wondering when – and why – she'd checked out the camper.

"When will they start shooting?"

"Three weeks, give or take."

Meg nodded. "Guess you've got lots of people asking about getting a part."

"Some, sure. They think it'd be an adventure. You want a part? I'd be—"

"Are you asking me?" She blinked in surprise.

He didn't like women who couldn't tell when he was joking.

"Everybody wants to be in movies," Pellam said, not looking at her directly, but studying her reflection in a round wall mirror. "Everybody wants to be rich. Everybody wants to be young. Everybody wants to be thin."

She – *Meg* he remembered her name (MAC-10, rocket, terrier, call Trudie, Meg, Meg, Meg) – she swallowed whatever she was going to say and instead offered: "I've got a son." Saying that seemed to make her more comfortable, established some boundaries. *Yo, men, secure the perimeter.* Pellam was getting tired of the visit. He had his present, she had her son and her husband's massive rings. Now he wanted her to leave. Meg said, "He'd love to be in a movie."

"You don't want him to be," Pellam said in a tone that said he knew.

"I don't know. He's really into California. We went to Universal Studios last year. He loved it. I did too."

"Universal Studios isn't Hollywood. Except in the most general of senses."

Meg said, "You have any kids?" Now her eyes did the heart-finger scan.

"Nope," he said.

A pause. "I think it'd be tough to have a job like yours and have kids."

"It would, true."

"Or," she said, "be married."

"Also true."

"So, you're not?"

"Divorced."

Meg nodded. He wondered if she was storing this information and, if so, in what kind of file.

"So, you just drive around and look for places to shoot movies?"

He thought for a moment and decided that described his life about as succinctly as anybody'd ever done. "Yep."

A luxuriant silence.

She handed him a piece of paper. "That's my insurance agent."

He put the slip on the bedside table, next to the bed-pan.

"My husband told me not to say anything to you . . . But, I had to come by."

(*"John, cops and insurance companies they're going to eat*

up your words like M&M's. Don't say a goddamn syllable to
the cannibals, got it?")

He told her, "These things happen."

"I hit a patch of leaves. I wasn't expecting to see somebody
in the middle of the street."

He said, "You've acted, haven't you?"

She laughed in surprise. "No. I did some modeling. Just for
a year. How could you tell?"

He said, "The way you carry yourself . . . I don't know. Just
an impression."

He felt she wanted to warm up, but was keeping the tone
conversational. "I lived in Manhattan for a while. I did some
fashion work. But I was too short to get good assignments. I
didn't like it anyway." She folded her arm across her chest and
looked for the door, seemed relieved that it was only six feet
away. "Why are you asking me these questions?"

"I always like to find out from the locals about locations I'm
scouting. It's—"

"Locals?" She tromped hard on the frown, but some of it
escaped.

He said, "I get the feeling you've lived here long enough to
give me an idea of what Cleary's really like."

Meg was grimacing. Whatever was behind the visit – Pellam
didn't have a clue what that might be – wasn't working out. On
cue, she looked at her watch. "I should go. There's someone
covering for me at the office."

"When I get out of here – they're paroling me tomorrow –
let me buy you lunch."

"No, I—"

"Not to worry," Pellam said. "I'll drive."

"Uh, I don't think that's a very good idea. I've got a lot going on. I'm very busy."

"People are busy in Cleary?"

Okay, it was a little over the line with that one. He'd forgotten you have to be real careful when you hit people in their home towns. Especially if you're from one that's a thousand times bigger than theirs. But come on, country folk, you gotta have a sense of humor.

She bristled. "Yes, people are busy in Cleary. There's more to this town than people like you'll ever see—"

"There, perfect," Pellam announced.

She frowned.

"Keep talking. You're giving me a feel for the place. That's just what I'm looking for."

"I should go."

He said, "No, you shouldn't."

"Anyway, I'm not a local. I've only lived here for—"

"Don't tell me, let me guess . . ." Pellam was feeling perverse (hell, why not? She'd run him over). "Ten years."

Her eyes flared. "What makes you think I've lived here that long?"

In for a penny, in for a pound.

"The makeup, the hair, the clothes—"

"What's wrong with—?" Her voice was high, indignant.

"Nothing. You just asked me—"

"Never mind." Meg unfolded her arms and walked to the door.

Pellam asked, "So when can we get together?"

"The word *never* comes to mind." She stepped through the doorway, gripping the knob hard then must've decided she shouldn't be slamming clinic doors and closed it silently. A second later it opened and she said to him, "And for your information, I've lived here for five years, not ten."

The door closed again, harder this time.

Ah, she'll be back.

Pellam heard her low heels tapping on the linoleum, then the grind of the front door and then nothing.

She'll be back. She's on her way now.

A car started.

She'll be back.

He heard a car strew gravel as it hit the road, then the whine of gears.

Okay, maybe not.

Bzzzzt.

Marty stuffed the moist square of the Polaroid into his pocket and squinted as he looked at a bald spot on the small mountain across a ravine. Acid rain'd eaten away at a lot of the greenery. It didn't look good at all. By the time Marty'd gone to college, schools were offering degrees in the environment. Marty could recognize acid rain.

He took four pictures, numbered them and slipped them into his pocket. All location scouts he knew used Polaroids, but Marty was an amateur photographer and would've preferred to use his old Nikkormat 35mm. The variation in the lenses – wide angle, telephoto – would give a better idea of what the scenery and locations looked like through the Panaflex movie camera. But the studio paid his salary and the studio said 'Roids.

So 'Roids were what they were going to get.

Marty wanted to be a cinematographer eventually. He knew

cameras. He liked the murmuring gears and heavy, oil-scented parts that fit together so well. He liked the perfectly ground disks of the Schneider lenses, set into their royal-blue velvet carrying cases. He liked the portable Arriflex 35mm cameras, which cameramen would carry around on sets like rocket launchers. He liked the robotic contraption of Steadicams.

He figured a couple more years of location scouting, then it would be about time for his break (a unit director would call out, "Holy Mother, the director of photography's on a bender – you, kid, get behind the Panaflex. Roll, roll, roll . . .") Until that happened, however, being a location scout would do. Especially being a location scout for John Pellam, where you tended to get a week of experience in the movie business for every day you worked.

Marty wandered back down the hill toward the rented Tempo.

Get the feel.

Marty worked hard at trying to get the feel. Pellam made him read the scripts over and over. Scripts are a bitch to read but he kept at it. Pellam would question him about a story. You gotta get the feel for it, he'd say.

The feel . . . that was the extra ten percent that Pellam – for all his bullshit and fire-me-if-you-want attitude – was always talking about. The ten percent that Pellam delivered. This was the essential lesson Marty had learned from John Pellam.

The day was getting hot. The sun was out. Marty looked at his watch. There were still thirteen locations he had to find but sun like this was too good to miss. Beer break. Marty went to the trunk of the car and took out a Miller. He opened it. He sat on the rear bumper as he flipped through the script for *Shallow*

Grave. He unbuttoned his shirt and let the sunlight fall on his tanned, skinny chest.

He liked sitting in the sun and drinking beer. He liked the country, liked the blond dry grass that hissed when he walked through it. When he was in California he usually stayed in a condo in Van Nuys, but he preferred to travel because there were no seasons in L.A. He loved fall. He wondered if there were more jobs for cinematographers in New York than in L.A.

He wondered—

The bullet hit the back of the car with a huge ringing slap a full second before he heard the rolling boom of the rifle shot. Marty jumped up, eyes wide, dropping the script, the camera and his beer. White, malty foam shot out of the gold can.

"Christ," he whispered as terror and relief oozed through his legs. All he could do was stare, openmouthed, at the hole in the car, remembering a newspaper story about a woman who was killed by a gunshot from several miles away, a hunting accident. "Christ."

He thought: that'd been four feet to the right . . .

The second shot, which he never heard, wasn't four feet to the right at all. It hit the gas tank pretty much dead center.

You could hear, as if on a soundtrack, a huge whoosh, as the flaming ball spread twenty feet in all directions.

You could hear Marty's horrific scream from the tangle of fire.

And, as the Ford burned into black metal, you could hear the honking of geese and swans, fleeing with their imperfect memory of the terrible explosion.

4

At first, Pellam thought the tragedy was his.

Leukemia. A tumor. Hodgkin's.

I'm sorry, sir. The X ray showed something else.

The doctor opened the door slowly. Pellam looked at the man's face and knew something bad was coming. The man sure had the technique down. Pellam had used it himself. When his father had died he'd been elected to break the news to a lot of people. He let the downcast eyes and endless loop of a sigh explain to them that terrible news was impending, before he said a word. The telepathic message of tragedy did a lot of the work for him.

Pellam saw this same expression in the eyes of the strong, young vet of a doctor, pausing in the doorway, looking at Pellam as if he were gazing at the last few seconds of his patient's good health.

"Evening," Pellam said.

Then he saw the deputy, a young man, similar in build to the doctor, baby-faced, crewcut, and he thought – his first fleeting thought – someone had stolen the camper. But their eyes explained too much. And at that moment, Pellam understood.

"Marty?"

The doctor looked at the deputy, who nodded.

He asked, "An accident?"

The deputy said, "I'm sorry, sir."

"What happened?" Pellam found himself breathless. The air had actually escaped from his lungs.

The deputy said, "His car caught fire. I'm sorry to have to tell you he was killed."

"Oh, God." Pellam closed his eyes. He felt an overwhelming, raw sense of loss. Images of the boy flipped through Pellam's head. Like still pictures. That was one thing about himself he'd always thought odd. For someone who worked in film, his memories were always static. Kodacolor snapshots. They never moved.

"Oh, God . . ." His voice faded. Suddenly, he thought of all the things he'd have to do. Who should he call? What should he say? There'd be hours of the grim, official business that he'd have to handle. Pellam, surrogate father to this poor young man. "What happened? A crash?"

The deputy, a boy not much older than Marty, but with that vest of self-assurance most cops seem to wear, said, "Truth be told, sir, appears he was doing some drugs. We found pot and some crack cocaine vials. He—"

"Crack? Marty? No, no, no . . ."

"We found the body next to the gas tank. We think some grass caught fire and he tried to put it out. Before he could, she blew up."

"He didn't do crack."

"Well, sir, I should tell you too that we got a call just before it happened. Couple men said they'd seen him selling some pot to a local boy. They—"

"No," Pellam spat out. "Impossible."

"They described the car pretty good, sir."

"Who was it? Who reported it?"

"An anonymous call. There was a foil package with a goodly bit of grass in it. And some crack. It was in the car. The glove compartment. It wasn't all burnt up."

Pellam lifted his hands to his face. He wondered if he was going to cry. He'd cried twice in the past ten years. Once was just after the funeral of a friend. The second time was when his ex had left. He'd been drunk on both occasions. He was sober now and he didn't think he was going to cry.

"If it's any consolation," the deputy said, "the coroner said it was fast." He looked at the doctor for confirmation that a fast death was better than a slow one.

The doctor handed him a paper cup. Inside were two pills, tiny white pills.

"They'll help you sleep."

Pellam shook his head but he didn't hand them back. He held the cup in both hands and stared at the two dots of pills, studying them carefully, noting the way the light, muted by the side of the paper cup, fell on them, how they were perfectly symmetrical, how they rested against each other – a kind of infinity symbol in three dimensions.

What Pellam couldn't tell them was: one of the things he was feeling was fury. He'd been after Marty for months to give up the pot. Pellam had done his share of controlled substances in his day, but had been shocked to find that Marty had smuggled a few nickel bags into Mexico. When Pellam had found them, he'd pulled the boy from bed, pinning him to the cold metallic sides of the camper just before dawn, demanding to know where the rest of the stash was. He owned up and handed it over to Pellam, who threw it out. Marty promised he'd abstain while they were driving together.

Would the boy have gone back on his word?

And crack? He'd never even mentioned that.

"Uhm, what?—" Pellam started to ask the deputy but his thoughts jammed. The men looked at him patiently. He remembered. "What should I do?"

The doctor said, "You don't have to do anything at all but get some rest. I still don't want you out of bed till tomorrow."

"But—"

The young deputy held teardrop-shaped sunglasses with haze-cutting yellow lenses – right out of a sixties biker movie. The sincere, well-scrubbed man hooked a thumb into a leather mesh belt and said, "The coroner's doing his report right now; we've already called the young man's family. And your film studio."

His family . . .

Hello, Mrs Jacobs. You don't know me, but I worked with your son . . . The two of us, we got our asses thrown out of a whorehouse in Nogales about three weeks ago . . .

The deputy continued, "We're making arrangements to ship the body back to Los Angeles. We figured you'd want to be traveling with him, sir, so we've booked you on the same flight. The local funeral home's agreed to transport the body to Albany airport. That'll be American Eagle flight 6733, day after tomorrow."

"If he's well enough to travel," the doctor said.

Your son, Mr Jacobs, was smoking a nugget of crack and got blown up . . .

"Of course," the deputy said. "Sure." The man leaned forward and Pellam saw a roll of dense fat encroach over the black belt of his Sam Browne harness, Vaseline-shined patent leather. The deputy said, "I don't like, you know, drugs much, sir. Especially if he was into selling them to some of our young people. But I'm truly sorry about your friend. What happened, wasn't fair. All outa proportion, you know what I mean?"

The man's battleship-gray eyes were tight with sorrow and Pellam thanked him. He looked again at the pills. The cup wasn't waxed and he found that his sweat had left fingerprints on the sides.

The doctor said, "Take those now. You need rest."

Pellam couldn't speak. He nodded.

"We'll leave you alone. You want some company or anything, my wife and I live a hundred yards up the road. There'll be someone here all night, a nurse. Just tell her and she'll get me."

"Thanks."

The men left the room. Pellam set the cup on the tabletop. He misjudged the distance and it hit the edge and fell to the floor. He heard one, or maybe both of the pills, rolling somewhere, endlessly. He didn't even look down. He lay back in bed and stared at the ceiling as the dusk turned into night and finally he slept.

The noise.

Sitting in the Winnebago, Pellam remembered the way the

boy would sit sideways in the camper's small bunk and swing his Adidas back and forth. The thud-thud, pause, thud-thud. A monotonous heartbeat.

God, it was quiet. Pellam cocked his head and couldn't hear a thing. A hum, but that was in his head. (Well, he heard Marty's voice and his laugh and the fake heartbeat of his boots but those were in his head too.) No airplane drone, no diesels. No children whooping as they played. Pellam sat in the driver's seat of the camper, looking back into the living quarters. The pain in his back was less when he sat upright. Standing was agony, unless he leaned. For some reason when he moved the pain wasn't as bad as standing still.

Ah, Marty . . .

He stood up. The tragedy tired him out more than the injuries did. He walked stiffly. He'd refused the cane the doctor recommended. There was a black scab on his head and the bruise now had some green in it.

While he still had the courage, he filled a Macy's shopping bag with the boy's belongings. He rested, sitting on the bunk in the camper, looking at the bag for a few minutes, the big brown-red logo, the white, spidery wrinkles. Pellam stood, emptied the bag and packed the contents back into his own leather suitcase, which he'd bought on Rodeo Drive eight years before, folding the boy's shirts and jeans and Jockey shorts as careful as if he were doing piece cleaning in a Beverly Hills laundry.

Then he sat and studied the suitcase for a half hour.

After he'd been released from the clinic a few hours before, the first thing he'd done was shave. He'd passed a mirror, and his face, with the uneven beard laced with gray, had shocked him. He looked like he was a badly abused 50. Then he'd called Marty's father. It had not been a good conversation. The man, a retired studio gaffer, blamed Pellam. He wasn't contemptuous, he wasn't snide, but throughout the conversation, Pellam could hear the pedal tone of suspicion – as if Pellam had supplied the drugs that had killed his son. Pellam wondered what the man looked like, what his house was like, what his relationship with Marty had been. The boy had complained about his parents a lot but most of the examples the boy cited made Pellam think: And the problem is what exactly? Marty bitched about the time they took away car privileges for a month after he'd passed out drunk in a HoJo's off the Eden's Expressway. And the time they made him go to a counselor when he went through a spell of cutting classes.

All high school stuff – bitching and moaning.

Pellam also asked to speak to Marty's mother. He felt a wave of relief when the boy's father said that wouldn't be a good idea. Then he'd hung up and lain back in the camper cot.

He clicked the heavy brass latches back and forth. The suitcase had cost him a thousand dollars.

Pellam felt the bottle of Demerol in his pocket, took it out and tossed it into one of the kitchen drawers. He needed something different. He slowly crouched down and reached into a cabinet. Out came a bottle of mescal, a quarter full, with a bloated white worm in the bottom. Pellam poured a double shot and drank the liquid down in two swallows. He coughed and felt the crackling wave from his chest up to his face and the nearly instantaneous deflating of the pain. He poured one more, smaller, and again began the slow crouch to replace the bottle. He set it in the back of the cabinet but it landed on something and fell forward. The

loose cork stopper fell out and a quarter cup of liquor spilled out
before he could snatch the bottle up again. "Damn." He managed
to save the worm. Pellam reached in the back and felt for what
the bottle had landed on. It was soft and crunched. He jerked
his hand back, thinking: Rat, mouse . . .

He looked. Just a Baggie. He reached in and pulled it out.
Filled with Marty's stash. He looked at it for a long moment
then wrapped it in paper towels, which he soaked under the
low-pressure water tap and wadded up. This he dropped into
a brown paper bag, crumpled that up and then stepped outside
and tossed the whole thing into a refuse basket.

Pellam hefted the suitcase, wheezing painfully from the effort,
and left the camper. He walked stiffly through the cold autumn
sunlight to the Greyhound depot, which took up a small portion
of a gas station on Main Street. He paid to have the bag shipped
to Marty's parents.

The clerk stroked the leather. "That's a fine suitcase."

"Yessir," Pellam said, and as it joined other luggage on a
baggage cart, walked listlessly outside.

He was reminded of the last time he went hunting with his
father – in his hometown, Simmons, New York, probably no
more than sixty or seventy miles from where he now stood.

Walking then through the same stubbly grass he now limped
over, smelling the same scent of damp foliage, bathed in the
same pale cast of light. Twenty-five years ago Pellam Senior had
struggled through the fields, lifting the long Browning shotgun
with an effort and missing even the slowest of pheasants. Two
days later the man had collapsed with the first of the heart
attacks that would eventually finish him.

Pellam associated the hunting trip with his father's death.

That memory came back to him now and would not leave.

He walked slowly, favoring his left foot to ease some of the dull ache in his back. Should've taken the damn cane the doctor had offered him, he thought again.

The top of the park had been roped off by the police. A thin yellow tape that said, "Sheriff's Department," every few inches stretched from one thick rusted pipe to another. There was a chain on the ground attached to one pipe; they could have used that to bar the entrance but Pellam guessed the cops wanted the chance to use all their crime-fighting gear. He walked around the pipe and started to climb toward the summit of this hill.

Pellam, breathing hard against the pain, reached the top of the drive and stopped.

Obliterated.

He walked to the center of the parking area – what had been grass and gravel was now just a pile of rich dark earth and the surrounding mess made by the dozer, whose tread marks he'd seen on the way up but hadn't thought anything of.

Obliterated.

In the exact center – probably just where Marty's car had been – there was no trace of scorch marks, no trace of footprints, no car treads. Just a dry foamy powder of dug-up dirt like a huge round grave. He stayed here for a long time. Mostly just walking around in slow circles, listening to the birds and the whiplashing wind in the leaves; there was really nothing to see. Nothing at all.

"What happened?"

"Happened?" the deputy asked.

They were standing outside the camper, parked on Main Street. The beefy deputy looked familiar. Pellam thought he was maybe the same one who'd helped him to the clinic after his accident. (What was the driver's name? May? Mary? No, Meg. That was it. Meg.) The law enforcer stood with his arms pushed out from his body by a lot of biceps muscle. He noticed the man's .357 had rubberized combat grips. He wondered if the gun had ever been fired anywhere but on a range. This deputy also had teardrop-shaped glasses though his had lavender-tinted lenses.

"I get to where the accident was," Pellam explained, "and the ground's all plowed over."

Lavender?

"Oh, that. What it was, they figured it would be, you know, discouraging for people to see where it happened."

Discouraging? "How do you mean?"

"Wasn't my decision. I don't really know. I just heard, what with leaf season here and all, it might hurt tourist trade."

"Discouraging?" Pellam asked in exasperation.

The deputy answered in a monotone. "It was kind of unpleasant. A bad fire, you know. Blood. We get a lot of hunters too. We—"

"Then why was the tape still up?"

"Tape?"

"The police tape. That'd discourage tourists too pretty fast, you'd think."

"Oh, the tape. You're right, sir. We forgot about it. But thanks for bringing it to our attention."

"You're welcome," Pellam said. "What happened to the car?"

"Car?"

The miniature troops with needles were climbing up and down Pellam's back, working hard. He thought about the Demerol. He thought about tequila, with or without worms. The pain was bad and he was losing patience fast. "My friend's car, the one that burned?"

"Yessir?"

"I'd like to take a look at it."

"Don't think that'd be possible."

"Why not?"

Not a nick in his deputy soul. The man was a real side of beef. "Well, sir, it just wouldn't."

"I see. That explains it." The men stood facing each other, the deputy scanning the street for crime. Pellam scanning the man's face. "If you could just tell me where it might be."

"I really don't know. I just know it was hauled away after the investigation."

"You do any forensics?"

"I really—"

"Got it," Pellam said. "Never mind." They both did the street scan this time. Pellam looked back and asked, "I don't remember what the company was. Would you know?"

"Company?"

"Where my friend rented the car."

"We don't have any Avis or Hertz here. Or nearby."

"It would be more helpful to know where he *did* rent it, rather than where he didn't."

"Sillman's Garage, I think it was. Up the road a quarter mile."

"Thanks."

The deputy said, "Kleman's Funeral Home's made all the arrangements."

"Thank you, officer. Appreciate it."

"Not at all, sir. I was to L.A. once. Me and the wife went to Disneyland. You know, the real one."

"Uh-huh."

"Suspect you'll be going back for the funeral. The mayor's got an airline ticket—"

"No, I won't be going."

There must have been a flicker somewhere in the brain, but there's wasn't one in the eyes. "No?"

"I'll be staying around for a while."

"Around here?"

"That's right."

"Oh. We expected you'd be leaving."

"Yeah, well, I won't be. Now, I'd like to see the police report. And—"

"Can't do it, sir."

"What?" Pellam felt the anger popping like fire-crackers.

"That's not public record material."

"Public record material?"

"That's right, sir."

"Well, I'm not public. I was his friend."

"Sorry, sir."

"How about the coroner's report? Is that public record material too?"

"Nosir, it's not. But all it says is he died as a result of injuries caused by a fire of his own making. I'm pretty much quoting."

"Officer, someone killed my friend. There were incidents of vandalism against our camper before he was killed and . . ."

"In Cleary?"

"That's right," Pellam said.

"I don't recall you reported them."

"We didn't. I didn't think anything of them until this happened."

"Yessir. Let me ask you, you drive into any small town, the local kids probably go fooling around some with your vehicle, don't they? Pranks. That's happened before, hasn't it?"

"Sure, but—"

"There you go."

"But it's never happened the day before one of my friends is murdered."

"Murdered? Nosir. The coroner said it was accidental."

"I guess there's not much more you can tell me."

"That's right, sir." The sunglasses went back on and the big man's eyes turned a delicate shade of purple. He said, "You staying around, sir, I'd be a bit careful. Already, these couple accidents. Maybe you're kind of a bad luck fellow."

Pellam said he'd be careful, but he was thinking there was a good chance the deputy was right.

———•◦•———

5

Alan Lefkowitz sat in his huge, completely immaculate office, rocking back and forth in a leather desk chair, and looked out the windows, which were also huge and completely immaculate. Beneath him the traffic on Santa Monica Boulevard flowed past Century City. His eyes were on this wide road, full of nice cars, but his thoughts were solely focused on Upstate New York.

President and principal shareholder of Big Mountain Studios, Lefkowitz, 52, put in at least ten sweaty hours a day working on his film projects. A law school graduate, a successful former agent, he took continuing education classes at UCLA and USC in accounting and finance – at an age when many of his friends (well, this was Hollywood; call them *colleagues*), also producers, were delegating the hard work to underlings and spending mucho time engaged in the "Development" work (that is: thinking in Palm Springs and drinking at the Beverly Hills Hotel).

Also on the asset side of the balance sheet: Lefkowitz had integrity. He'd pretty much resisted Hollywood's strongest gravity, which pulled producers toward teenage comedies, buddy cop movies, special effects – fat science fiction and horror films. His own orbit wasn't as lofty as his favorite directors, Bergman, Fassbinder, Kurosawa and Truffaut, but in his heart he wanted to make quality films.

With film schools pumping out students who learned *cinema* (not, no, never *movies*), there was no lack of independent directors in the U.S. making wonderful, small, serious flicks. But Lefkowitz's particular talent was that he worked within the system. His films were mostly financed, and wholly distributed, by major studios, one of which he presently had a five-movie housekeeping deal with (this being one of the better gold rings in contemporary movieland). Balls, a temper and an ability to convince people that he had vision had managed to get him into bed with this huge entertainment conglomerate, which was putting up 80 percent of the money for any five pictures he wished to produce.

Good muscle tone, a beach permit for his Mercedes, and a housekeeping deal for five flicks. It didn't get much better than this. But, although he could legitimately be spending this lunch hour reflecting on his good fortune, what Lefkowitz was in fact obsessing about was New York, the Empire State, while he swung back and forth in a three-thousand-dollar leather chair.

The reason for this meditation sat in front of him on his desk (which was huge but not at all immaculate): a battered, red-covered script, marred with doodles and numbers and words. It was the first flick in the five-movie deal. A dark and lyrical film called *To Sleep in a Shallow Grave*. A picture that had no buddies, no car chases, no wisecracking teenagers, no karate fights, and not a single actor magically turned into a dog, baby or person of the opposite sex.

The property had had a strange history. The film was in turn-around – another studio had bought the script and started production. A month later, though, it had been canceled. Lefkowitz, who'd lusted to do the film ever since he'd read the book it was based on years before, immediately snatched up the rights. But buying a turn-around property meant paying a premium; he had not only to pay for the script itself but he also had to reimburse the first studio for its production expenses. So what should have been a small art film became overnight a big-budget monster.

Then a famous rule in Hollywood proved true: If anybody wants it, everybody wants it. Last week, two other studios started bidding for the film.

Loyalty in Hollywood is a moving target and Lefkowitz's studio would have sold the property out from underneath him in a minute, except that under his contract he had an absolute right to make the movie.

Absolute, that is, *provided* the film met a complicated series of production deadlines. It now seemed there was a serious possibility that these deadlines might be missed. Already the company was two weeks behind schedule and Lefkowitz knew that the studio lawyers had notified the production execs that if principal photography didn't begin in three weeks, all bets were off. Lefkowitz would be in breach, and *Shallow Grave* would disappear from his company faster than a gold chain on the streets of New York.

Lefkowitz was reflecting on this when the assistant producer, a handsome, intense thirty-year-old, walked through the door.

Since he'd been working for Lefkowitz, the young man, who'd been so eager and talked so flippantly about ball-busting when he'd accepted the job, didn't look so young anymore. He definitely wasn't as eager. And the only balls he thought about regularly were his own.

"He's calling at three," the AP announced.

Lefkowitz examined his Oyster Perpetual. Five minutes. "Tell me what happened."

The assistant producer began, "Marty—"

"Who's Marty?"

"Jacobs. Pellam's assistant."

"Okay."

"He was killed, and—"

"Jesus."

"Pellam ended up in the hospital. I'm not sure but the way the sheriff explained it they seem to be separate accidents."

"What happened to Marty?"

"The car blew up."

"Jesus. What about his family?"

"The sheriff called and he told them. I made a call for your office. You don't have to do anything, but—"

Lefkowitz said, "We'll send flowers. You know that florist, the one I mean?"

"Will do."

"I'll write a note too. How's Pellam?"

"I'm not sure. All I know is I got a message saying that he was going to be calling in at three."

"We should get mobiles in all the honey wagons. It's crazy we don't. Look into that, okay?"

"Youwant, yougot."

"Any chance we'll get sued?"

"By who?"

"Marty's family?"

"I don't know . . . But there's something I've got to tell you, Alan. It gets kind of worse."

"How could it get worse?"

"The mayor of the town where it happened? Cleary? He called. Crazy man. I'm talking PMS. They won't issue permits."

"Oh, Christ in a tree. Oh, Christ."

"It's like a real small town. They found the stuff—"

"What stuff?"

"Aw, Marty had a little grass on him. They said some crack too, but I don't think—"

"Brother," Lefkowitz whispered. He looked out at the huge, immaculate highway. He closed his eyes. "Why, why, why? . . ." He spun around and faced the AP. "Any chance we can buy our way in?"

"I tried. Thousands. I practically gave him head."

"And?"

The AP swallowed. "He called me a ghoul. Then he called me a prick. Then he hung up on me. It's cratered, Alan. The whole's project's cratered."

Lefkowitz felt numb. A moment passed. Finally he asked, "Pellam's okay, though?"

The phone rang. Both men looked at their watches. It was three. The AP said, "Why don't you ask him?"

Pellam leaned his head against the glass of the phone booth. Cleary still had booths with squeaky, two-panel doors. He looked at two initials carved into the aluminum; otherwise there was no graffiti. One set of initials looked like *JP*. He listened to the buzz of the phone ringing. He felt the vibration of the healing skin under the bandage on his temple.

Alan Lefkowitz came on the phone himself, something he had never done. No secretary. No AP. Just the soft voice of a tanned, fit, eccentric, multimillionaire producer.

"John, how are you? What happened?"

He sensed some real sympathy.

"Fine, Lefty. I'm okay." Pellam then told him in general terms about the accidents – Meg's running into him, Marty's death.

Lefkowitz said, "The permits. What happened?"

"Permits? What about them?" Pellam was squinting. No, it wasn't *JP* written on the phone booth wall. It was *JD*. Below that, in marker: *Tigers, they're number one!!!* One thing about the country: teenagers were literate. In Manhattan he'd seen a similar sign. *Debbo and Ki there the best!*

"They're not issuing permits. The mayor, or somebody. Didn't anybody tell you?"

Pellam felt the shock. He burned with a wave of sudden fever. A week's work, wasted.

Marty's death, wasted.

"I didn't hear. Did they say why?"

Lefkowitz said, "They found some shit on him. I don't know, pot or something. You guys . . ."

"Alan, Marty wasn't smoking when he died. I don't know what happened but it wasn't that. I found his stash. It hadn't been opened."

"Whatever . . . You know I don't have any choice."

"It wasn't Marty's fault." Pellam focused outside the glass

and found he was staring directly into the window of Dutchess County Realty. The awning was down and the lights inside were on. There was nobody in the office.

"Well, I'm sorry, John. But you understand."

"Sure." Then it occurred to Pellam that there were two conversations going at once. He said, "Actually, no, Alan, I don't understand. What're you talking about?"

"I've got to let you go."

"Alan, what are you saying?"

"I'm saying you're fired, John."

"What?" *Just like that?*

"I thought that little incident a few years ago would have taught you a lesson."

In a low voice Pellam said, "What the hell do you mean by that?"

"I'm back at square one, thanks to you and Marty."

"I'm telling you Marty was murdered. It was a setup."

Lefkowitz seemed distracted. "Get the wagon to the New York office. We'll have your check waiting for you."

"Just—"

Lefkowitz said, "Sorry, John. I got no room for mistakes with this project."

He hung up.

"—like that?"

The first thing Meg Torrens did when she woke up: she put her two-carat diamond ring on her index finger then lay back in bed for fifteen minutes and tried to think about nothing.

It was a form of meditation she'd read about somewhere. It cleared your mind, made you healthier, relaxed you, made you more creative. It didn't always work, but even if not, the discipline required – working with your brain like an unruly puppy – seemed helpful. Marginally helpful. *Mademoiselle* helpful. *Better Homes & Gardens* helpful.

Beside her, Keith stirred slightly. His breathing was slow.

She glanced at him, closed her eyes.

Thinking about nothing.

A bird trilled in the distance, a truck shifted gears on the grade of Lampton Road.

Nothing, nothing, nothing.

An instant before the alarm rang, she sensed it in her mind. An electronic *Bzzzzt*. Meg opened her eyes and just as the Seiko went off, reached over to tap the off button. She patted Keith on his solid shoulders. He was ten years older than Meg and had some serious businessman fat on him. But she didn't mind that. His legs and butt were thin; you could get away with a lot of belly if everything else stayed in line. He had a broad, handsome face, the face of an actor who played kindly merchants and railroad owners. His hair was dense and unruly and he forced it into shape with spray and split it with a ruler-straight part. Meg regularly talked him out of dye; she thought salt-and-pepper was sexy.

Keith reached up and squeezed her hand, muttering something. She moved closer to him, smelling the warm body sleep scent puff out from under the bellows of the sheet and comforter.

The tip-off was his wristwatch.

Keith groggily pulled the Rolex off his wrist and dropped it heavily on the bedside table. When he took off the watch she knew what was coming.

His hands began to wander.

"Honey . . ." she said, something of a protest. But let herself be pulled over to him.

They kissed. She pulled off the violet Victoria's Secret teddy he'd bought for her several months ago, offering the box shyly, as if he was worried she'd be offended.

The familiar routine began. He kissed her long, on her mouth, her chin, working downward. He lingered at her neck, taking her S-link chain in his mouth. He often did this and she wondered if the gold had a taste that he liked. Then his lips found her collarbone and he moved down toward her breasts and, slowly, slowly, to her contracted nipples.

When they made love Keith was energetic, simple, effective.

Meg was ready for him. Although from time to time she let her hands explore herself when she was taking a shower she hadn't done so since the last time they'd made love, a week ago. So now, even though it was morning, even though she wanted to bathe first, to brush her teeth, even though she didn't feel beautiful, even though she had to wake Sam in the next few minutes to get him moving in time for his schoolbus – despite all that, she felt the low kick inside her.

Meg smiled, kissed his chest and nipples, rolled him over on his back. She stroked him then moved down his belly. She felt her own passion swell when he began to grow inside her mouth.

This is what their romantic life had become – usually mornings, usually spontaneous. And Meg Torrens had no real complaints about it. True, they weren't youthfully passionate. But who is, after ten years of marriage? The compensation was that neither of them demanded too much from the other. Sex was comfortable, like browsing through antique stores or trying out new recipes. Diverting pleasures. Silent and a little anonymous. They'd learned not to intrude on each other's fantasies.

He nearly came and he held her head still. Then he sat up, rolled her over and kissed her breasts again, moved down. Licked her navel. He moved further down her trim body.

After five minutes she shuddered violently under the clever effort of his tongue and fingers. She lay gasping and smiling in the near darkness, trying to cement the moment.

Keith waited a gallant minute or two before mounting her. She held him fiercely and she moaned the way she knew he liked but was too shy to ask her for. She bit his ear. She dug nails into his back. She pressed her face against his soft, gray hair, through which a residue of sweat was building.

She curled her legs around him, she moaned again. Then, suddenly, her eyes snapped open.

The intrusion was like a slap. A spray of cold water.

No!

The memory of the sound wouldn't go away.

Bzzzzt.

She couldn't place it, but it intruded unrelentingly. It was spoiling the entire moment. She hated it.

No, no, go away, please.

Then, she remembered. At the same instant Keith gripped her furiously and squeezed the air from her lungs. She felt the contractions and the fierce tensing of his hips.

That was the intrusion – a sound.

Playing in her mind, over and over, was the satisfying whir of the film as it shot out of the man's Polaroid camera. She pictured his narrow face, she heard his voice. She saw the glossy dark scar. *A machine gun. An Oldsmobile. You've lived here how long?*

Keith rolled off. She pressed her legs together tightly and stretched. They lay together for five minutes. (Nothing, nothing, think about nothing!) Then slowly Meg sat up. A *local?* she thought angrily. He thought I was a local?

Who'd lived here *ten* years?

"Love you," Keith said.

"Me too."

She sat for a moment then saw her face in the mirror. A confused, frightened look in her eyes. She smiled at her husband and forced all thoughts of the location scout out of her mind. She swung out of bed and walked into the hall.

The bathroom was carpeted in black shag. The shower curtain was black with red roses on it and the walls were pink. (Meg couldn't decide whether the decor was eighteenth-century country or Victorian bordello.) She shook her head and tossed her light blonde hair with her fingers. It stuck out wildly in all directions from yesterday's spray and the electric curlers she set it with. It would take half an hour of diligent work to turn herself into a blond, bouffanted, real estate agent.

She fixated on the mirror. Her lips had always bothered her. They were nearly flat planes and she used two subtly different shades of lipstick to give them dimension. And, when she remembered, she would keep the bottom lip curled forward slightly. This tended to make her look more pouty than sensuous, but, in her experience, men liked pouting women as much as sexy ones.

Out of the shower, drying her thin legs and waist, Meg stepped on the scale automatically, though she'd never weighed a pound over 105 since a month after Sam was born. She combed her hair straight, pulled on her robe.

She called down the hall, "Sam, let's go, honey."

In the bedroom Keith was still in bed. He seemed asleep. As she passed he groped playfully for her butt. She slapped his hand gently then tugged at his arm. "Up, up!" she called. "The world awaits."

He groaned.

Meg walked down the stairs. She didn't put on her slippers until she stepped into the kitchen. She liked the touch of the carpet on her feet in the morning.

Fifteen minutes later, rolls were warm, coffee was hot. Meg was sipping from a heavy mug and wondering where they got the crazy names for kids' breakfast cereal when Sam came thumping down the stairs. He was his father's son in many ways. In the morning he was groggy, puffy faced, his sandy hair going at odd angles. But unlike Keith (a pudgy boy forty years ago, a pudgy man now), Sam was lean and tall.

And brilliant. This gift *was* from his father. If Meg had said prayers, she would have thanked the generic all-powerful spirit she nearly believed in that Sam had received the gene for Keith's brains, not hers.

Meg Torrens, with two years' community college, was going to be the mother of Samuel K. Torrens, Ph.D., *cum laude*.

Keith came down the stairs slowly, wearing knife-crease gray slacks, a white dress shirt, a green-and-black striped tie.

She poured coffee. He said, "Thanks, darling," and started working on a sweetroll.

They paid the premium for the *New York Times* but Keith preferred the Cleary *Leader*, which if you read it regularly would really scare the hell out of you, and make you think that Dutchess County was filled with nothing but murderers, child molesters and the mournful classmates of teenagers who'd driven the family car into trains while tanked up on their father's vodka. Today was Tuesday, publication day, and he read the thin paper hungrily, boning up on local gossip.

"Hey, Mom," Sam said, sitting forward on his chair, making valleys in his cereal. "What happens when a duck flies upside down?"

Meg knew that success as a mother, just like success as a politician, is largely dependent on cheerful insincerity. She turned to him, thought a moment, then frowned. "I have no idea. What?"

"He quacks up!" He laughed. Meg did too and wiped a bit of Smurf off his cheek. Keith grunted a laugh and ruffled the boy's hair.

Sam dodged away and shook his hair back into place. "Dad!"

Keith looked at him for a moment, an affectionate gaze, then turned back to the paper. There was a shyness about Keith, even with his wife and son, and he didn't look up as he said, "If I don't have to work, how about going to the game on Saturday?" It was as though he was afraid they'd turn him down. He added, "They're playing . . ." He looked at Meg. "Who're they playing?"

The high school team's standing and upcoming opponents were pretty much common knowledge in Cleary. Meg said, "No game this weekend, remember? It's the festival. If you're taking time off we can all go."

"Yeah!" said Sam, his voice breaking.

"Sounds good."

Meg said, "Maybe I should enter my apple butter."

Keith said slowly, "Well, sure. You could."

He and Sam looked at each other.

She said, "It wasn't *that* bad."

"It like tasted good, Mom. It really did."

"Maybe," Keith said delicately, "next time, just some food color."

"Critics." Meg turned to the *Times* classified real estate section and added up the commissions she would have made last year if she were selling houses in Scarsdale or Greenwich instead of Cleary.

At seven-thirty: the bus arrived and Meg pitched Sam his pro-wrestling lunch box. He hugged her then disappeared out the front door.

Keith said, "That guy ever call the insurance company?"

Meg asked, "What guy?"

"Your accident? That guy with the movie company."

Bzzzt.

"Oh, him. I'd forgotten about him. I don't know. I'll call Jim. Find out."

Keith looked at his watch, muttered, "Damn," and walked quickly up the stairs. He returned ten minutes later; he'd added spit-shined shoes and a navy blazer to his uniform of the day.

They brushed cheeks and he walked out the screen door. She called, "Bye, honey."

Keith said something to her and lifted his hand but she missed his words. They were obscured by a sound that started running through her head again, the whir of the Polaroid, which this time, try though she might, she could not force out of her thoughts.

———•═══•———

6

"Mr Pellam."

Pellam smiled and shook the man's hand; glancing around him.

The scene was something out of a really bad movie – one that Alan Lefkowitz wouldn't have come close to. He was in a little, close-smelling town-government office. A lumber yard calendar on the wall, a dead plant in a drought-struck flower pot, a few yellowing files, a map dated 1964. The smell of bitter old coffee, papers, musty cardboard.

And at the desk: a local pol – looking just like Oral Roberts – with a tight grin he no way in the world meant.

"You're the mayor, that correct?"

"Hank Moorhouse." Silver hair, baby-blue suit, shiny pale green shirt and striped brown and yellow tie. Jowls and chicken skin. His eyes were bloodshot. "Mayor and town magistrate. First, let me say how sorry we are about what happened to your friend. Is there anything I can do?"

Pellam discreetly studied Moorhouse's Sunday-go-to-meeting

outfit. "I'd like to see the coroner's report on my friend's death. The deputy—"

And damn if the man wasn't nodding and looking over his desk. He pulled a file out from underneath a stack of papers. "Sure thing, sir. Here you go."

Pellam opened it. On top of the report were pictures of Marty's body – taken at the scene of the fire and during the autopsy. It was like a jolt of electricity seeing those photos. He closed his eyes for a moment then glanced at Moorhouse's impassive face and shuffled the glossy pictures to the back. He read the short, badly typed report.

The cause of death was shock and loss of blood due to massive burns. There was evidence of some alcohol in the blood stream but no drugs.

"How do you figure he was killed doing drugs if the coroner didn't find any in his system?"

Moorhouse sniffed a cautious laugh. "Oh, well, that's easy. Pretty clear he was killed before he had a chance to smoke anything."

Pellam handed the file back. "I'd like to see the police report, if it's possible."

"Sorry. That's not public—"

"—record material."

Moorhouse said, "Nosir. That's correct."

"Did you consider the possibility he was murdered?"

"That's not my job, sir. The sheriff and the coroner make that determination. Tom – he's the sheriff – he's out of town for a day or so. And as for the coroner, well, what does that tell you?" Moorhouse tapped the file. "County doc seemed to think it was pretty straightforward."

Pellam asked, "What about the permits?"

Moorhouse swivelled back in his green leatherette chair. "Don't need to see me about that. Town clerk can issue them."

"He can?"

"Yep. Deer'll cost you twenty-five. Bear's protected. Geese—"

Pellam smiled. "I understand you decided not to issue obstruction permits to my movie company."

"Oh, that. True."

"Why?"

Moorhouse pulled an inch of Scotch Magic tape off a dispenser, rolled it up and began chewing it. "Your friend, if he'd got himself killed in a car crash or racing out into the street to rescue a little girl we'd put banners up and welcome your outfit to town. But the boy was smoking crack—"

"He wasn't smoking crack. He never did crack. I traveled with him for months."

"Well, we found crack vials – pot there too."

"I doubt it was his."

"Somebody walked up and dropped a foil-wrapped package full of hash in a burning car?"

"If the police found it there then, yes, that's exactly what happened."

"What'd you be suggesting, sir?"

This man, like the town deputies, was getting some serious mileage out of "sir." The word seemed to have a different meaning every time he said it.

"He couldn't have had any with him."

"And why would you be so sure?"

"I just am."

"Yessir, well, doesn't really matter. It's in our discretion to issue permits or not. We chose not to. Nothing more needs to be said. We're a self-sufficient community."

Pellam blinked, wondering what on earth that meant.

"I'm saying we don't need your movie here, sir. We don't need your Hollywood money."

"I'm not suggesting you do."

Moorhouse held his hands up. "So. That's it. There's nothing more to be said."

"I guess not."

Moorhouse's wattles stretched as he broke into a shallow smile. He opened his desk. "Now, we've got a ticket for you . . . Ha, that'd be an *airline* ticket. Not parking."

"Oh, I'm not leaving."

"You're not . . ."

"Leaving."

"Uh-huh. I see."

Pellam said, "Real pretty around here. The leaves and everything."

"We do get tourists from around the world."

Pellam said, "I can understand why."

"So, you're just going to look at some leaves for a while?"

"Well, see without those permits I'm out of a job. So may as well take a bit of a vacation."

"Vacation." The Scotch tape got chewed and the eyebrows moved a fraction of an inch closer. "That's wonderful. I'm glad our little burg made an impression on you. Uhm, one thing I'd mention, for your benefit. You've got that camper of yours. Which you can't park on the town streets two to six a.m. You'll get yourself a ticket, you do." The grin tightened. "That's parking. *Not* airline. Ha."

"And I'll bet that's enforced pretty well."

"Tom and his boys do their best."

Pellam walked to the door. He stopped. "The car?"

"Car, sir?"

Damn, gotta learn how to say that. *Sir, sir, sir, sir* . . . It seemed very Zen. Like a mantra.

"The car Marty was in. The one that burned. You still have it in custody, don't you?"

"Believe it's been sold."

"In two days?"

"Sold for scrap."

"But how?"

"Selling a car's easy, sir."

"I mean, there'll be lawsuits, won't there? There'll be some kind of investigation."

"The police investigation ended with the coroner's report. You curious, you'll have to ask the rental place."

"Obliged for your help . . ." Pellam opened the door. He turned back and nodded. "Sir."

Meg Torrens listened to the familiar squeak of her chair as she sat back. It was the oldest chair in an old office, a teacher's dark oak chair with an elaborate spring mechanism underneath a carved seat that matched no posterior she'd ever seen.

"Wex," Meg said, "I can promise you, they aren't going to go with less than R-1. This is Cleary P&Z you're talking about."

Wexell Ambler sat across from her and looked unhappily at the survey in front of him.

The midmorning lull was in full swing at Dutchess County Realty. In residential real estate evenings and Saturdays were the hectic times though that was an adjective Meg doubted could ever legitimately describe business in Cleary (No, Mr Pellam, you are one hundred percent on point there: people *aren't* busy in Cleary. Never have been, never will be). The small office, littered with three desks and unmatched chairs, scarred bookcases, an eclectic assortment of lamps, which were always illuminated because the window awning had been frozen in the down position for a year. The room was decorated with one yellowing ficus tree, some primitive paintings of houses one broker's daughter had done in grade school and a huge roll-up map of Cleary and environs, which made the town look more impressive than it ever could in person.

Ambler twisted the survey several ways and studied it. None of the positions cheered him up.

Wex Ambler was a tall man – six four. Lean. In his early fifties. He was thin on top, with a few renegade tufts of fine hair going in different directions. He had a long face and he continually reminded himself to keep his chin high; otherwise his neck flesh became a small wattle. He played golf, he jogged two miles a day and was a member of the town council. He believed (one of the few things he had in common with most of the rest of the local population) that he was the wealthiest man in Cleary. He owned Foxwood, the one apartment complex in town, and was the most successful real estate developer in this part of the county. (Real estate and death of a rich relative being the only ways people in Cleary could come by real money.)

Meg's co-broker of the day, a horsy, blond woman named Doris, was ticking off items on her to-do list with a tiny flick of a mechanical pencil. "Ah, huh," she said with each accomplishment. Meg fired a look of irritation at the self-congratulations – Doris missed it completely – and she turned back to Ambler.

"They're not . . ." Ambler searched for a word. "Progressive."

Meg laughed, her expression saying: You just figured that out about Cleary?

She knew that Ambler had told a number of people – his ex-wife, his associates, even virtual strangers – that his life goal was not to amass a huge reservoir of money. What he loved was the entrepreneurial process itself. It didn't matter what he did, as long as the challenge was there. The process held more intrigue and excitement than the capital gains did.

Still, he told her now, "The difference to me between three-quarter acre lots and two acres . . ." He looked up, calculated. ". . . is about eight million dollars. Total. For all lots."

"But that's pretax," she said seriously, frowning. She was trying to joke.

Ambler wasn't amused. "A variance'll take forever."

Meg said, "It's the best land north of the city. It's—"

"Meg," Doris interrupted her jotting. "There. That's him. Didn't squash him so bad, looks like."

She looked up and watched a thin man in jeans walk down Main Street.

"Is that? . . ." Meg asked.

"Yup," Doris said.

Ambler's eyes followed him. "Who?"

Doris turned to him with an excited face. "Didn't you hear? The man from the movie company. Meg ran into him in her car." She smiled at Meg and continued to tick away on her list.

But Ambler said, "I know. I heard. I heard you went to his hotel room."

Meg blinked. Doris's head shot up. She stopped ticking.

Ambler shook his head. "I meant his hospital room."

Meg's eyes flared. "I went to see how he was."

Doris said, "You didn't tell me that."

Meg said, "Did you hear about his partner?"

"No," Doris asked.

"The accident?" Meg continued.

"What accident?" Ambler looked at her.

"I don't know much about it. Just that he was smoking dope and it blew up. Killed him."

"My God," Doris said, "the fire in the park?"

"That was it, yeah."

Ambler said nothing. He stared out the windows.

Doris said, "Tough luck, honey. You know, Mr Ambler, last week, after those boys showed up, all Meg was talking about was trying to get an audition . . ."

"Doris," Meg barked.

Doris said to Ambler, "Meg did some modeling in Manhattan, you know. She was in *Vogue* and *Self* a couple times. *Woman's Day*."

"I think I knew that," Ambler said.

Doris continued, girlishly. "I know you were trying to get an audition, but—"

"Enough!"

"—running him over's a hell of a way to do it."

Meg mouthed *Bitch* at Doris, who blinked and retreated to her ticks.

Ambler's eyes left hers and he looked out the window, staring across the street. Meg noticed this. She zeroed in on Pellam who stood in front of Marge's, opening a Styrofoam coffee cup.

He said, "What's he doing here?"

Meg answered, "They were looking for places to shoot a movie. He's a location scout."

"No, I mean, why hasn't he left town? If his friend died . . ."

Doris said, "Well, I talked to Danny, the guy works afternoons at Marge's? He said he heard from Betty in Moorhouse's office that he's staying for a while."

"He is?" Meg and Ambler asked simultaneously.

"That's what Betty told Danny."

"So they're going to do a movie after all?" Ambler said.

Doris said, "Dunno."

Meg stared out the window, sighting on Pellam through the reversed letters. She kept her eyes there and said, "Look, Wex, I hear what you're saying but look at some of the features. It's practically flat; you're going to need zero grading. And clearing? Only a quarter of the whole package is trees and they're shallow-root pine. You don't even *have* to touch that, unless you build with leaching fields toward the trees."

"I'm not saying I don't want those plots. I'm saying I don't want two-acre zoning. If I had my way I'd want half acre."

She frowned. She said, "Why don't you just do fifty by seventy-fives? Burn out the trees and Lefrack it? Put in cinder block." There was irritation in her voice.

They both realized they'd been negotiating while they were looking out the window. They simultaneously turned to face each other. Ambler stood up. Meg frowned. She wondered if she'd offended him. He said, "I'll have to think about it."

"I've got another developer interested," Doris said.

"Who?"

"Ralph Weinberg."

"Oh. Him," Ambler said. "You'd rather sell to a . . . to someone like him?"

"His money's as good as anyone's."

Ambler was quiet for a moment. "I can't think about it now. I'm sorry."

• • •

TO SLEEP IN A SHALLOW GRAVE/
BIG MOUNTAIN STUDIOS

FADE IN:

EXTERIOR DAY, GRAVEYARD, BOLT'S CROSSING,
NEW YORK

CREDITS ROLL, as we see VARIOUS ANGLES on the cemetery. Uneven tombstones of granite, chipped and broken, thumbed down by the weather. The grass is anemic, the lighting bland, ghostly, like the bones buried here.

Pellam tossed back the bourbon and bent over his typewriter.

He had stopped by the funeral home to pay for shipping Marty's casket back to L.A. but had found the charges had already been taken care of, courtesy of Alan Lefkowitz. He'd spent a few silent minutes alone with Marty in the back room of the funeral home that had arranged for the shipment. A loading dock, really. He'd wanted to say something. But could think of absolutely no words. He found a Bible in a small chapel near the room where the casket rested. He looked for three or four minutes to find a passage that he liked. Nothing applied. He put the Bible back, touched the smooth, heavy coffin, and returned to the Winnebago.

Outside, it was a windy night, and the camper rocked slightly, reminding him of a boat, though he'd only been on water once or twice in his life. Subterranean noises rose from his stomach. The dinner of ham with fruit sauce he'd eaten at the Cedar Tap wasn't sitting well.

He returned to his typewriter, a small German portable. He hammered away.

> *. . . the graveyard is on a plateau. One hill eases down to the cemetery from the crest of the piney woods. On the other side the land glides down to the river. From that point of stability you go into the town itself. An old cannon is small and over painted, just like the park benches. The storefronts are bleached out and full of antiques no one wants, hardware that no one needs. The town has managed something remarkable – absorbed fatigue and turned it into a fuel that runs a thousand small-town dreams.*

> *ANGLE: A flagpole rung by its wind-blown rope like a bell.*

> *ANGLE: A roaring 4x4 with exhaust bubbling driven by a YOUNG MAN, who grins at a TEENAGE GIRL. He's your perfect citizen of Cleary: snotty, confident, comforting as*

*long as you share his race and ancestry. We FOLLOW
the truck to –*

*LONG ANGLE: A motorcycle coming toward us, a man
in his thirties driving slowly. There's something ominous
about him. He –*

The car door outside the Winnebago startled him. He'd seen
the lights through the curtain, but, absorbed in writing, hadn't
noticed they weren't continuing around the curve and disappearing.

"Hey, Pellam, you in there? I saw the light." A woman's
voice.

He opened the door.

"Hi there," he said and let Janine in.

"I was just passing by . . . You know." She laughed and set a
shopping bag on the table. She surveyed the rooms. "Reminds
me of, know what?, an airplane."

What was that smell? It entered with her. He thought of newly
mown grass. He looked outside then shut the door and locked it.

"This is luxury," he said. "At the studio they call these honey
wagons."

"Why's that?"

"There are several theories," he said. "None of which I really
ought to go into."

"Look, I heard about your friend. I'm so sorry."

"Thank you."

"What happened?"

Pellam believed that grief, like joy, was best explained
simply. "Car accident."

"That's so sad. Terrible." She looked like she meant it and he wondered if she was going to start crying. He really hoped she wouldn't. She said, "What I was saying the other day, about Cleary? You read about car crashes every week in the *Leader*." She surveyed him and nodded toward his thigh (scary about these small-town rumors – man, they spread fast). "How're *you*?"

"Right muscle. Wrong leg. I'll be okay."

The sorrow in her voice was gone; he was grateful that she'd expressed it but hadn't overdone the emotion.

"I'll give it a massage. I studied Rolfing."

"Maybe later. It's a bit tender right now."

She studied the camper carefully. Her eyes lingered on the one decoration: A New York Film Festival poster of Abel Ganz's *Napoleon*. She kept giving faint little laughs, as each new thing she noticed surprised her.

"I heard they aren't going to do the movie here."

"True."

"But you're staying?"

"True also. I got fired."

"No! Why?"

"It's Hollywood."

"What a downer." She didn't look real down, though. She touched his arm. "I'm sorry about the movie but I'm glad about you."

He didn't respond.

She waited a few seconds then let go and looked around again. "Don't you get claustrophobic?"

"It's not bad."

"I'm not disturbing you?" Though as she said it she was

sitting down in the small dining alcove, making herself at home.

There are times to say, Yes, you are, and times to say, No, when asked that question.

He said, "No, not at all."

"I brought you some dessert."

"Dessert?"

"I remember you liked dessert. The cake at Marge's? When you picked me up? On Monday?" Her eyebrows raised with every sentence.

"I remember, yeah."

Picked her up?

"Terrible cake," he added.

"Could've warned you. My desserts aren't terrible."

She unloaded the bag. Carefully wrapped in foil was a small package. Next came a thermos, two mugs, a jar of honey.

"Tea. Herbal tea. Rosehips and lemon grass. It's very relaxing." She opened the foil. "And brownies."

"Ah, brownies." Pellam looked at them closely. Then he grinned. "Wait. Are those . . . ? They aren't really, are they?"

"Uh-huh. They're a little bitter but, hey, so's peyote, right? They're worth it, though. Man, I'll tell you . . . It's not as strong as a Thai stick, but then again you won't wake up with a cough. You have a plate?"

He dug into the cabinet. "Plastic."

"Shame on you. Disposable? What'd nature ever do to you?" Janine cut the brownies – she'd also brought a knife. He tried one. It tasted bitter and left bits of soggy vegetation in his mouth. The tea was awful but you needed it to wash the grass down.

"Honey?" She held up a jar.

"No." He sipped the weed water. He glanced at the bottle of whisky. Was tempted. But he figured that Janine might feel that making liquor was an unnatural thing to do to plants.

"Really great," he said. She'd already finished her piece of brownie. He chewed down the rest of his.

She looked at what he was typing. "You mind?" She pulled it forward and read intently. After a few minutes she gave another of her breathy, surprised laughs. "This is fantastic. It's like poetry. Is this the way they write scripts?"

"It's the way I write scripts."

"I didn't know you were a writer."

"I write scripts that nobody reads, just like . . ." He stopped himself. He was going to say, *the way you sell houses that nobody buys.* Good line, wrong woman. ". . . everybody else in Hollywood."

"I hear you. But aren't you, like, fired?"

"It's a crazy business out there," he said without explaining further.

She read a few more portions. "Damn, Pellam. Poetry."

"The movie's good but it could be a lot better. Also, Guild scale for script doctoring is obscenely high."

"Know what it reminds me of?"

Renoir? Fellini? David Lynch?

Pellam asked, "Who?"

"Kahlil Gibran."

What? He tried to smile. Wasn't he that romance poet? Pellam hadn't read him but he believed that they used his verses in Hallmark cards.

She looked at him wide-eyed. "I really, really mean that."

"Well, thanks."

"The descriptions are fantastic."

He explained, "I think the setting in a film is another lead character. Setting a scene one place instead of another will produce a totally different movie. Like casting Denzel Washington in a lead versus Wesley Snipes. Same lines, same direction, but a different film."

Kahlil Gibran?

"You write like this, why're you just a location scout?"

"Just?"

"You know what I mean."

He did know what she meant. "I like traveling around. I don't like meetings. I don't like California. I don't own a suit—"

"That sounds like you're reciting catechism."

"In nomine Zanuck, et Goldwyn, et spiritus Warner."

"Ha. There a message in this movie?"

"The advertising department will say it's about betrayal and passion. Mostly, it's a love story, I guess."

She squinted and licked honey off her reddish finger. "You guess?"

"Love's a funny thing to pin down." Pellam broke off another piece of brownie. No buzz, no tiny people stuffing cotton in the crevices of his brain. He was disappointed.

She was surveying the inside of the camper again. She opened drawers and nodded. "You don't mind, do you?" Fully prepared to keep going, he sensed, if he'd said that he did. But then she came to a cabinet and opened it. Started to pull out a couple of battered scrapbooks.

He was up fast and lifted them, gently and laughing, out of her hands.

"Oops, sorry," she said, "I'm being nosey, huh?"

Pellam smiled and put the books away.

She looked at him for a moment. "You know, I was thinking about this today. You seem awfully familiar. There's something about you . . . Have I read anything about you?"

"Me?"

Janine shook her head. "Maybe," she said seriously, "it was in a former life."

He'd heard this one before.

Sometimes they said, "You and me, I think we're soul mates."

Sometimes they just said point-blank, "Can I come with you in the camper?"

Sometimes they never said anything but looked at him with hungry, hurting eyes. That was the hardest.

Pellam said, "Past lives, huh? Maybe you were a pioneer woman and I was a cowboy." He told her the Wild Bill Hickok story.

"Holy shit, that's terrific, Pellam, a gunslinger."

"His name – I always have to set this straight – was James Butler Hickok. Not William." He blinked and looked at the brownie. It seemed to be floating in the air. He broke off another piece and ate it. "Anyway, he was a . . ." His mind stopped working for a moment. He retrieved the end of his sentence. ". . . relative. I mean, an ancestor." He added, "On my mother's side."

Janine's eyes danced with enthusiasm. She maneuvered her taut hips out of the booth and stood up. Where was she going? There weren't many options in the camper. She asked, "He was the one with the wild west show? With Annie Oakley?"

"No, no, no – that was *Buffalo* Bill. William Cody. *Wild* Bill was a gunfighter. Fast draw and all that. Just like in the movies. Buffalo Bill hired him for a while to be in the show but he wasn't a very good entertainer. He was good at shooting people. That was about it. So maybe you knew Wild Bill in a former life."

"Oh, but your former lives aren't the same as your ancestors. But maybe you were a sheriff that Wild Bill killed and you came back—"

"He didn't kill sheriffs. He was a scout and a federal marshal."

"Okay, then an Indian warrior he killed. Or a cattle rustler. Maybe I was a squaw. And we've met a couple of times in the past . . ."

Pellam lost this train of thought completely. She had disappeared into the back of the camper. He heard her voice, muffled. "This is very comfortable." Pellam heard the bedside light click on. "Cozy, you know."

"I guess." He was moving unsteadily toward her. He said, "Maybe I was the lover of the wife of the cattle rustler . . ." Pellam stopped speaking.

Janine was lounging back. Pellam found he was staring at her breasts. She noticed his eyes and he said quickly, "Nice pin. You make it?" He pointed to a round moon face necklace made of sterling silver. It had a coy feminine face.

She leaned forward and held it out to him. He tried to focus on it. "It's a bestseller at my store." Then she frowned.

"What's the matter?"

"Well, here I bring you brownies and tea, and you don't even ask me to get comfortable."

He clicked the bedside light out. The moonlight came in through the blinds and the cold illumination was almost as bright as the lamp. "Sorry. What can I do to make amends?"

"You can start by helping me off with my boots."

She lifted her leg, and he took her calf, taut in the tight denim, in his left hand and gripped the heel of her boot. He looked down.

They were cowboy boots.

7

"How many you want?" Billy asked the boy.

Before he could answer, Bobby said, "Have four."

"What's your name again?" Billy asked.

"Ned. And sure, I'll have four."

The pancake somersaulted through the air like the bone in the movie *2001*, the bone that became a space station. What the pancake became, after Bobby maneuvered the plasticized Grand Union paper plate underneath it, adjusting for the trajectory, was just more of the boy's breakfast – flapjacks, sausage, eggs and buttered toast.

"That was, you know, totally fresh," the boy said, his eyes whipping up and down, replaying the flip. Billy nodded toward his brother and said, "Nobody flips 'em like Bobby."

Another flip. Ned, a strapping, seventeen year old, was having five pancakes, it turned out, not four.

Bobby looked shy and pleased about the good review of his talent. He didn't say anything. He wiped his hands on his Kiwanis-supplied apron.

Billy and Bobby were twins. They were about the same size as the boy, a little under six feet and maybe a hundred eighty pounds. But less of them was muscle than in the kid. They were thirty-five. They wore their dark hair similarly, Carnaby look: with long bangs. A fringe came over their ears in a slight curl. They shampooed with coal tar soap and always had a medicinal smell about them. Today, they wore brown. Bobby had on a white shirt because he'd volunteered to cook at the Kiwanis Breakfast. Billy, just hanging around and helping whoever needed help, wore a beige short-sleeved shirt printed with designs that looked like chain links.

"Whatsa time?" he asked the boy, who looked at a big, gleaming watch (birthday present, Billy thought).

"Almost eleven."

"Near quitting time for us," Bobby said. He scanned the site of the breakfast – the basement of the First Presbyterian Church of Cleary – and motioned to a nearby paper-tablecloth-covered card table. "Why don't you sit over there. We'll join you."

"Well, sure," Ned said, turning his round, red-scrubbed face to where they pointed.

Bobby made himself and his brother plates of pancakes and sausage, then plastered the stacks with smears of Parkay. He added a couple extra sausages to his and poured syrup on both plates.

He called across the room to Earl Gibson, the manager of Cleary Bank & Trust and president of the Kiwanis, and asked if it was okay for them to quit and have something to eat. And Earl came by, pumped their damp hands and said, "You bet." Then he thanked them both for doing such a good job. "Whatsyer secret, Robert?"

Bobby winked at the boy and said, "What it is, they get aerated when I send 'em up."

"He makes 'em good, Mr Gibson," Ned told Earl.

Billy said, "Aunt Gee-mima, watch yo black butt. My bro Bobby's in town."

They all laughed and the twins sat down with the boy.

The twins loved to volunteer. They were Little League coaches and they worked regularly at the Cleary Boys' Club and the Future Farmers of America. Their favorite volunteering was for this, the Fall Kiwanis Pancake Breakfast, and the Jay-Cees summer barbecue and, though they weren't married and had no children, the PTA's regular potluck suppers (nothing beat the combo of food and volunteer work).

Ned was one of those teenagers that could talk easily with adults, especially adults like the twins, who knew sports and weren't too geekish to tell an occasional Polack joke or one about girls' periods or boobs. The boy's rambling monologue was up and running by the time Billy and Bobby focused on it.

"Oh, man, I heard it was like totally awesome. Sid, he's kinduva dweeb but, you know, he can be okay sometimes, he was driving by and seen the cloud."

"Cloud?" Billy asked, eating a huge mouthful of pancakes.

"Yeah. Of smoke. He goes, 'It was totally black.' I thought he was a hatter, man, really. Like I go, 'Excuse me, I mean, *excuse* me, but gas doesn't burn black.' But then I figured it must've been tires. You hear about that illegal dump over in Jersey? They had like a million tires there and they caught fire only nobody could put it out."

"Missed that," Bobby said. He frowned. "Did you hear about that?"

Billy said, "Didn't hear about it."

Ned continued. "So what is I went by the park. Stan was there and he wouldn't let us get too close. I mean, the body was gone and everything but the car – you should've seen it. Totally nuked. Awesome!"

Bobby said, "I didn't hear about any car, what happened?"

Ned said, "The guy was freebasing or doing crack. And, man, it went up like an M80. Like what *is* freebasing?"

Bobby shrugged and finished his pancakes. He took half of one off his brother's plate. "I don't know."

"What happened to the dude who was driving?" Bobby asked.

Ned said, "Torched. Like this sausage." He grinned and held it up on a white plastic fork. He put the whole link in his mouth and chewed slowly.

"He was the guy from the movie company, right?"

Ned said, "Yeah, I guess that screws up the chance of 'em making a movie in Cleary. The other one's still here, though. His buddy."

Billy said, "I'd like to be in a movie."

Ned said, "Yeah, both you guys together! I don't think I ever saw twins in a movie." He wiped up syrup with his finger and licked it off slowly. "I think it'd be totally fresh to be in a movie. Only, you know what bothers me?"

"No telling."

"Well, think about it. In a love scene, okay? Some guy's kissing Sharon Stone or Kim Bassinger or some fox, he's gotta have a hard-on, don't you think?"

Bobby said, "You'd think."

"Man, that'd be totally embarrassing. I'd try to think about making a play at second or something but I bet I'd still get a hard-on. Oh, man, what if I *came* while I was kissing her, right in front of everybody? God, I'd die."

The twins glanced at each other. Neither of them looked like they'd die under those circumstances.

Billy said, "I think it would've been fun, have a movie made here. Then go out to the mall, to the Multiplex over in Osborne, and see Main Street up there on the screen."

Ned said, "Oh, you know what'd be great? When they kiss on screen, you know, the girl's gotta kiss you whether she thinks you're a dweeb or not. It's like in the script, so what I'd do is, I'm holding her and the director says, 'Roll it,'—"

"'Action,'" Bobby offered.

"Yeah, right, 'Action,' and what I'd do is I'd tongue her so fast, bang, just like that! And she'd have to put up with it. She'd have to look like she enjoyed it."

"But then you'd get a hard-on," Billy said, "and be all embarrassed. Was there anything left of it?"

"Of what?" Ned sucked his fork.

"The car?"

"Just the metal parts. They were all twisted and burnt up but—"

"So where's that car now?" Billy asked.

Ned said, "Jimmy and me wanted to go take a look at it. It's at Sillman's garage. They're the ones that rented it to him."

Bobby said, "What you think it's worth?"

"Worth? It's pretty totaled, man. It's like nothing's left of the back half. The engine might be okay."

Bobby looked at his brother. "Maybe we should take a look at it."

"Can't hurt."

Bobby looked at the boy's empty plate. "Hey, you want any more?"

"They're closed up," Ned pointed out.

"Hell, for you, we'll open the kitchen."

"Well, just pancakes and sausages. I don't want any eggs."

"Coming right up," Bobby said just as Billy started to say the same thing.

Wexell Ambler's house was on Barlow Mountain Road just South of Cleary. The yard ran at a shallow incline down to what was called a lake on the local maps, though it was really just a pond. A hundred years ago Samuel Bingham, the Hartford insurance magnate, wanted to surprise his wife on her fortieth birthday by giving her something she didn't already own, which didn't leave many possibilities. But he noticed a low-lying spot on their seventy-acre estate and an idea occurred to him. He dug out three hundred apple trees and dammed a small stream that ran through the property.

The result was a shallow, weedy ten-acre lake, now surrounded by houses of the sort Ambler owned: half-million dollar colonials (Ambler's was the oldest, built in 1746) and contemporaries. All two-acre-plus lots. Ambler's ex-wife had landscaped the place; it was trim and simple. Pollen-dusty hemlocks, azaleas, rhododendrons, boxwood. She'd given up on tulips and annuals. ("The damn deer can find their own entrées," the woman had said shrilly.)

Standing now at the edge of this pond, Ambler whipped his fishing rod back and forth, trying to drop the tiny dot of burgundy fly into the yellow plastic hoop floating thirty feet away. Each time he'd flick the willowy rod he came close to his target but there was an uneven breeze and he was having problems compensating. Although he'd hunted all his life and fished frequently with a spinning reel he'd only been fly-fishing for a year, and learning it was hard as hell. Still, he kept at it, patient, squinting at the hoop, which looked white through his yellow-lens glasses.

The footsteps came up slowly behind him. The steps were deliberately loud (and, he decided, male); someone was walking heavier than necessary to announce himself. So he wouldn't startle Ambler.

He glanced over his shoulder at the young man. "Mark."

"Howdy, Wex."

The man wore blue jeans, a plaid jacket, a blue down vest, engineer boots. He was in his late twenties, heavy. His thin lips curved into a sincere smile. His sand-colored moustache was irritatingly meek. He had brush-cut hair, parted in the middle. Put him in a polyester suit and he'd be a model Kmart manager. He didn't look like what he was: a facilitator. Ambler didn't particularly like the young man; on the other hand, labor and accounts receivable problems at Ambler's construction company had nearly vanished since he'd hired Mark.

The boy was chewing tobacco and Ambler hoped he'd spit ugly so he could dress him down for it. But he just kept the wad in his mouth like a New York Yankee pitcher and looked happily across the lake.

"Catching anything?" Just a salutation. Snappers, snakes and algae were the only living creatures in this lake. Everybody knew that.

"Nope."

"I've asked around. Seems like it's right. About that guy."

"He's staying around."

"Yessir."

"What for?"

"Asking questions about his friend was killed."

"Goddamn."

"You don't have to worry, Wex."

"Any chance at all that somebody saw you?"

"No. I'm sure."

"How sure?"

Mark was completely patient. It was funny how calm and patient truly dangerous people could be. "No one saw me."

"When I heard the car burned up I thought it'd be destroyed."

"I wrapped the stuff in foil. It was in the glove compartment. That may have helped."

"Helped? What do you mean?"

"I don't mean helped in a good sense. I mean, that may have kept it from burning up. There was hash and some crack vials."

As if he didn't want to hear the details Ambler asked quickly, "When you called the sheriff there's no way to trace it? Maybe they could do a voice print."

"Tom doesn't have that kind of equipment, Wex. You know that. Anyway, he was out getting his haircut. I left the message with Gladys. She doesn't even know my voice. Said a couple of us had seen him."

"I shouldn't have told Moorhouse to plow the ground over."

Ambler thought of something else. "What about fingerprints?"

Mark didn't say anything, just stared at the band of colorful trees across the pond.

Ambler said, "I'm sorry. I'm sure you thought of that. I just thought Pellam would have left. It's upsetting."

The fly went wide and caught in some reeds. "Damn," Ambler said. He pulled out his complicated fishing knife, with a hook remover and scaler on it. He was going to cut his line but then thought maybe a Canada goose might get tangled. Ambler was wearing two-hundred-dollar L.L. Bean shoes. He had no idea where his wading boots were. He sighed and started walking into the lake to free the line. He felt soft muck under his shoes. Bubbles of soft air rose around his legs.

Mark said, "You want me to do that?"

Ambler said, "No."

He walked unsteadily to the weeds, unhooked the fly then returned slowly to the shore.

"I know the kind of man he is."

"Who?"

"The man from the movie company. He's not leaving till he gets some answers." Ambler sighed.

"You know him?"

"I know his *kind*," he said impatiently.

The young man looked out over the lake, squinting at a phalanx of geese coming in for a landing. It was a wistful look – as if he wished he were sighting down the barrel of a long ten-gauge shotgun, leading a bird by ten feet. "You want me to keep an eye on him?"

"Yes, I do."

A moment passed. A swan floated past. Ambler knew that

however beautiful they were they were also mean sons of bitches.

Finally Mark said, "You want me to do anything else?"

Ambler glanced at him then dropped to his knees and began to undo the tangled fishing line.

"You're the place rents cars?" Pellam asked the young man.

The kid wore dungarees and stood under a yellow Monte Carlo, which was head high on a lift. The garage had two bays and a small office, the whole place stinking of grease and gasoline and burnt coffee. Pellam's eyes watered from fumes.

"Yessir." He was changing the oil and apart from his fingernails there didn't seem to be a fleck of grime on his body anywhere.

"That's a good trick, staying that clean."

"I don't work that hard."

Pellam yawned. He was tired. Winnebago beds are small and Janine was a big girl. Also, she was an energetic lover. A bit desperate too. It unnerved him the way she kept promising him how much she liked sex with him, how good he was. He didn't believe women were capable of that many orgasms in a two-hour period. At least not in a Winnebago bunk.

He woke up once in the middle of the night and found her crying. He'd asked her what the matter was. She said angrily he wouldn't understand. He sensed he was supposed to pry an explanation out of her but he fell asleep and woke at seven to find her foraging in the small fridge and making a huge omelette she ate out of hunger and he downed from politeness.

Pellam now asked the well-kempt garage man, "You Sillman?"

"Nosir, just work here is all."

"Is there a Sillman?"

"Yessir, but he's down in Florida."

Pellam walked to the front of the bay and looked again for the wreck. He wasn't sure he wanted to see it. It didn't matter because, although he saw a lot of decrepit cars, he didn't see any burnt wrecks.

"I understand you rented that car that got burnt up. The one the other day?"

"Oh, yeah. That was terrible, wasn't it?"

"You know what happened to the car?"

"Was here yesterday. Out back. Then she got sold."

"Sold?"

"That's right, sir. For scrap."

That *sir* again . . . Pellam asked, "Didn't anybody from the insurance company tell you not to?"

"Me?"

"Well, somebody."

"I don't know, sir. Nobody told me not to do anything. I heard that Mr Sillman settled with the boy's family. Paid 'em some good money. I heard a hundred thousand."

Man, for a town where nobody seemed in a hurry, some things got done real fast.

"Why would Sillman settle? Everybody's saying it's the boy's own fault."

"I'm not a lawyer, sir. Just a mechanic."

Pellam asked, "You know who bought it?"

"Nope."

"Who would?"

"Sillman. He's the one who sold her."

"I thought he was in Florida."

"Clearwater."

"But you said—"

"Oh, he left at noon."

"And that's all you know about it?"

"That's about it, sir."

"And Sillman'll be back when?"

"Probably next month."

"It's a stupid question but I don't suppose you know where I could reach him?"

"Clearwater's a big town."

"Stupid, like I said. A month, hm? He always take a vacation that long?"

"Oftentimes he does."

Pellam said, "This garage business .... must do pretty well, a man can take a month off."

"You'd be surprised, sir. By the way, that's a nice camper you got yourself. You wanta fill?"

"Not today," he said.

Pellam walked over to the three men playing poker, sitting in the back of the Hudson Inn's sour-mash- and beer-scented bar. "Mind if I sit in?"

A little uncomfortable at first, this crew. Then he bought a round of Bud, in the tall bottles. Then he bought another and things loosened up. Fred was the easiest to talk to. Close to seventy, with a red, leathery face. He hadn't been a farmer, which would have been the safest guess, but had worked railroads all his life, retiring early from Amtrak ten years before. Pete – in his mid forties – ran an insurance agency from his split-level a mile outside of town. Before the first hand was dealt, Pete started hanging on everything Pellam said. Agreeing too often, nodding broadly. He'd say, "Wait!" a lot and have Pellam repeat himself, to make sure he understood what was said. The other of the foursome was Nick. Twenty-one and as blasé as anything Cleary had ever produced. He'd roll his eyes, saying, "Shee-it!" and offered a sneer of a smile that Pellam came to decide wasn't as mean as it appeared. It was just part of the topography of his face. Pellam pegged him as a searcher. A successful high school linebacker going to fat as he cast about for a career.

Fred told the others that Pellam was descended from a famous gunfighter. "Wild Bill Hickok."

Pellam closed his eyes for a moment. "Now where the hell'd you hear that?"

Fred shrugged. Pete's eyes widened another few millimeters and said, "Holy Moly." Nick said, "Bet five."

Janine, of course. It had to be Janine. "See you," Pellam said. "Raise five."

Pete said, "Hey, I saw that film. Who was in it? Jimmy Stewart? I don't remember. He was one of the best shots in the west, Wild Bill. He was your classic gunfighter. He shot . . . who was it? I don't remember. Maybe Billy the Kid. Just . . . it was incredible. See your ten. He got shot in the back . . . Oh, hey, sorry, Pellam." He looked down, blushing at his faux pas.

"Christ, Pete, I never knew the man."

"Well, you know."

Fred said, "Dealer sees your ten. Shot in the back. Hey, Pellam, that why you're sitting facing the door?"

He laughed and said, "No." He didn't tell him that the reason he'd picked this chair was so that he could look across the street into the window of Dutchess Realty Company, where Meg Torrens sat, her white blouse ill-defined but evident in the dimness of the office. He'd decided a real estate broker could give him a good run-down on the cast of characters in Cleary – and who might not want a movie made here.

"Shot in the back? Man, fucking cheap shot," said Nick, and tossed in more chips. "Call you."

They played for nearly an hour, Pellam steadily losing fifty bucks, most of it to Fred.

Pete was still staring at him in an irritatingly eager way when Fred said, "Ha, Pellam, you're a poker player. You ever get a deadman's hand?" Then turned to Nick. "You know what that is?"

"What's that? Like so awesome it blows everybody away, a royal flush?"

"That's what Wild Bill had when he got shot. Full house of aces and eights. You ever get that, Pellam?" Fred stacked up his ample inventory of battered chips.

"Not that I can recall."

Nick got up to hit the john and Pellam asked Fred and Pete, "Got a question. Say somebody had a wrecked car. Where'd they sell it for scrap around here?"

"She run at all?" Fred asked.

"Nope, just for steel."

The local men looked at each other. Pete said, "Couple places. I'd go to Stan Grodsky's yard, out on Nine."

Fred said, "He's a Polack and he'll rob you."

Pete blushed again. "He asked who'd buy wrecks. Stan buys wrecks."

Fred said to Pellam, "He'll rob you."

Pete said, "*I* got a good deal there one time."

"Says you."

"Yeah? I got me a hundred bags of Sakreet at three dollars per."

Fred said, "They were forty pounders, not sixties, and how much was solid on the bottom?"

"Not much at all."

Fred scoffed.

As Pellam wrote down the name, Fred grimaced. "There are a couple others. Bill Shecker's Army & Navy, over on 106, about three miles north of here."

Pete was thinking furiously. "Oh, there's also R&W. They're out on Nine too. That's Nine also, I mean. Not Ninety-two."

Fred nodded. "Yeah, forgot about them."

Nick returned. The table was stacked with bottles, a forest of glossy brown. The bartender cleared some away and the game resumed. Pellam watched the cards flying out from under Nick's thick hands.

They played for another twenty minutes. Then Pellam saw motion across the street. Hard to say, vague in the dusk, but it might have been a pretty blonde in a white blouse wearing too much pancake makeup and fleshy pantyhose, locking up a small-town real estate office at dusk. He looked at the three jacks in his hand and folded. He stood up.

Everyone at the table looked at him.

"I'm beat."

Fred said, "Tough work losing money."

Nick frowned. It was too early to leave. Pellam was breaking gambler protocol. "Suit yourself."

"Maybe sit in tomorrow."

Pete said, "Come by sometime. Anytime. I'd like to get your opinion on what we were talking about before. You know."

Pellam had no clue. "Sure thing. Evening, gentlemen."

By the time he got to the sidewalk Meg had finished locking the door and was moving toward her car.

He felt a presence at his side. It startled him. Someone took his arm.

Janine kissed his neck. "It's Cecil B." She squeezed his biceps into her breast, "I just closed up shop and was going to stop by your camper and say hi. How are you, darling?"

"Doing good," Pellam said, forcing himself not to look toward Meg's receding form.

She squeezed his thigh, mindful of the bruise, and said, "You don't look as sore as last night." A sly grin. "I was thinking, love, you still haven't seen my house. Come by and I'll make you dinner. I'll even cook meat, you want."

"How about a rain check? I've got to send a package off to my studio. I'll be working all night."

"I've got an awareness group tomorrow and women's crisis intervention the day after. Maybe I can . . . Oh, hell, then my old man's coming by. He's bringing his new cycle over to show me . . ." She stood back and examined his face. "Hey, you're not jealous, are you?"

"Not a bit."

"That's a good boy." She held his eyes in a vice grip, then leaned forward suddenly and kissed his mouth. Hers was partly open. He recoiled for an instant in surprise, then returned the kiss.

Janine said, "Then the apple festival's on Saturday and I'm working a booth. How would Sunday be?"

"Sure. Good."

Where was Meg? He'd lost her. Goddamn, why'd she worn a black jacket? He couldn't see her. He looked back at Janine, who was saying, "You better not get cramps anywhere but in your writing hand." She punched him playfully on the jaw, though bone connected with bone and he blinked. She said, "And you better not stand me up. Mama doesn't like to be stood up."

"Yes, dear." He smiled and stood hard on the sarcasm.

Not far away Meg's Toyota fired up. He heard the bubble of the exhaust and saw the gray car back out of its stall. He said, "Well, much as I hate it, better go do some work. Sunday, then?"

"I close the shop at four. Why don't I come by the camper after? We'll drive home together. How's that?"

"Sounds great."

He kissed her cheek, broke away. As he started toward the Toyota he saw the little car speed away. The brake lights flashed as it made a fast turn and then was gone.

"Damn."

Pellam slowed his walk. Stopped and headed back toward the camper.

Thinking about junkyards.

He walked to the end of the deserted block and turned the corner onto the side street where the Winnebago was parked.

Thinking about getting something to eat.

Thinking about—

He nearly walked into the car. The little gray Toyota, idling at the curbside.

When he put his hands on the roof and bent down to the window, where she sat holding the wheel in both hands, staring straight ahead, she said, "You're alone."

"Nope. I'm with you."

"I thought you maybe had a date."

"Date?"

"Weren't you walking with . . ." She debated and the catty side won. ". . . Ms 1969?"

"Business," he said.

"Ah. Business."

Pellam asked, "How about a drink?"

He knew she was going to say no but he was curious what form it would take. There were a thousand different ways a woman says no to a man and they all have different meaning.

"I can't. I'm going out with the girls tonight. Bridge."

"How about poker? I can get us into a game up the street."

She laughed. A moment passed. "I wanted to say I was sorry about your friend. I heard about the accident."

"Thank you."

"I also wanted to apologize."

He cocked an eyebrow toward her, and she added. "For the other day. In the hospital."

"Naw. I was out of line," Pellam said. "I hate hospitals. They put me in a bad mood."

"No . . ." She studied the tachometer. "I was rude."

A hotrod car went past, exhaust popping as it slowed for a stop sign, then took off again.

She said, "There's something else."

He smiled. "Is there?"

Meg swallowed and tried to put up a shield against the flirt.

"It's kind of last minute. But you interested in coming over for dinner?"

"You cook like you drive?"

She blinked and tried to think of a comeback. He could see her thoughts racing. But she decided not to play the wittiest-comeback game. "About eight. That's extremely fashionably late around these parts. In fact, it's about bedtime."

"I'll bring some wine."

"No, you don't have to."

"No bother."

Meg gave him directions. He memorized them and repeated them out loud. He said, "See you then," grinning. She gunned the engine. He stepped back and she spun the car into the intersection, scattering gravel. She'd kept it in gear, the clutch depressed, while they'd talked. Planning a fast getaway.

Meg glanced back and, unsmiling, waved. She drove into the darkness.

8

M eg Torrens, mixing fresh dill weed into sour cream, heard her husband upstairs, moving slowly.

Keith Torrens liked to dress for dinner.

He'd be laying out his clothes on the bed. He'd picked that up from some episode of *Masterpiece Theater*. Almost anybody else in Cleary mentioned that they are going to dress for dinner, it'd make them sound like an idiot. Or it'd be a joke about changing out of sweats. But Keith was a natural at that kind of formality. Meg found it charming. He was moody some and quiet. But he was a scientist. He was brilliant. His mind was different from everybody else's.

Meg liked smart men.

She liked formal men.

She liked successful men.

And Keith was that. She'd never met anyone so devoted to his own business as her husband. He'd always wanted one, a business of his own. Keith the dreamer. Even as head of research and development at Sandberg Pharmaceutical outside of Poughkeepsie (not a job to shake a stick at, she'd reminded him on the dozens of occasions when he wanted impetuously to quit), he'd obsessed about being an entrepreneur.

At first he hadn't been sure how to go about it. First, he'd considered a consulting firm. But that smacked of laid-off middle management. Then he considered for-hire research laboratory. But that was pretty much for losers and academics and – more troublesome – it wouldn't give Keith the income he wanted as badly as he wanted his name on a corporate office.

Then one day, two years ago, he came home and announced he was going to do it.

"Do it?" Meg had asked uneasily.

"I'm quitting."

"We've been through this a dozen times," she'd reminded.

"Dale's got cash."

Keith's friend from Sandberg and his intended business partner.

"How much cash?" Meg had inquired.

"Enough."

And she knew there was no deterring him.

So with a $185,000 mortgage, a son destined for MIT and a wife who in a good year made twelve thousand in commissions, Keith took the plunge.

In a whirlwind of eighty-hour weeks, Keith, Dale and their lawyer bought their way out of stiff noncompete contracts with Sandberg, and opened a company.

It hurt her some that he wouldn't let her in on the deal. Not that she wanted to have anything to do with the technical part, of course: setting up the factory, the financing, hiring employees.

She knew she wasn't smart in those ways. But Meg thought she was a pretty good broker and when Keith bought property through another realtor it really stung. Why, one night she'd even taken a phone message from the bastard, a competitor.

Another broker!

"Honey," she'd said, "that's what I do for a living. Why didn't you ask me?"

And he'd looked at her, surprised, and then forlorn. She could see that he hadn't even thought about using her. He'd confessed that he'd blown it. He'd apologized, looking miserable. Like a boy who'd forgotten Mother's Day. Oozing contrition. She'd smiled and forgiven him.

Brilliant. But sometimes he just didn't *think*. That was so peculiar. How could that be?

Sam wheeled through the kitchen. "Hey, Mom, you know why the dinosaurs went extinct? An asteroid crashed into the earth and this poison gas killed them all." He sniffed the dip. "Yuck." He vanished.

Did that really happen? How could all the animals on an entire planet get killed at once? Did we have to start over again in evolution? Maybe civilization would be millions of years more advanced if not for a single asteroid . . .

Meg filled the dip bowl and set out crackers like flower petals on the plate. She finished setting the table and wandered through the downstairs rooms.

She'd decorated the house herself. Laura Ashley wallpaper – tiny flowers like an airbrushed spray of blue. A three-inch border of burgundy paper around the walls, below carved molding. Braided rugs. Most of the antiques had been bought on a single occasion, at an auction in Vermont. Country rustic some of them, painted and distressed, and a lot of Victorian. (And a whorehouse of a bathroom, she kept thinking. Gotta change that.) Dried flowers, wreaths, vases and doilies were everywhere. On the living room walls were photographs from the 1800s, mounted on sepia paper. She'd bought them in a local antique store for a dollar each and mounted them in old frames. She sometimes told visitors they were her ancestors and made up elaborate stories about them.

Meg dimmed the lights in the sconces and stood looking for a moment at the romantic ambience. She shook her head. She turned the lights back full and trotted up the stairs.

Keith was sitting on the bed, putting a shine on his shoes. Now he examined the loafers like a diamond cutter.

Until she began to undress. One glossy shoe dropped in his hand. He was grinning.

"Hey, boy," Meg said, "we got a guest in twenty minutes. Get that thought out of your mind."

He dropped his shoes, stepped into them, kissed her chastely. Left the bedroom. Meg tossed her clothes onto the hamper, slipped into her robe.

Do Do a Do . . .

She stepped into the bathroom.

Don't Do a Don't . . .

In the shower, her hair protected under a translucent shower cap printed with somber seagulls (a Christmas present from Sam), Meg felt the stinging water and wondered about the Don'ts for this evening.

It became a private joke, Meg's and Keith's, after she'd told him about a movie she'd seen in high school hygiene class. "Don't Do a Don't, and Do Do a Do" was the theme of the film, which warned about sexual risks in such delicate euphemisms that nobody could figure out exactly what the Don'ts were.

She decided that tonight's Don'ts were: Don't talk about the movie, about his friend's death, about Hollywood . . .

Which made her wonder why she'd invited him in the first place.

When she got out of the shower she heard the comforting sound of her husband flipping through the Moebius strip of TV channels downstairs.

She laid out a black angora sweater with a star in pearls above her left breast and black slacks with a razor crease. She sat at her dressing table. She spread the heavy foundation powder over her face and began working with blue eyeshadow. Her hand paused.

What's so Cleary about me?

Five years, not ten, Mr Pellam.

Bzzzt.

Meg walked into the bathroom and cleaned off the makeup with Ponds. From the back of the toilet, she pulled a recent *Vogue* magazine and began flipping through it.

"Hiya," John Pellam said.

In her heart, Meg knew that every man from Hollywood believed fidelity to one's wife was an idea so odd it could be a headline in the *National Enquirer*. But Pellam's weak handshake and chaste cheek kiss told her she may have found an exception.

His eyes, however, did a complicated reconnaissance of her face and she almost laughed as he tried to figure out exactly what was different about her. She could tell he decided it was the French braid of her hair.

Keith did the same scan and said, "New sweater, darling. Looks super." He'd given it to her two Christmases ago.

Pellam was wearing black jeans and a gray shirt, buttoned at the neck, without a tie, and a black sports jacket.

He was smiling steadily, looking around the house and talking to Keith. She heard her husband say, "You look like you're recovering pretty well from your little run-in with my wife, excuse the expression. Ought to be a town ordinance. Everybody *else's* got to wear crash helmets when Meg drives . . ."

"All right, buddy boy," she said, offering a wry smile, "you want to talk fenders? You want to talk body work."

Keith rolled his eyes. Said, "Okay, sometimes I run into things, true."

"You found the place okay?" she asked Pellam.

"Perfect directions."

Keith was looking out the door. "Oh, a Winnebago?" He stepped out on the porch.

"Home sweet home." To Meg, Pellam said, "Brought you a present." He handed her a small, flat bag. "Oh, yeah," he said. He added to it a paper-wrapped bottle, which turned out to be one of her favorite merlots.

Meg looked at the small bag. "What's this?"

Pellam shrugged.

She opened it and began to laugh. "Honey!" she called to Keith. Pellam cracked a grin. She held up a bumper sticker: *So many pedestrians. So little time*.

Keith laughed hard. "That's a good one, sir. That's very good." He said, "Come on. I'll show you around."

Meg glanced up the stairs. A small face was looking through the newel posts at the landing.

"Sam, come on down here."

Her son jumped down the stairs.

He walked right up to Pellam and stuck out his hand. "How do you do?"

Megan felt a burst of pride.

Pellam smiled – maybe at the formality and at the firm shake. Meg knew that childless men and women tended to think of kids as, more or less, pets. Meg had worked hard with her son. He was polite and direct. Meg said, "Meet my son, Sam. Sam, this is Mr Pellam."

Keith said, "Come on upstairs. Sam, we'll postpone your home-work long enough so you can show Mr Pellam your room."

"Yeah!" the boy said in a high voice.

The male contingent of the dinner party vanished upstairs.

Meg walked into the kitchen and poured glasses of Pellam's wine for the three of them. She sipped hers and stared at the Winnebago. Should she join them or not?

No, something told her to stay here.

Ten minutes later the creak of footsteps had worked their way back to the top of the stairs. Pellam's camper was next on the tour itinerary. Sam started to burst out the door but Keith made sure he was wearing his jacket. Meg offered wine to the men. Pellam took his, nodded at her with a smile. Keith glanced at the glass but shook his head. "I'll have some later." He was a hard liquor drinker mostly. Scotch.

"Mom, I showed Mr Pellam the computer, then my burglar alarm and my metal detector . . ."

Pellam said, "He made it himself. I can't believe it."

Sam said, "Dad helped."

"But not much," Keith said.

They all moved toward the door. Keith said to Meg, "We're getting a Winnebago tour."

She said, "Dinner's ready."

"Honey," he said patiently, "it's a Winnebago." And a glance at Sam's face told her a cold dinner was worth it.

As they walked onto the porch Sam asked, "Hey, Mr Pellam, do you like bombs?"

"I've worked on a few."

"Huh?"

"Movies."

Meg laughed.

Sam continued, breathlessly enthusiastic. "Sometime maybe I could show you these practice bombs. They're at this junkyard. They're really neat. Mom won't let me buy one but . . . wow, that's so neat. Can I sit in the driver's seat?"

"You can even honk the horn," Pellam told him.

"Cool."

At the dinner table, Pellam looked out over the spread of osso bucco, mashed sweet potatoes, green bean salad, broccoli. How'd she made all this in the two hours since she'd intercepted him downtown?

Sam was in bed, Keith was serving and Pellam kept looking around him. He felt as if he'd never seen a house before.

Keith adjusted his tie and lifted his wine glass. "To my wonderful wife and her superb dinner."

The conversation meandered. Washington politics, Los Angeles smog. Pellam asked Keith what he did.

"I own a little company that makes over-the-counter products. Cough syrup, aspirin, things like that."

"He's too modest," Meg said. "Keith keeps tap dancing on Bristol-Meyer's face. It's an uphill battle but he's getting there slowly."

"It's tough for us small boys. But I like the challenge. That's what's great about growing a business. The competition."

"You a corporation?"

"Uh-huh. You have to be, with all the personal injury suits now. My single biggest overhead expense after salaries is insurance."

"You have a partner?"

Silence. Meg stirred. Pellam had asked something awkward. Keith said, "Dale Meyerhoff. We worked together at a pharmaceutical company near Poughkeepsie. He died not long ago."

"Died? Oh, I'm sorry."

"Car accident," Meg offered.

Keith said, "Last year. It was quite a shock."

Pellam realized that they'd dealt with the loss a long time ago but they were uneasy now for *him* – probably worried that the reference would remind him of Marty. He said, "So you do everything, hm?"

Keith said, "I had a lot of learning to do. Dale – my partner – was sales and finance. Me, I'm just a chemist basically. A scientist. A nerd, you know."

"Studio I used to work for did a film about a chemist one time."

"Really?" Keith smiled. "Usually you just see movies about cops and monsters and private eyes."

"I guess it wasn't really a chemist. It was called *The Surrey Alchemist*. We made it in England. It had very limited distribution over here."

"Witches and sorcerers."

"Alchemists were considered scientists at the time," Pellam said. "We did a lot of research. Turning lead into gold is called base alchemy. True alchemists practice sparygia."

He noticed Meg checking out the plates, pushing bowls toward Pellam when the helpings got too close to empty. Keith seemed fascinated with the story and wasn't eating.

"Sparygia?" Meg asked.

Pellam said, "It means extracting basic properties from things, usually plants. What an alchemist does is try to find the essence of something and that essence supposedly had powers beyond just the chemical composition of the material."

Keith said, "I remember from a scientific history course I took at MIT. What's the movie about?"

"It was based on a real story. In the late 1700s, in England, there was a rich man named James Price. He was like a lot of the wealthy then. You know, dabbling at science. Maybe he was a little more than a dabbler since he got named a Fellow of the Royal Society. He was also kind of a crank. A little bizarre. He set up a lab in his home – in Surrey, out in the country. He does all this secret work then calls a meeting of his friends and fellow scientists. He brought them into his lab, where he'd set up a display – the three basic ingredients of alchemy: mercury, nitrate and sulfur—"

Keith laughed. "Hey, you know what those are?"

Meg said, "Let him finish."

Pellam said to Keith, "What?"

"A formula for a bullet. Nitrate and sulfur are in gun-powder and fulminate of mercury's in the firing cap."

Pellam laughed. "Wish I'd known that. It would've been a nice metaphor for the flick. Anyway, Price also had some other ingredients – something secret – in covered boxes. He got this crowd together and made a grand entrance. He looked awful, though. Sick and pasty, exhausted. Then he mixed a white powder with the three basic ingredients and turned them into an ingot of silver. He did the same thing with a red powder and produced gold. The metals were tested by a metalsmith and were supposedly genuine."

"Then he sold the ingredients on late-night cable TV and made a fortune," Meg said.

Keith hushed her.

Pellam continued, "But here's the interesting part. Price kept up the alchemy and made a huge amount of gold but after a few months his health began to fail. Finally, when the Society insisted he do another experiment under observation, he agreed. Three members of the Society rode to his laboratory one morning. He invited them in, set up his chemicals and drank a cup of poison. He died right in front of them – without revealing what the powders were."

Keith, tilting back his chair, then said, "What was it, a hoax? And he had to kill himself?"

"We left it up in the air. It's tough to make movies based on true stories. You have to pamper reality."

Meg laughed at this.

Keith suddenly squinted at Pellam. "You seem real familiar."

Pellam said, "Really?"

"Were you ever famous?"

Meg said, "Keith—"

Pellam said seriously, "In my mother's eyes."

Meg laughed. Keith shook his head. "It'll come to me." He squinted again in recognition but apparently the thought vanished; he began talking about his company, new product lines. Stories only a businessman would love. Pellam nodded and ground his teeth together to squash the yawns. He was pleased that Keith wasn't a movie hound and hadn't asked for one iota of Hollywood gossip. On the other hand he was a major bore. Pellam hardly listened to a word he said – until he realized Keith was talking about someone dubbed Miss Woodstock, who knew the astrological sign, as well as a few other intimate facts, of every single man in town. Meg leaned forward and with a coy smile caught Pellam's eye. He knew what she was up to and kept his eyes on Keith until she disappeared into the kitchen of dishes.

The womenfolk gone it was time to talk about serious stuff. Keith lowered his head and asked, "Have you talked to the insurance agent? About the accident?"

"Not yet. Meg gave me his name. The doctor said he'd have a bill ready for me in a couple days. He was waiting for the X-ray lab's bill."

"If you have any problems, you come to me, okay?"

"Appreciate it."

"How long you think you'll be in town?"

"Don't really know. I—"

Meg returned. "Coffee's almost ready." She sat down.

"So tell us, you married?" Meg asked.

He'd told her. In the clinic. Maybe the question was for Keith's benefit, to show that she hadn't known. It meant a bit of intimacy existed between them. Pellam's eyes swept over her dress. The pin on above her breast. She looked a lot younger today. The makeup was better. Maybe she had to wear realtor camouflage when she was selling houses.

He realized he was staring at her and still hadn't answered the question.

"Nope," he said. "Was divorced a few years ago."

"That's right. You'd mentioned that."

Oh. A bad memory. That's all.

"There's a girl I've been dating off and on. Nothing too serious. Her name's Trudie." (Damn! He'd forgotten to call. He would tomorrow. Definitely.)

A timer bonged in the kitchen. As Meg rose Pellam glanced at the pin on her dress again. Thought of Janine's pin. And her breasts. She'd had a moon. Meg was wearing a sun.

"Dessert," Meg said, walking back in from the kitchen with a tray.

Keith said, "Meg's a whiz with desserts."

She set the tray down.

"Brownies," Pellam said.

"You like brownies?" she asked.

"Can't get enough."

The beige car pulled off the highway and into an asphalt parking lot, which was slowly turning into black gravel.

Sleepy Hollow Motor Lodge.

"Here we be," Billy said.

The twins got out of the car and Bobby snagged a big bag from the backseat. "Heinekens," he said, proud he'd bought imports in Gennie Ale country.

They inhaled deeply and Bobby said, "Fall. I love it."

Billy looked at his watch. "Late."

Bobby walked past him and opened the door. Inside was an ugly square room, too hot, too brightly lit.

Billy followed him in.

"Toasty," Billy said. He opened a window.

"Fucking hot. Heh."

Neither of them really liked the hotel that much. Cheap, plastic, tacky. It reminded them of Brooklyn, where they'd been born, or Yonkers, where they'd lived until their junior years in high school, when their father had been laid off from the Stella D'Oro bakery and had moved the family up to Dutchess County. He'd bought what he said was an antiques business, but which turned out to be – to the young twins' delight – a junkyard.

They'd finished high school. Bobby, just barely, though he was captain of the rifle team. Billy, with a B average. When their father died they inherited the family's lime-green split-level and the junkyard, which they renamed after themselves, Robert and William. They'd promised each other that they'd only marry another set of twins – which didn't make room for a lot of matrimonial material in Dutchess County – so their social life was pretty limited.

They had a few other business dealings that took them to New York every couple of weeks and they were always glad to hightail it back to their house, which happened to be in the first tract of land that Wex Ambler had ever developed in Cleary. It was a nice house. Big and filled with the things they loved – dark still life paintings of dead birds and rabbits, prints of leaping fish, carved wooden statues of horses and bears, a Franklin Mint model car collection. The twin leather recliners, Sears Best, were aimed right at a huge stereo TV. Within arm's reach of Billy's chair was a Better microwave, which was perfect for heating nachos and chili during *Jeopardy* or *The Tonight Show*.

A perfect home for two boys on their own.

Exactly what this dingy hotel was not.

Billy expressed this sentiment, as he stepped on a silverfish in the bathroom.

His brother shrugged. "We don't have much choice. Can't do this at home."

"Don't mean I have to like it here."

Bobby shrugged in reluctant agreement. Then sat down on the bed and opened two beers. The twins drained them. Billy turned the TV on, grumbling that the remote was broken.

In five minutes there was a knock on the door.

Billy opened it. Ned, the boy from the pancake breakfast, stood there, in jeans, a T-shirt and a varsity football jacket.

"Ned, hey, how you doing? Come on in."

"Hey, guys, what's up?"

"Nothing yet," Bobby laughed, beating Billy to the punch by a millisecond.

Ned frowned, not getting what seemed to be a joke. "Kinda hot in here," he said.

"Yeah, a little. Funny weather."

"Hey, totally fine place here. Totally." Ned looked around.

The twins exchanged wry glances as Ned studied the brown and orange shag, the laminated brown furniture, the prints of flowers bolted to the wall. Looked like he was examining the grand ballroom of a Fifth Avenue hotel.

They cracked open more beers and turned on a rerun of the *Bill Cosby* show.

Bobby said, "He's stupid in this one. Cosby, I mean. He just mugs for the camera and counts his money. I liked him better in *I Spy*. That was some real acting."

"I never saw it," the boy said.

"On before your time. These two CIA guys. White guy, he was Robert Cummings—"

"Culp," Billy corrected.

"Robert Culp. Right. And Bill Cosby. Man, it was a good program. They knew some real shit karate."

"Course, *this* show's got Lisa Bonet," Bobby pointed out.

Billy called, "Hey, Ned, would you get a hard-on kissing Lisa Bonet?"

"I get a hard-on *looking* at Lisa Bonet."

"Hot as hell in here," Billy said. He took off his shirt and wiped sweat from his face with it. Underneath he wore a sleeveless T-shirt. "Hey, Ned, you're one strong dude. See if you can turn the heat down."

The boy pulled off his red and white jacket and dropped it on the bed. He wrestled with the radiator knob for five minutes until he was crimson-faced from the effort.

"Damn, it's frozen."

"Aw, forget it," Bobby said. "We'll just sweat." He unbuttoned his shirt to his navel – no tee underneath – and flapped it to cool himself. The twins dropped into the room's two chairs. Ned started to sit on the floor but Billy said, "Naw, take the place of honor." He nodded at the bed and Ned flopped onto the spongy mattress. Bobby handed him another beer. They watched TV for a half hour.

Bobby said, "Hey, you want to try something?"

Ned said, "I guess. I don't know."

Bobby pulled an envelope out of his pocket, a small manilla envelope. He rattled it. "Surprise."

"What's that?" the boy asked.

He opened the envelope and showed the contents to the boy.

"The hell's that?"

Inside were two dozen bits that looked like rock candy.

"It's sweet," Bobby said.

Billy gently shook the envelope until three or four spilled into the boy's hand. He lifted them and smelled.

"Don't smell like much."

"Yep."

"We're gonna eat fucking candy?"

"Sure, why not?"

Billy and Bobby each took one. The boy lifted his palm to his lips but they touched his wrist. Billy on the right, Bobby on the left. "Uh-uh. Just one at a time."

"Huh?"

"Just one."

The boy dropped the others back into the envelope. Then lifted the single crystal to his mouth. He ate it slowly.

"It *is* sweet. It's—" He stopped speaking. His eyes went wide then suddenly his lids drooped. "Man," he whispered. "This is totally fresh. Man." He brushed at his ears as if they were clogged, a dumb grin on his face. "What the fuck is this?" His words faded into a giggle. "Man. Excellent."

They knew what was happening – how the soft cotton was expanding into the crevices of his mind, the warmth, the coming feeling starting at the fingertips and flowing along the skin like a woman laying slowly, slowly down on your body, dissolving into a warm liquid, flowing, melting . . .

"You happy?" Bobby asked.

The boy giggled. "Man." He opened his mouth and inhaled as if he were tasting air.

Billy caught his brother's eye and a slight nod passed between them. Bobby closed up the envelope and slipped it into the boy's jeans pocket, where his hand lingered for a long moment.

9

T he third on his list.

The R&W Trading Post on Route 9, which the poker-playing boys had been kind enough to suggest to him, was the one. The time was 9 A.M. and a faded sign promised the place was open.

Pellam parked the camper in the small lot and walked back along the shoulder, which was gravelly and strewn with flattened Bud cans and cello wrappers from junk food. Occasional cars and pickups zipped past and he felt the snap of their slipstream.

The Trading Post stretched away behind a gray, broken stockade fence, which was decorated with some of the artifacts that were waiting to be traded: A rusted Mobil gas sign, a blackface jockey hitching post, a cracked wagon wheel, a whiskey aging barrel, an antique wheelbarrow, a dozen hubcaps, a bent plow, a greasy treadle sewing machine mechanism. If R&W had put the premier items here in the window Pellam wasn't too eager to see what lay behind the fence.

But that didn't interest him anyway. What had caught his attention was what rested at the far end of the lot, where the chain-link gate opened onto the secrets of the Trading Post: the rental car responsible for Marty's death.

There was a small shack in front of the fence. It leaned to the left at a serious angle, like a Dogpatch residence. When Pellam knocked no one answered. He strolled over to the jetsam of the car.

The wreck was scary, the way bad ones always are – seeing the best Detroit can do, no longer glossy and hard, but twisted, with stretch marks deep in the steel. The front half was pretty much intact but in the back the paint was all blistered or missing and it was filled with black, melted plastic. Pellam could see the gas tank had blown up. The metal had bent outward like foil. Inside of the car nothing remained of the seats except springs and one or two black tufts of upholstery, sour as burnt hair.

Then he found the holes.

At first, he wasn't sure – there were so many perforations in the car. Parts where the metal had burned clean through, dents and triangular wounds where shrapnel from the tank had fired outward. But, crouching down, studying the metal, he found two holes that were rounder than the others, about a third of an inch in diameter. Just the size of a .30 or .303 bullet – which wasn't to say that some hunters or kids hadn't left the holes there after they found the wreck (Pellam himself had spent a number of lovely, clandestine afternoons playing Bonnie and Clyde with his father's Colt .45 automatic and an abandoned 1954 Chevy pickup). But still—

"Help you?"

Pellam rose slowly and turned.

The man was in his thirties, rounding in the belly, wearing overalls and a cowboy hat. He had a moonish face and weird bangs.

"Howdy," Pellam offered.

"To yourself," the man said, grinning. His hands were slick with grease and he wiped them ineffectually with a wad of paper towels.

"This your place?"

"Yep. I'm the R of R&W. Robert. Well, Bobby I go by."

"Got a lot of interesting stuff here, Bobby."

"Yep. Used to be all Army-Navy but surplus ain't what it used to be."

"That a fact?" Pellam said.

"You don't get the deals you used to. My daddy, owned the place before us, he'd buy some all-right from Uncle Sam. Compasses, Jeep parts, tires, clothes. World War Two, you know. Bayonets, Garands, M-1s. Originals, I'm talking. I'm talking creosote and oil paper."

The man's eyes strayed to the wreck. "I got a better set of wheels, you're interested."

"Nope, just happened to notice it."

"I bought it from a garage over in Cleary. A hundred bucks. There'll be something under the hood I'm thinking I can salvage, then sell 'er to somebody for scrap. Could clear three hundred . . . But if you're not after a vehicle what would you be looking for?"

"Just sight-seeing."

"You're not from around here," Bobby said, "but your, you know, accent. Sounds familiar."

"Born over in Simmons. Only about fifty miles away."

"Got a cousin lives there." The man walked back toward the shack. "You need any help, just holler. I don't mark prices on nothing, too much trouble but you see something you take a liking to we'll work something out. I'll listen to any reasonable offer."

"Keep that in mind."

"You price stuff too high," Bobby explained, "people just aren't going to buy it. Never make money unless you make a sale."

"Good philosophy."

This time it was the sheriff himself.

Pellam hadn't even set foot on the asphalt of Main Street before the man was next to him. He smelled of Old Spice or some kind of drugstore aftershave. Unlike the deputies he was tall and thin, like a hickory limb. He wasn't wearing any *Cool-Hand Luke* law enforcer sunglasses either.

"How you doing today, sir?"

Sir, again.

He was wearing that smile, that indescribable smile the whole constabulary seemed to have. Like Moonies.

Pellam stepped out of the camper and answered, "Not bad. How 'bout yourself?"

"Getting by. Hectic this time of year. Crazy, all these people come looking at colored leaves. I don't get it myself. I'm thinking maybe we should open a travel agency here, take tours of people into Manhattan to look at all the concrete and spotlights."

Pellam grinned back.

"Name's Tom Sherman." They shook hands.

"Guess you know me," Pellam said.

"Yessir, I do."

"You're back in town now," Pellam pointed out. "I heard you were away."

"Some personal business. How you feeling, sir, after your little accident?"

"Stiff is all."

"Wanted to let you know, we probably wouldn't be inclined to cite Mrs Torrens for anything. Unless you were thinking of filing a complaint . . ."

Pellam was shaking his head. "No. She's taken care of the medical bills. I'm not looking to make a profit."

"Well, I think that's fair, sir. You don't see much of that. I was reading in *TIME* about people suing people over all sorts of things. This woman – I saw this on TV – *Sixty Minutes* maybe, I don't recall. This woman, what she did was she opened this package of cereal and there was a dead mouse inside and she sued the company and got, I don't know, a half million dollars. She didn't eat it or anything. She just looked at it. She said she had dreams about mice for a year. That a crock, or what?"

"Uh-huh. Say, Sheriff, there's something I wanted to talk to you about."

"What's that?"

"I saw the car my friend was in."

"Your friend? Oh, right – the car got itself blowed up."

"There were two bullet holes in it."

"Bullet holes?" Not one strand of lean muscle in his cheek changed position. "I doubt that, sir."

"I've hunted since I was twelve," Pellam said.

"We went over it real careful and we didn't find any sign of nothing a'tall."

"Two," Pellam said, "by the gas tank."

His face still didn't budge. "Oh, you mean, in the back. Those the holes in the back about three, four feet apart?"

Pellam said, "Believe they were."

The sheriff nodded. "Firemen."

"What?"

"When they got there, the car was still on fire and the trunk was closed. They used this pike, I don't exactly know what it is, a big rod kind of thing with a hook on it to pop the trunk. They do that with a burning car. Open it up as much as they can. They got a lot of good equipment. Always using the Jaws of Life to cut people out of wrecks."

"Oh."

"Where'd you happen to run across this car, sir?"

"Saw it out by the highway. At the junkyard a mile outside of town."

The sheriff looked down at his feet, shoes expertly polished with more Vaseline. "Uh, one of the things I was looking for you for – I wanted to mention: it might not be such a good idea, you doing what you're doing here."

Pellam said, "What would that be?"

"You know, I get the feeling that you don't like the fact your friend got himself killed doing drugs and you're trying to show something else happened."

"Investigation was pretty fast."

"Pardon?"

"The coroner's inquest, your investigation. All happened pretty fast."

The impassive, sunglass-less face nodding slowly. "Maybe you'd be used to city police work. We don't have a thousand homicides a year in Cleary, sir. We get a crime, or an accident, and we take care of it quick."

"I appreciate that. But I doubt my friend was doing drugs . . ."

"Mr Pellam, we don't have an evidence room, like you see on TV, you know. But we have this file cabinet and sitting inside it right now is a foil package with what must be a couple ounces of hashish. Now, I—"

"But—"

"Let me finish, sir. I was in Nam. I've done some smoking in my day. And I should add I've got no axe to grind with movie people or with you or your friend. We found the dope, we found a lighter, we found a brush fire. You yourself can see where the evidence points."

"I've never heard of a car getting blown up because somebody was smoking nearby."

"Well, you think about that Negro comedian a few years ago, set himself on fire."

"Marty wouldn't be freebasing coke in a state park at noon."

A faint smile. "Oh? Then when would he be?"

Pellam leaned forward. He spotted a cautious flicker in the sheriff's eyes. "Listen, Sheriff, let me line it up for you. And you tell me what you think, okay? My camper's vandalized with threatening messages. Then my friend dies in a pretty curious way. And in forty-eight hours the place where it happened is dug over, the car gets sold to a junkyard and the man who rented the car to him goes off to Miami."

"Clearwater. Fred Sillman goes to Clearwater every year."

"I don't honestly give a shit what his leisure schedule is. My friend didn't die the way everybody keeps saying he did. And if you aren't going to find out what happened I am. Simple as that."

"We did our job, sir. We found some facts about your friend that weren't so nice. I'm sorry about him and I'm sorry about your job but there's nothing to be gained by you staying in Cleary."

"You telling me to leave town?"

"Of course not. You're free to visit, to sight-see, hell, you can even buy yourself a house here – I understand you know a local real estate broker pretty good – all I'm saying is, you're not free to be a policeman. And if you start troubling people I'm going to have to get involved."

"Your concerns've been noted." Pellam tried to imitate the smile. It didn't work too well. He had better luck with: "Have a good day, sir."

Wexell Ambler was going to visit his lover.

He walked out of his house – supposedly on his way to a meeting – and strode toward his big Cadillac, parked in the U-shaped driveway. He was looking forward to sitting with her in the Jacuzzi in the glass-enclosed deck of his house in nearby Claverack, New York, from which they could watch the Catskill Mountains in the distance – now a stunning wash of color. He could look forward to enjoying fresh coffee and tasting some of her cooking.

Thinking about making slow love in the hot tub or in the large Shaker bed he'd bought for her because she'd mentioned that she liked the simple lines. She was a strange woman. He often compared the two of them, his ex-wife and his mistress.

And tried to decide what were the differences and what were the similarities. They both were attractive, dressed well, knew how to carry on a conversation at the country club. His wife was more intelligent but she was also less imaginative; she had no spark, no humor. She let him get away with anything. His lover challenged him (perhaps, he now reflected, this made him feel younger. Uncertainty was a quality brought out by one of the first girls he'd been in love with).

He'd just gotten into the Caddie when his housekeeper ran to the door and signaled to him with a wave.

"It's Mark," she called. "Says it's urgent."

Ambler said, "Have him call on the car phone."

He backed the car out of the driveway and waved to her affectionately once more.

Waiting for the call. He was thinking less about what the beefy young man would have to say and more about the woman he was on his way to see.

Ambler was a religious man (on the executive committee of the First Presbyterian Church), and although he understood that Calvinistic predestination did not absolve him from choosing the right path, the moral path, nonetheless the religion instilled in him a tendency toward helplessness on those moral questions the answers to which he did not like. He tended to throw his hands up and follow his instinct.

So although he knew what he was doing was immoral, he felt an addiction to his mistress, and could more or less successfully conclude that he had no control over the matter.

He packaged the infidelity carefully, though. For instance, he never thought of the word "cheating," which gave the whole matter a blue-collar taint. And he always thought of his paramour as a mistress or lover, rather than girlfriend or "the woman he was seeing on the side." (Dignity was important to Wex Ambler.) He never risked embarrassing his lover just to satisfy his own passion and went to crazy lengths to keep the affair secret.

The one problem, though – one he hadn't counted on – was that he'd fallen completely in love with the woman.

Ambler, who was fifty-two, was not so old that he had forgotten love makes people stupid – and in his philosophy, as well as his profession, stupidity was the number-one sin. He had guarded against love but unlike religion and unlike money and unlike power, love had a mind of its own.

It had nabbed him, but good.

At his insistence, their get-togethers had become more and more frequent. And he now felt his center giving, falling further toward her. He was growing hungrier, even desperate – while *she* seemed increasingly aloof.

Was there anything more foolish than a middle-aged man in love? And was there anyone who could care less about that foolishness?

Ambler smelled leaf dust and warm air from the Caddie's heater and wished he were already at the cabin.

The phone buzzed. The noise always disturbed him; it reminded him of the alarm a hospital monitor would make when a patient went into cardiac arrest. He snatched up the light receiver.

"Yes."

"I talked to Tom," Mark said.

"Yes. And?"

"The guy's turning into some kind of private eye."

Ambler concentrated on driving. The roads were narrow and wound in tricky meanderings past horse and dairy farms. He had a tendency to wander onto the shoulder if he didn't think about his driving. He asked Mark, "What do you mean?"

There was a pause and he heard Mark spit. A young man chewing tobacco – it was stupid. Maybe he did it to darken his moustache. Mark continued. "He's been asking a lot of questions about his friend and the car. He was down to R&W."

"The junkyard."

"Right. Looking at the wreck of the car."

Ambler felt the car bobble as the right front tire dipped noisily off the asphalt. "Damn." He forced the car back onto the road, overcompensating. It slipped over the broken yellow line before he got it steady again.

Mark asked, "What should we do? I was thinking maybe we could offer him some money. You know, bribe him to leave."

"Then he'd think I had something to do with the accident."

"Not necessarily." When Ambler didn't answer, Mark said, "But maybe."

Ambler said, "I've got an idea. I don't want to talk about it on the phone. Come see me."

"Now?"

"I'll be busy for a while. I'll call you."

They hung up, and it took Ambler the rest of the drive to the cabin to shake off his concern at Mark's news. In fact, it wasn't until he turned into the leaf-packed driveway and saw his lover's car sitting obliquely in the turnaround of the cabin that his spirits lifted. He climbed out of the Caddie, eager and buoyant as a seventeen-year-old en route to a homecoming date.

10

The Cleary Volunteer Fire Department had a long history of proud firefighting and a photo gallery to prove it.

Dozens of faded pictures of hand-pump, horsedrawn wagons, even a few of bucket brigades, were scattered on the walls of the tiny office – as if the company had had a Matthew Brady protégé on staff to record every major fire before, after and including the big one of 1912. The firemen seemed to have been arranged by the photographer and Pellam wondered if they'd actually stopped working momentarily, smoothed their pushbroom or handlebar mustaches and posed for the leisurely exposures.

"Afternoon," said the man sitting at the desk, rocking back in a metal chair. He was in his early thirties, wearing a black T-shirt over good muscles, blue jeans, a New York Mets cap.

"How you doing?"

"Not bad."

Silence

Pellam looked through a glass window at a big, yellow Seagrave fire truck. "Got some nice equipment there."

"Town don't scrimp, I'll say that."

"You all volunteer, huh?"

"Yep. There's pay for one man on duty to take calls twenty-four hours."

"He must get pretty tired."

The man snagged the joke right away and fired back with, "But makes a hell of a lot of overtime."

Pellam said, "I'm the one with the movie company."

"I know."

"You mind if I ask you a few questions?"

"Nosir."

"You on duty when that car blew up? The one in the park?"

"That your friend's car?"

Pellam said, "That's right."

"I answered that call, yessir. All of us did."

"You tell me what happened?"

"You mean what caused it?"

"Whatever you can tell me."

The man said, "There was most of it in the coroner's report."

"This isn't official or anything like that. I'm just curious. He was a good friend."

"Yessir, I understand." The fireman squinted up at the spotless, red-enameled tin ceiling. "I recall the back end of the car was burning pretty good when we got there. Somebody'd driven past and called it in."

"You know who?"

"Nope. I think it was a call from a pay phone. Anonymous."

"You showed up and then what happened?"

"No hydrants, course, so we had to use the tank on the truck to get things cooled off enough to get close to your friend. Then half the crew started on the brush fire with extinguishers and shovels. That was about it. We got the body away from the wreck and finally got the fire out. He died right away. It was pretty quick."

"The gas tank had blown up?"

"Yessir."

"You opened the trunk?"

"We popped it open, that's right."

"How do you do that?"

"Usually, we just pop out the cylinder, then reach in and flip the release bar. But the steel'd been pushed outward, so what we did was whack it a couple times with a pike. That jarred the bar and popped it open."

"Why'd you open the trunk?"

"The sheriff wanted us to. To see what was inside. Anyway, it's standard procedure. In case there's cans of gas or oil. Also, your spare'll burn for hours you don't douse it good."

"You find anything interesting?"

"Sir?"

"You said the sheriff wanted to look inside."

"I don't know. I was at the hood."

"You have one of those pikes handy?"

He wasn't yet uncomfortable under this questioning but he was growing warier. "They're mounted on the truck, sir. We're not really supposed to let civilians into the house, you know."

Pellam nodded. He looked at the truck through a greasy

window. The pikes looked blunt and heavy. It didn't seem they'd leave holes as small as the ones he'd seen in the car. "What're they made out of?"

"Steel of course."

"One last question. Why was the area dozed over?"

"Sheriff ordered it. Somebody called him up and told him to, I heard. I don't know why."

"You don't know who called, do you?"

"Sure don't."

Pellam thanked him then said, "Aren't you going to ask me?"

"Ask you what, sir?"

"Whether we're going to be making a movie here?"

The man shrugged. "Don't make a lick of difference to me, sir. I work in feed and grain, not movies."

At noon, Meg Torrens walked out the door of the Dutchess County Realty office, set the hands of the *Be Back At* clock at 1:15. She looked around the square. Pellam's Winnebago camper was parked opposite. She looked up and down the street, then crossed over and circled the camper. Taking in the tan and brown paint, the battered fenders, the mud stains, the chips in the windshield.

What the hell was she doing here?

Going shopping on my lunch hour, that's all.

And when was the last time, my dear, you bought anything in one of these rip-off antique stores? Three, four years ago, wasn't it?

She imagined herself in one of the campers, on location. She imagined what it was like to be in a movie. The modeling she'd done had been pure effort – exhausting. And she'd been treated like a dim-witted cocker spaniel. Making a movie would have to be different, she believed.

She caressed the metal skin of the camper. Noticed the faint remains of some graffiti on the side. It looked like two crosses.

Meg slung her leather bag over her shoulder and strolled up and down the street, looking at sights she'd walked past for years and never noticed. A cornerstone dated in late September, 1929 – could that have been Black Thursday? A painted wooden barrel on the side-walk emblazoned with the number 58 in red paint. One building was topped with a weathervane in the shape of a whale – why here, a hundred fifty miles from the ocean? Another was decorated with a beautiful round stained-glass window.

Meg was gazing into the window of Steptoe Antiques when she heard slow footsteps. A voice asked her, "Could use seconds on the brownies."

Meg turned, looking blank at first, the way she'd rehearsed in case this happened. She said, "Should've eaten them while you had the chance, cowboy."

Pellam stepped next to her to look at what she was examining. "How're the driving lessons coming?"

"'Bout the same as your photo classes."

Meg pointed to a tattered rug hanging on the wall in the window. "See that? Price tag looks like it says sixty. Wrong, that's six hundred. They'll sell it for that too."

"What's that supposed to be on there, a dog?"

Meg looked at it closely. "Could be. Maybe a cat. I don't know."

"Dinner was nice," he said. "I enjoyed it."

She lifted an eyebrow. "I did too." She'd chosen the pronoun carefully.

"Your house is beautiful. That was the first dinner I'd had in a house, I mean a real house, in over a year."

"No kidding," she said, though she wasn't surprised. "Sam's done nothing but talk about you. You better make good on that promise."

Pellam said, "The practice bombs. I haven't forgotten."

They walked past another real estate office. Pellam looked at some of the listings.

Meg's voice dropped a half octave. "I've got some wonderful properties, Mr Pellam. Owner financing is available . . ."

They laughed.

Eyes were on them. Cars slowed as they passed. Meg thought, *Go to hell.* But the defiance was shaky. She felt vulnerable, like the time she found herself at a Florida resort wearing a new bikini that turned out to be more see-through than she was comfortable with. As she did then she now crossed her arms over her chest.

"I guess I better get going," she said.

Pellam touched her arm. She froze, then stepped back casually. He said, "I'd like to ask you a question. In confidence."

Her thoughts raced but she just nodded slowly.

He asked, "There any reason why somebody might not want a movie made in Cleary?"

"We say no to drugs."

"Beg pardon?"

"There's some talk that there might be bad influences if your company came to town."

"Okay, granted. I've heard that before . . . But let me be a little blunter. There any reason why somebody might kill my friend to keep a movie from being made here?"

Meg turned to him, her mouth open in shock. "You're serious, aren't you?" She turned back to the window. "That was a stupid thing to say. Sure, you're serious."

"This is off the record?"

"Sure," she said.

"Okay, Marty did have some pot. Except, it was in the *camper*. Along with the rolling papers—"

"What's that?"

"Rolling papers? Cigarette papers."

"Oh. Right."

"So it *wasn't* in the car with him when it blew up. Somebody planted those drugs on him."

She shook her head, but noncommittally, as if he were a lawyer taking down her reactions.

"Then I looked over the car a little while ago."

"You did?"

"And I found two bullet holes in it."

"Bullet holes?"

"I think so. Near the gas tank. I think that's what happened. Somebody shot the tank, it exploded and then they planted the drugs and left before the fire truck got there."

At first she thought this was impossible – in Cleary. But then she remembered the darker side of the town. The murders of those businessmen, the occasional rapes, two high school boys had driven into a tree at eighty miles an hour – they were both stoned on heroin, of all things.

He continued. "I was hoping I could talk to Keith. Maybe

there's a test he could do. On the metal. See if they were bullet holes."

Meg said, "Why don't you talk to Tom? Didn't he investigate . . ." Then she understood. "I see. You think he's involved in some way, do you? The sheriff?"

"I just want to keep it low-key."

Nodding. She opened her purse and handed him one of Keith's business cards. "Well, sure. Give him a call. He liked you."

Across the square she saw a couple staring at them. The woman leaned toward the man; there was an extended whisper going on. Meg felt the burst of discomfort again.

Life in a small town . . .

I've lived here for five years, Pellam. But it feels like ten.

"Lunch?" he asked.

She hesitated. Yes, no, yes, no . . . she said, "Uh, I don't think so."

"Why not?"

Don't Do a Don't. She said, "Because this is Cleary."

He nodded and said, "Got it."

"Good luck, Pellam." She walked to the coffee shop.

"Uhm, one thing . . . All I'm interested in is lunch. Nothing more or less than that."

Meg lifted her hands and dropped them to her sides with faint slaps. "You maybe have the most honorable intentions in the world . . ." She paused, and for a millisecond tried to read his face for his reaction to this. She couldn't tell. She added, "but Cleary's still Cleary."

"Suppose that doesn't change."

"Not in your life or mine," she said and walked into the diner. The screen door snapped shut with a wooden slam.

M&T Pharmaceutical was a one-story cinder block square outside of Cleary. Prefab. It was surrounded by a gravel parking lot, in which sat thirty or forty cars – a lot of old ones, Torinos and Novas, as well as newer Japanese imports. And, Pellam noticed, pickup trucks galore – many of them with back windows smeared from the noses of excited hunting dogs.

Near the main entrance were several marked parking places. *Mr Torrens* was the first. Beside it was an empty space with a sign that had been painted over. It was probably the spot reserved for Keith's late partner. This had been L.A., Pellam thought cynically, that space would have been appropriated five minutes after the funeral.

It was late afternoon, dusky, and just as he eased the Winnebago into two of the visitor's slots, a sodium vapor light on a pole in the middle of the parking lot came on. He walked past the company sign, a swirling design of an M and a T, backlit.

A young receptionist, hair shooting up in a frothy tease, smiled and shoved the Juicy Fruit into the corner of her cheek.

"Hello, Darla," Pellam said, reading the name off her gold-plate necklace.

"Help you, sir?"

"John Pellam to see Keith Torrens."

"Yessir, have a seat."

Pellam sat and thumbed through a pristine copy of *Chemical Week*. In three minutes, a grinning Keith Torrens walked into the reception area.

"John." They shook hands. "Good to see you."

"Thanks for taking the time."

"Come on, I'll give you the fast tour."

Factories generally depressed Pellam – the regimentation, the way machines dictated where people stood and what they did (reflecting some kind of fear, he decided, that if it all fell apart, he'd end up on an assembly line somewhere twisting sheet metal screws into Whirlpools for the rest of his life). M&T, though, was a surprise. It was bright and clean. Filled with spotless white tile, brilliantly lit. The workers wore white jackets, pants and shoes and transparent bluish hats, like shower caps. It looked like a kitchen. Many of the people were bent over conveyor belts, checking machinery, packing cartons, reading computer screens. The machinery was stainless steel and white.

"Quite an operation."

Keith said, "I'm a small guy. To compete with the Pfizers and Bristol Meyers-Squibbs, you've got to be efficient. That's the key word." Light brown cardboard cartons rose to the ceiling on small elevators and moved along a conveyor overhead until they vanished into the shipping department.

Keith was so excited to show off his company that he talked very quickly; that speed, together with the loud pulse from a dozen different kinds of machines, made it impossible for Pellam to catch more than a few phrases. Still, he smiled and nodded enthusiastically.

They finished the tour and ended up outside Keith's office. "It's small but we're proud of it."

Pellam said, "I'll buy your cough syrup next time I get the flu."

"I'll give you enough samples to last for two years." He vanished into a corridor.

Five minutes later – throat lozenges, cough syrup, nasal spray stuffed in Pellam's jacket pockets – they walked into Keith's office, a large sparse room, done in cheap paneling. Keith seemed like the sort who'd sink most of his money into the factory itself. Pellam shut the door and said softly, "I'd like to ask you a favor."

"Meg said there was something on your mind."

"I'd appreciate if you'd keep this off the record."

"Surely."

Pellam said, "It's about my friend. The one who was killed."

"That car accident."

"I'm not sure it was an accident."

"No?"

"I found the wreck and I noticed what looked like two bullet holes in the back. The sheriff said they were caused by the fire department but I checked out their equipment and I don't think that's it."

"Bullet holes." Keith was frowning.

Pellam shrugged. "I was wondering if there was any way somebody could look at a hole and see if it was definitely made by a bullet. Someone like you?"

Keith said, "Possibly. What do the holes look like?"

"The ones I saw were about a third of an inch, so that would mean they're about thirty caliber."

Keith said, "Deer round, so it might be copper jacketed."

"Could be, sure."

Keith was looking up at the ceiling. "Any chance you could find the bullets in the car?"

"Let's assume they disappeared."

"Got you." He nodded knowingly. Then reflected. "The car burned, right?"

"Right."

"If," Keith began slowly, "they were just lead bullets, the odds are that any residue would have been burned away. Lead oxidizes at a very low temperature. Copper, though, that's a different story. It has a real high vaporization point. And going through sheet steel in a car? Yeah, I'd guess enough would have come off in the holes to find traces."

"Now, next question—"

"I'd be happy to."

"I wasn't going to ask you to go to the trouble. Isn't there something you can show me to look for?"

"After about four years of inorganic chemistry, sure. But why don't we just spend a half hour right now? I'll take some samples and we can have it back here in the lab in no time. We'll run it through the chromatograph and spectrometer. Where's the car?"

"Out at a small junkyard on Route 9."

"R&W?"

"Yeah, that's it."

Keith frowned. "I thought it would've been impounded or something."

"See why I'm a little curious about what's going on?"

The camper, followed by Keith's Cougar, pulled into the R&W parking lot, much of which was piled high with twisted copper piping. The pudgy man Pellam had spoken to yesterday – Bobby, he recalled – stood looking at it like a proud father, his hands on his ample hips. He wore bib overalls and a seersucker hat, like a train engineer's.

Pellam and Keith climbed out, walked up to him.

Keith said, "Hey."

"Hey, Mr Torrens. How you doing?"

"Not bad. How's business?"

"Lookit this," Bobby said proudly.

Keith nodded.

Pellam examined the tangle of pipe. "Not bad."

"No shittin'." He laughed at the obvious statement.

Three men, staring down at ten cubic yards of pipe. Nodding, impressed the way men always are at good finds.

Pellam glanced along the front of the fence toward the charred wreck. It was lit by bare incandescent bulbs in mechanic's hand-held light baskets.

With an odd formality Bobby stuck out his hand. "How you doing, sir? You're that movie guy, right?"

Pellam blinked. "That's right. We're here about what I was asking you before. The car?"

"Car?"

"I was talking to you about that wreck." He nodded toward the remains.

The man frowned. "Don't believe so. No."

Pellam glanced at him. "We were talking about that car down there. The wreck."

The man lifted his hat and greasy bangs dropped onto his forehead. "Don't recall that."

Oh, I get it.

Pellam sighed, reaching for his pocket. He found a bill and was starting to pull it out when the man said, "Bobby."

"What?"

"You were talking to my brother. Bobby. I'm Billy."

Oh. The W in R&W. Got it.

Keith laughed. "Billy and Bobby're twins."

Billy said, "But don't let that stop you." He accepted the twenty.

"You mind if we take a look at the wreck?"

"If you're in the market for a car," Billy said, shrugging, "I can do better'n that. But help yourself." He turned back to his precious pipe.

They walked toward the burnt-out car.

Pellam whispered to Keith, "Twins?"

"You do horror films for your company, I'll bet you could get 'em pretty cheap."

They walked around the wreck. Pellam stopped suddenly.

"It's gone."

Keith blinked and leaned forward. Someone had used an acetylene torch to cut off the trunk and rear portions of the fenders.

Pellam called, "Excuse me . . ."

Billy tore himself away from his pipe. "Yessir?"

He wandered slowly to the wreck.

Pellam said, "What happened to the metal here? The back portions?"

"Whatsat?" Billy called.

"Look here," Keith said.

"Shit, it's gone," Billy said.

"I got the gist of that," Pellam said.

"Shit." The twin put his hands on his hips and looked around, like he was searching for a dropped quarter.

Keith said, "Bobby start to cut her up?"

"Naw, he's not into like heavy work. Damn now. Who'd come by and steal half a burnt car?"

Keith and Pellam walked back to their vehicles. "I'm sorry. Wild goose chase."

Keith said, "It's pretty funny, though. You go out to look at the car and find what looks like evidence. Next thing, you come back and that part's gone."

"Yeah, funny."

Billy stood in the shack, waving goodbye to Keith Torrens and the movie man. He picked up the phone and punched in a number. Bobby answered on the first ring. He must have known it was Billy because he just picked up the phone and said, "So what is it now?"

"Hey, guess who was just here."

"Lessee, Elvis's ghost, singing 'Love Me Tender.'"

"Naw," Billy said, "but wish it was. That'd be a fuck of a lot better for you and me."

—◆◆◆—

11

" A re you all right?"
   Wexell Ambler's lover didn't answer him.

After a moment, he gripped her buttocks tighter and dug his nails, which were long for a man's, into her flesh. She whimpered. He remembered to relax his grip somewhat.

"Does it hurt?" he asked. "Does it—"

"Wex, oh—"

"—hurt?"

She whimpered again and pressed her forehead against his pulsing neck.

When they'd begun seeing each other it had been awkward. Several problems.

First, neither had ever had an affair before and they didn't know what you did and didn't do. Surely affairs had special protocols – How do you make dates? Do you even call them "dates"? Do you shop at different grocery stores to avoid chance meetings when you're with your spouse? Or is it better to see each other casually like that and avoid arousing suspicion?

Second, there was a funny type of jealousy at work. He accepted that his lover was married but he was occasionally stung by the thought that she'd learned a certain technique – a touch or kiss – from her husband.

Third, neither of them was twenty-five any longer. Ambler had worked in the building trades when he was young and still hunted and fished – the history of physical effort had helped slow the inevitable effects of gravity and sedentary life. But there was no denying that muscle was giving way to fat, that erections that used to last an hour began to fade after fifteen minutes, and that he'd be no good for twenty-four hours after he came. His hair was thin (though in some slight compensation, not too gray) and he'd developed a jowl that he kept poking at as he'd pass the large oval mirror in his dining room until his wife commented on it and he immediately stopped the habit.

Oddly, though, his lover, who was more than ten years younger than he was, had been even more self-conscious than Ambler. Her body could easily pass for a thirty-year-old's, yet she always shut the lights out and drew the shades before she undressed.

But despite these worries, they had quickly fallen into a comfortable pattern and they soon found themselves making good, sweaty love for the first time in years.

Today, in the dark tangy-wood-scented bedroom, Ambler pinned her to the stark oak bed and pressed into her – hard, hard. Almost cruelly. He wasn't sure why. He knew he had a reputation for being a cruel man in business and at other times, but he would never think of being cruel to anyone he loved. But as he felt himself coming closer to the moment, he wanted to hurt his mistress. He wanted her to admit she was in pain but that she didn't want him to stop.

"Does it hurt, love?"

"Yeah," she whispered, her mouth saying the hot word against his skin, a centimeter from his ear.

She gasped twice, then whispered something he couldn't hear, then she said, "Don't stop. No, don't stop. I like it." The words were lyrical grunts. He smelled the aroma of her perfume and sweat.

"You like it . . ."

"Don't stop."

". . . to hurt?"

"Oh, Wex . . ."

Afterwards they lay together. Unlike when Ambler had made love with his wife he and his lover often began to talk immediately, right after they had caught their breath.

Today, though, he kissed her forehead, whispered, "Darling," and then they lay with their own thoughts for five minutes, half dozing.

"He's still here, I heard," Ambler said casually.

"Who?"

"That man from the movie company."

"I heard."

"What do you suppose he wants?"

"Taking time off after his accident, I suppose."

Ambler asked, "They aren't going to make the movie here, after all?"

"Why don't you like him?"

Why do you say I don't like him? But Ambler didn't say that. He said, "Look what happened. With the drugs and everything."

"Wasn't his fault."

"Movie people."

"Are just like everybody else," she countered.

"You're glad he's staying, aren't you?"

"Wex, what's this all about?"

"Drugs and—"

She said, "You take it on your shoulders to be the moral protector of the town and you scare all these people into thinking that the big bad world is going to gobble them up alive."

That made him nervous. He considered. No, there was no way she could know about what Mark had done. She wouldn't be here if she suspected that. He said, "You give me more credit than I deserve."

"You bully people."

"As if I could bully the whole town of Cleary." After a moment, he said, "Did you talk to him about a job?"

"No."

"Would you?"

"I considered it. I thought—"

He scoffed. "You thought you'd be Lana Turner."

"I'm wasted here. My life is wasted. I should . . ."

"You should what?" he asked, edging back toward desperation.

"Nothing."

"You're life's not wasted at all."

"I feel like I'm just drifting."

"How can you say that? You've made *my* life something wonderful."

The lines fell like a lead sinker. She squeezed his shoulder but he was glad for the darkness. His face burned with embarrassment.

He asked, "Have you ever thought about moving?"

A pause. "I've thought about it."

"You'd just leave, without talking to me about it?"

"Don't put words in my mouth. I didn't say that. I've got a lot of possibilities."

"Some of them involve me, some of them don't. I see."

"Wex." There was a bony edge to her voice. Ambler didn't believe he'd heard this sound before. He wondered if they were going to have their first serious argument. That would be very bad – in light of what he was planning to tell her.

She continued, "Don't disrupt things. Between us, I mean."

"Is something wrong?"

"No, nothing's wrong. What do you mean?"

This was sounding like the conversations he used to have with his wife. Before he fell out of love with her.

He backed off. "You just seem . . . I don't know."

She said, "We were just having a discussion. Don't take it personally."

"You're the one who seems to be picking a fight."

"I am not."

After a moment he felt her stiffen and draw away from him. Only millimeters – but it was enough so that he refused to do what he instinctively wanted to and touch her leg in a chaste way, seeking forgiveness for his vague crimes.

The day wasn't going as he'd planned. Not at all. He wished

they hadn't made love. It tilted the balance of power against him. Men and women. Never changes.

He felt a shudder of pain and anger course through him.

There was silence for a long moment. He debated then wiped his sweating palm on the sheet. "Can I ask you something?"

She didn't answer.

Ambler said, "We've been seeing each other now for, what? Six months?"

She said a neutral, "About that."

"I was thinking . . . I'm not good at this." (The same way he hadn't been very good at asking her out the first time, he recalled.)

She softened. He knew that she had a weakness for chivalrous, struggling men. "What are you trying to say, Wex?"

At least the terrible edge was gone from her voice.

His mind went blank, then he blurted: "I think we should get married."

He wanted to be light about it. He wanted to joke. Like middle-aged couples on sitcoms. Snappy comebacks. Rejoinders. Mugging for the camera. He couldn't think of a single thing else to say.

And from her: Utter silence. As if she'd even stopped breathing.

It couldn't have been that she'd never considered this before, could it? Was he so far off base that he'd completely misjudged? His heart pounded. He actually heard it.

Her hand touched his arm. "We said we'd never think about it."

"That was before." He looked futilely for some appropriate milestone in their relationship – the twenty-fifth time they'd had sex? The twelfth candle-lit dinner together? The sixtieth time they'd laughed at a private joke?

She sat up and reached for the night table. The light snapped on. It was a low bulb, which she'd asked him to put in the lamp. He knew she hated bright lights.

Meg Torrens pulled the comforter around her shoulders and said, "Oh, Wex."

And in his name, spoken through a loving, gentle smile, he heard the word No as clearly as if she'd shouted it.

● ● ●

TO SLEEP IN A SHALLOW GRAVE/
BIG MOUNTAIN STUDIOS

EXT. ROAD TO BOLT'S CROSSING, NEAR FOREST – DAY

ECU: JANICE'S FACE. It is not aged so much as weathered. You can see in it the hampered beauty of a woman at forty. An earth mother. She was at Woodstock. She cried at Woodstock and got stoned there. The long hair falls across her face, subdividing it into patches of ruddy skin. She brushes it aside. The wind pushes it back.

MEDIUM ANGLE: SHEP. He's leaning against his motorcycle. The lights should be gelled magenta to put an aura on the chrome, harmonizing with the sunset that's approaching behind them. He's torn. He's told her he's leaving, and he wants to go. But also wants desperately to find something

about her that will keep him from leaving. Is it pity? Or is it
something more genuine, more mutual? He doesn't know.

Pellam sat in his hot camper – though he was really in Bolt's
Crossing, not Cleary, New York.

Which was where he needed to be at the moment.

In Bolt's Crossing, there was no stinking hulk of a car,
punctuated with scorched tufts of upholstery shooting outward
like patches of hair.

In Bolt's Crossing, the only people lying still in funeral
parlors weren't dead at all and in four scenes would be prowling
around in flashbacks, lusting and ornery and laughing.

In Bolt's Crossing, people like Marty never died.

CUT TO:

MEDIUM ANGLES, CROSSCUTTING between Janice
and Shep

JANICE

I took a chance you might be here.

SHEP

(Avoiding her eyes)
Brakes gave me some trouble. Thought I should fix them
before I left.

JANICE

I was thinking about what you said. Last night?
About me.

SHEP

I was mad. I—

JANICE

You were right. I keep looking for answers in the past. If I'm not careful, there won't be any future left.

Pellam pulled the sheet out of the typewriter with a satisfying buzz of the platen. He wrote *Insert 58A* across the top and slipped it into the script, which he'd unfastened. It was now just a stack of a hundred fifty sheets of wrinkled paper, filled with his handwriting and interleaved with inserts like this one.

He put his hand on it, then picked it up and riffled the pages, feeling the thin breeze on his jaw.

He walked to the front of the camper and sat in the driver's seat, looking out the grimy windshield. Now he wasn't seeing the cinematographer's stunning dusk in Bolt's Crossing but the winding country road that led into Cleary.

The Winnebago's engine turned right over. He drove downtown, parked and stepped out into the brilliant sun. Blinking his way along Main Street he found a stationery store that did photocopying. He gave them the script and asked for a copy. The polite acned teenage boy behind the counter told him the job would take about twenty minutes. Pellam offered to pay now but the boy said, "No, sir, no hurry. Want to make sure you like the job."

Pellam hesitated then said, "Sure," remembering that he wasn't in Los Angeles or New York and that there was no reason to be suspicious of politeness.

He wandered out into the street, blazing with its raw sunlight, to get a cup of coffee. He saw Marge's across the street but, thinking of the day he and Marty had gone there, decided against it. Also, he preferred to go someplace where he wasn't so well known. He didn't want to be adored by the help, he didn't want to talk about Marty, about parts in movies, about Hollywood.

He walked into a drugstore, with its snaking turquoise lunch counter and chrome-and-red vinyl stools.

"Hey, Mr Pellam." From one of the clerks – a middle-aged man Pellam had never seen.

So much for anonymity.

And for hostility too. Whatever the official opinion about drugs and movies, the half-dozen people in the place all glanced at him with meaningful, eye-involved smiles that said, *I'm not asking but if you want to haul me off to Hollywood and put me in a sitcom episode of your choice, go right ahead.*

He nodded, walked to the pay phone and tried to make a credit card call. His company card number had been canceled. He sighed and billed it to his personal card. After five minutes the assistant producer came on the line. The boy was in high spirits.

"Yo, hombre. You better hope Lefty don't have a homing device set up. 'Cause he do, there's a scout-seeking missile aimed for your crotch this minute."

"He hasn't unfired me, huh?"

"Whoa, boy. You came real close to cratering that movie but I think it's going to fly. He bent over for one of the money cows and I guess it worked out okay. Shysters said Marty's accident was a force majeure. So he's got another couple of weeks."

"You got a location?"

"Not yet, but they've got a free-lancer down in Pennsylvania. Season's later. Gives 'em more time to shoot."

Pellam said, "Pennsylvania's all wrong."

"I'll connect you with Lefty. You can tell him."

"You sound pretty calm."

"I'm medicated."

"I'm going to do something and I need your help."

"No." Cheerful, cheerful, cheerful. "Absolutely not."

"Listen to me. I'm going to—"

"John, clue me in – are you trying to get *me* fired?"

"Every assistant producer gets fired. It's a rite of passage."

A sigh. "Okay, talk to me."

"I doctored the script."

"What script?"

"*Shallow Grave.*"

"Hmmm. Why?"

"I want you to get the changes to Bob. Is he still directing?"

"Pellam, are you mad?"

"Don't show them to Lefkowitz. Only the director. *Repetez apres moi.*"

"No."

"Answer my question. Has Lefty fired Bob?"

"No, and he can't. He's in too deep. His deadline problems are almost as bad as his herpes."

"Good. I'm sending it by Express Mail."

"John, no."

"To you."

"John, there's no way they're going to hire you back."

"That's not what I care about. I don't even want a credit. It's too good a story to screw up with that half-assed script. Get it to Bob and don't let Lefty see my changes."

"John—"

"Bye."

"—no."

Before he sat down at the lunch counter Pellam noticed a rack of sunglasses. His had met the same fate as his Polaroid, thanks to Meg Torrens's little Toyota. He decided to buy another pair. He noticed some mirrored teardrop shapes. He tried them on, checked them out in the mirror.

He smiled. Perfect. Yep: *Cool Hand Luke*.

The middle-aged man behind the counter said, "They're you."

"How d'I look? Like a small-town sheriff?"

"Yessir, you could man a speed trap any day with those."

"Take 'em," Pellam said.

"You want the fake leather case?"

"That's okay."

He sat at the counter. The clerk didn't seem much interested in a Hollywood career and just talked to Pellam about traveling, of which he'd done a great deal. He told Pellam how he and his wife had taken this year's vacation in Peru and Chile.

"The air is the thing you don't think about. The altitude, you know. You walk a couple blocks – well, they don't really have blocks but you know what I mean – and you've gotta lie down and take a nap. It's exhausting! I mean, I thought I was in good shape. I can chop a couple cord of wood and no problem. But I was beat. And there are all these little old women steaming along like it's nothing to them and trying to sell you pottery and these blankets and jewelry. They see money and they run right at you. They sprint! In air like that. It's all what you're used to." The man summarized: "Everything's relative."

"Suppose so," Pellam said, and listened to the history of Machu Picchu.

Pellam checked his watch, said, "I've got to pick up something."

"We did the Orinoco too but I didn't see one crocodile." He grimaced.

"Life's full of disappointments." Pellam stood and put his deputy glasses on.

"No disappointment at all. Sally and me're going back in October. We'll find one. I promise you that."

Pellam wished him luck.

———•✦•———

12

P ellam parked the camper in the driveway of the Torrens house
(the word "homestead" came to mind). Meg stepped out onto
the porch, then smiled and jumped down the few steps to the walk
that led to the driveway, wiping her hands on a scallopy apron and
looking just like a housewife out of a 1960s sitcom.

A housewife, however, in a tight, blue silk blouse, the top two
(or was it three?) buttons undone.

Eyes up, boy.

My God, she's got a freckled chest.

Pellam just loved freckles on women.

"What brings you here, Pellam?"

"Came to borrow something."

She blinked. To joke, or not to joke? "Butter churn?"

"Naw."

"Bear grease for your muzzleloader?" she asked.

Gotcha.

He smiled indulgently. "As a matter of fact," Pellam said,

"you're talking to one of the only people in the state of New York that's fired a Sharps .54."

And she didn't miss a beat. "A Sharps? Forget about it, boy. That's a drop-block breechloader, not a muzzleloader."

Gotme.

She laughed hard at his jolted expression. "Girls usually melt at gun talk, huh?"

He said, "Nobody in the goddamn world except me and born-again gun nuts know about Sharps anymore."

"I never fired one but my daddy had one. He collected guns. I've got myself a Springfield breechloader in the den."

"No." He laughed. "A forty-five seventy?"

She nodded. "Carbine. With a saddle ring and everything."

"Damn, what a woman. You ever fire it?"

"What good's a gun unless you fire it? But try getting the black powder smell out of your silk undies."

"Not a problem I have."

"Sam and I take it out to the range sometime. Hard to find ammo, of course."

"That's what I wanted to borrow."

"Ammunition?"

"Your son."

"The bomb expedition?" she nodded.

"Yep. It okay?"

Meg said, "You ever known any parent to mind when somebody says he'll take your child off your hands for a few hours?" She called Sam then turned back to Pellam. "Oh, before I forget . . . The Apple Festival is Saturday afternoon. You interested in seeing it?"

"I guess. You'll be there?"

"It's a family thing."

What was that supposed to mean? *You'll be there it's a family thing.* He waited a second for more messages; when he got none, he said, "Sure. Look forward to it."

Sam appeared. "Hey, Mr Pellam, we gonna look at bombs?"

"You bet, Sam."

"All right! Can we go in the camper?"

"That's the only wheels I got."

"Can I, Mom?"

"Sure, just be back by six for dinner."

"Mr Pellam, these are the greatest. They got red ones and green ones and they got mortar shells that Dad says they don't have powder in them anymore and hand grenades . . ."

"Do not, under any circumstances, buy him anything."

Pellam laughed, "Yes, ma'am."

They got into the camper.

"Hey, Sam, you know, one thing'd be fun?"

"What, Mr Pellam?"

"Why don't you bring your metal detector along?"

"My metal detector?"

"I have this collection?" Pellam said. "And whenever I'm in a new town I like to add to it."

"I collect dinosaurs. And baseball cards. And pro-wrestling cards, of course." Sam jumped down out of the Winnebago and ran into the house.

Energy. Where do they get it?

He was back in two minutes.

"You need batteries?"

"Nope. They're recharged. I used ni-cads. What do you collect, Mr Pellam? Coins?"

He said, "Bullet casings."

Sam said, "Wow."

As it turned out, Pellam liked the bombs as much as Sam did.

This particular junkyard was a lot classier than R&W. He remembered it from the poker boys' list. It sold mostly what the name promised: Army Surplus, which seemed to be in pretty good supply despite what Bobby (or Billy) had said. Vehicle parts, cartridge boxes, portable latrines, tools, tents, flashlights. All solid, olive-drab, functional. A lot of things that you couldn't use for much other than paperweights: Bombsights and old altimeters and doughboy helmets that wouldn't even make good planters.

But the bombs, yeah, they were great. All different colors. Different shapes. Some pointed like rockets, some rounded like old-time airplane bombs. Jesus, they were huge. Pellam cautiously tapped one. Hollow.

Sam said, "They're just practice bombs. You don't have to worry."

"I wasn't worried," Pellam said quickly.

"You looked like you were afraid it was going to go off."

"Ha, ha."

Sam showed him mortar shells, concussion grenades and bayonets, mean-looking things with deep blood grooves up the side. Most of them were still wrapped in sticky creosote.

Despite what Meg had told him, he wanted to buy the kid a bomb. They were only fifty bucks. Then he admitted he really wanted one for himself. One of the deep blue ones. He wanted to mount it on the front of the Winnebago.

No – what he really wanted was to buy one and mail it,

C.O.D., to Alan Lefkowitz, c/o Big Mountain Studios, Santa Monica Boulevard, Century City, California . . .

Then Sam decided it was time to look for bullet casings. They climbed back into the camper and drove ten minutes out of town, parked and started hiking.

They walked through the woods, following what was a pretty clearly marked trail. The boy had a box over his shoulder and carried a short metal rod with a disk attached. He had a headset around his neck. They were by themselves. The day was very quiet. Sam kept looking up at Pellam as if he expected him to say something brilliant.

"You think you're going to find bullets here?"

"You never know."

"Like from hunters?"

"Right."

"You hunt, Mr Pellam?"

"Yep. Haven't for a while. My father and I used to go out all the time."

"Where's he live?"

Pellam glanced at him. "He died few years ago."

"Like Grandpa Wold."

"That's your mother's name? Wold?"

"Un-huh. She's got a gun, my mom. Grandpa gave it to her. It's an old one. Mom and me shoot it sometimes down by the river. Wow, it makes this totally loud noise, really loud. And it knocked me over nearly."

He set down the metal detector and illustrated shooting the gun and falling backwards. He lay on the ground, still.

Pellam looked down at him, alarmed. "Hey, you okay? Are you all right?"

"Sure!" He jumped up. "My dad doesn't hunt much. We go fishing sometimes. What'd you hunt?"

"Pheasant, duck, geese."

Sam asked, "You like football?"

"I used to play."

"Yeah, I knew it! Where? Pro, I'll bet."

He laughed loud. "Pro? I'm about a hundred pounds light for that. Naw, just in high school."

"Quarterback, right?"

"Receiver. I figured it was better to get jumped by one or two big guys instead of four or five."

"What's it like to score a TD? Running over the line. I like the way, you know, how they run over the line and then drop the ball like it's nothing to them. That's so neat! What's it like?"

"I didn't score that many. I wasn't that good."

"Sure you were!" the boy countered. "I'll bet you saved the team. When was that? A couple years ago?"

"More like twenty."

Sam rolled his eyes. "Holy cow, you're older than my mom. You don't look old."

Pellam laughed. He'd forgotten how completely kids nuked your careful adult delusions.

"Hey, Mr Pellam, can we like practice passing sometime? My mom tries but she's a girl and all, you know. Maybe you and me could practice, you could give me some tips. My dad, well, he's busy a lot of the time. All he cares about is his job."

Pellam knew enough not to get into that one. He said, "We'll see."

"My mom'd like it if you stayed around for a while. She likes you, I can tell."

Or into that one either.

They came to a ridge that overlooked the parking lot where Marty had died. The lot was about two hundred yards away. There was only one other high point that Pellam could see that had a view of the lot and that one was five hundred yards. Not an impossible shot with a good scope but this would be the more likely spot for a sniper. Also, this faced the rear of the parking lot, and, if Marty had parked head in, would offer the car's gas tank as a target.

Still, it'd be a bitch of a shot in any kind of breeze, and on a warm day – as that day had been – heat waves from the valley beneath would have blurred the line of sight.

"Okay, Sam, go to work. Find me what you can."

The boy wandered back and forth for ten minutes, retrieving two mashed Coors cans and a quarter ("It's yours, son"). Suddenly he shrieked and ran up to Pellam with a .22 long rifle cartridge in his hand.

"Nope, too small. I'm looking for centerfire. You know the difference?"

"No, sir."

"Firing pin hits a .22 on the rim of the shell. So they're called rimfire. Bigger calibers hit the percussion cap in the center. They're called centerfire."

"Wow, that's neat."

"Come here, I'll show you." Sam frowned, then his eyes went wide, as Pellam opened his jacket and pulled a gun from his waistband. It was an 1876 Colt, steel with dark rosewood grips

"Wow," the boy whispered.

Pellam kept the gun pointed at the ground. "Always pretend a gun is loaded, even if you know it isn't, and always pretend that it could go off at any minute. So you never point it at anything unless you're prepared to shoot it. Got it?"

"I got it. That's a cowboy gun."

"It's a Colt Peacemaker, a .45." He opened the thumb cover and with the ejector rod eased the shell out. He held the end up for the boy to see. "There, that's the cap in the center. The pin on the hammer hits the cap and that sets off the powder. The old-time guns like this use black powder. Like the one your mother's got. Newer guns use smokeless."

"Can you take me shooting, Mr Pellam? Please?"

"Let's talk to your parents about it. Maybe."

"Shoot something. Will you?"

"Not now, Sam. It's not a toy." He put the gun back in his waistband. "Let's find me my cartridges."

With even more enthusiasm the boy swept the detector over the ground. Pellam wasn't paying much attention to him, he was looking at the dark patch of plowed-over earth in the distance, the parking lot, where Marty'd died a horrible death. He didn't notice the boy stoop down and pick up something then come racing over to him.

"Look what I found, Mr Pellam. Look!"

Sam dropped the two cartridges into his hand. They were .30 caliber, though the length was odd, stubbier than a .30-'30 or .30-'06, bigger than a Garand. They couldn't have been from a carbine like an M1 because a short-barreled rifle wouldn't have been accurate enough for a shot of this range.

"Good job, Sam." He patted the beaming boy on his shoulders. "Just what I'm looking for." He dropped the cartridges into his pocket.

"You show me your collection some day, Mr Pellam?"

"You bet, Sam. Time to get home."

"Aw . . ."

Together they walked down the mountain, swapping fishing stories.

That night, Sam upstairs, and Keith still at the company, Meg Torrens ate a turkey sandwich with cold cranberry sauce and drank a glass of white wine, reading the headlines and the first paragraphs of all the stories in the *New York Times*.

She heard the clicks and tiny pops of the hundred-year-old house, the muffled roar of the furnace coming on – something reassuring about the way its simple brain kicked the machinery on and coursed hot water through the pipes. It would shut off and there'd be moments of complete, muffled silence.

She finished the Arts section, dropped the paper and walked upstairs to Sam's room.

"Hi, Mommy."

She walked to his computer.

"Tell me again. You dial, then what do you say?" Meg looked at the computer.

"Aw, Mom," Sam said. He was tired, it was nearly nine. "It's a modem. Nobody says anything. You just get a tone. That means you're on-line."

"Show me." In the master bedroom the clock radio played a sad country western tune, an old Patsy Cline song.

Sam bent over the keyboard and typed rapidly. Meg and Keith spent thirty dollars a month for access to a current events database, which Sam had learned contained a sports submenu; they'd ended up with huge overages one month when he'd printed out the starting lineups of every baseball team since 1956.

He picked up the phone, dialed, his mouth twisted with exasperation, though Meg knew he was tickled to show off this esoteric knowledge. A squeal came from the phone. He held it toward her like a ray gun. "Zap, zap, zap!" And pressed a button on a small box. The computer screen came to life.

"You're on-line, Mom. What do you want to look up?"

"A name. I want to look up a man's name."

She typed in some characters. The response come back in five seconds. Meg scrolled through the text. "How do I print it?"

"You either do a screen dump or download the whole file."

Where did they learn this stuff?

"Just tell me what to push."

"Here." Sam happily hit a button, and the raspy matrix printer began its satisfying sound.

Reminded her of the Polaroid.

Bzzzt.

The sound lasted for some time. There was a lot to print.

———•••———

13

A pples.

A thousand apples, a hundred thousand. A million.

Pellam'd never seen so many apples in his life. And in so many forms. Apple pies, fritters, turnovers, apple butter, jelly, pickled apples and candied apples. You could dunk for them. You could buy them fresh by the bushels, buy them dried and painted and glued together into wreaths and wall hangings shaped like geese and pigs.

There were girls dressed up like apples. All the boys seemed to have round, rouge cheeks.

A woman tried to sell him a chance to win a Dutch apple pie by tossing a ring onto a board with apples nailed onto it.

"I don't really care for apples," he told her.

The football field was filled with more than a thousand people, milling through the booths, playing the games and examining the junk for sale – sweaters, wooden trinket boxes, clocks made from driftwood, ceramic, macrame. Janine had a jewelry booth. Pellam had homed in on it right away, waited until she was busy making a sale, and did the obligatory appearance. All she had time to say was "Dinner tomorrow, remember?"

He nodded.

"At four. Don't you forget, lover boy." She winked and blew him a kiss.

Pellam estimated half the crowd was tourists, half was locals. No one older than seventeen seemed exactly sure why they were there. The tourists were catching the tail of some indigenous upstate experience – *the country, the country!* – and holding on for a while, buying vases, jewelry, decorations, food to take back to their Manhattan apartments. The Cleary moms and dads were gossiping and doing some serious eating. The kids, of course, were the only ones really enjoying themselves because for them it was nothing more than tons of apples. And who needed more than that on a nice fall day?

No more 'Roids. He'd left the camera in the camper. Now, he was just another tourist scoping out the leaves, the booths, the scenery.

The Toyota showed up five minutes later, racing through the parking lot and skidding to a stop on the crumbling asphalt. Meg saw him right away and waved. Keith wasn't with her but Sam was. The boy waved energetically. He wondered if Sam had said anything about Pellam's tendency to collect lethal weapons.

Like the other night at dinner, she looked ten years younger than the upstate matron who'd visited him in the clinic. Her hair wasn't teased and stiff but was tied back in a ponytail. She wore tight jeans and a dark paisley high-necked blouse under a suede jacket. A silver antique pin was at her throat.

The boy stayed close. "Hi, Mr Pellam."

"Howdy, Sam."

"Hello," Meg said to Pellam. He nodded in reply.

They were suddenly enveloped in a large crowd of Izod-shirted Manhattanites. The men with curly dark hair, the women in black stretch pants. Everybody had great forearms and calves, courtesy of the New York Health and Racquet Club.

The gang passed and they found themselves alone.

"You made it," Meg said.

"Wouldn't miss this for the world."

"Here," Meg called. "A present."

She pitched him an apple. He caught it left-handed.

"I hate apples," he said.

Sam grinned. "So do I."

"Cleary still a small town?" Pellam smiled.

She frowned.

He asked, "Won't they talk, we walk around like this?" They circled on the fringes of the festival.

"Let 'em," Meg said. "I'm feeling rebellious today. Phooey."

Sam was running sorties to the booths but always circling back to study Pellam with casual awe. Then he'd be off again, hooking up with some buddies from school, conspiring, looking amazed and devious and overjoyed – and always on the move.

"Energetic, aren't they?" Pellam watched an impromptu race.

Meg said, "There's nothing like children for perspective. What they teach you about yourself is the best. Somebody said that the most honest and the most deceitful, the cruelest and the kindest of all people are children." She laughed. "Of course, that's only half true when you're talking about your own kids."

"You think about it, there are very few good movies about children," Pellam said. "Sentiment, mostly. Or revisionism – directors trying to patch up their own childhood on celluloid. Or trying to put adult values on kids' shoulders. Cheap shots, you ask me. I'd like to see a movie about the ambivalence of being a child. That would be a good project."

"Why don't you suggest it to your studio?"

Former studio, he thought, and didn't answer. Meg jogged away quickly to keep Sam from climbing a fence.

Pellam found himself in front of a turkey shoot booth, where you could win stuffed birds, chocolate turkeys, and a fifteen-pound frozen one by plinking tiny sponge rubber ducks – painted to look like turkeys – with a battered Sears pump action .22. Pellam called Sam over to him.

"What do you want, son, one of those little stuffed turkeys or a candy one?"

Sam looked shyly at his mother, who said, "Tell Mr Pellam what you'd like." She looked up, grinning. "This, I've got to see."

"I guess chocolate, okay?" His eyes on Pellam.

Meg said, "If he can win it you can eat it."

"But maybe not all at once," Pellam said. "It looks pretty big."

The booth attendant took a dollar from Pellam, who asked, "How many to win one of those chocolate turkeys? The bigger one?"

The man loaded the skinny gun. "Six hits out of ten."

"Okay." Pellam leaned forward, resting on the chest-high bench, and fired four shots slowly. They all missed, kicking up dust in the sandbag bullet trap.

Sam laughed. Meg did too.

Pellam slowly stood up straight. "Think I've got the feel." He quickly lifted the stock to his cheek. Six shots – fast, short cracks, as fast as he could work the slide. Six ducks flew off the board.

"Holy shit," the booth man whispered. Then he blushed. "Oh, beg your pardon, Mrs Torrens."

Pellam handed the gun back, and Sam took the candy, staring at him. Eyes wide. "Wow."

"What do you say, Sam?"

"Holy . . .," the boy began slowly.

Meg warned, "Sam."

". . . cow. Wow, thanks, Mr Pellam. That was like totally fresh. I mean, totally."

Meg said, "Sam . . ."

Sam said, "Mom thinks I don't speak English."

"I know fresh," Pellam said. He looked at the candy. "I hope that it is too."

Sam peeled back the foil and bit off the bird's head. "Wow," he said through a mouthful of chocolate and walked away, looking back every fourth or fifth step. Another story was about to circulate.

They wandered on. She said, "I thought all you knew was muzzleloaders."

"I drive the L.A. Freeway. You gotta know how to shoot."

"Where'd you learn?"

"My father," he said.

"Where'd you grow up?" she asked.

"Simmons."

She turned to him, "No! Not just across the river?" She nodded west.

"The very same."

"It's a lot like Cleary."

"Little poorer, little scruffier," Pellam said. "And we don't get the tourists for the leaves. It's mostly pine."

They walked in silence for a moment, kicking through the tall grass at the edge of the football field.

"Keith couldn't make it?"

"He'll be coming by later. He's at his company."

"It was good of him to help me the other day."

"He said somebody'd stolen what you were looking for."

"Yep. We got outflanked."

They walked for a few minutes then, as if Pellam had asked about her husband, Meg said, "Keith's changed. When his partner died, it affected him. He got an edge to him."

"Really? I didn't sense anything like that."

"I wasn't sure he'd help you. He doesn't like things that are out of his own, you know, orbit. I'm glad he did."

They were being examined – dozens of heads turned conspicuously away while eyes followed them.

After five minutes of looking at booths, he said, "Why did you leave Manhattan?"

"Keith got a job with a drug company up here. I wasn't getting modeling work and just couldn't break into acting. I had a baby. I always wanted a house."

"And you like Cleary?"

She gave a nervous laugh and looked away. "It's tough for

me to give you an answer. And it won't matter if I live here for another twenty-five years. I'll never know the place well enough to talk about it. These places, towns like this, they're born into you. The roots go way back. You come any other way, you're just a houseguest. You may be the life of the party, you may even get yourself elected to the town council, but places like Cleary don't become part of you. It's in the genes or it isn't. It's not in mine."

Applause not far away. A new Miss Apple had been crowned. Pellam saw a couple of kids gravitating toward him and Meg. Word was out that the location scout could shoot out a sponge duck's eye at fifty feet. The boys kept their distance as Meg and Pellam circled the field. The ripe, rich scent of decomposing grass came to them.

"Your hair looks nice that way."

Her fingers reached toward her ponytail then she stopped the acknowledgment and lowered her hand. Her eyes fled from his and she concentrated on something on the horizon. They walked to the festival's zoo – a sad collection of cows, goats, geese, ducks and a pony – before she said, "Is that why you and your wife broke up?"

"Uh, why's that?"

"Sorry, I was just thinking about you traveling around."

"There were a lot of reasons. Sure, the job had a lot to do with it."

"You were away from home six months, eight months—"

"I didn't travel as much then."

"I'd love to travel," she said. "Maybe do some acting. Not be a star necessarily. Character acting maybe. I'd even like your job."

Even your job.

Just a location scout.

"I don't think you would."

She said, "Well, I love my house. I wouldn't give that up. But seeing all those new places . . . It's like going on vacation, but having a purpose. I think that'd be wonderful."

Women said that. *My* house. Never our house. He remembered his wife saying just those words. Of course, in the end, that was how it worked out. It did become her house. Self-fulfilling prophecy, he guessed.

". . . I guess what I'd want is Sam to come with me for maybe a week or two at a time." After a moment, she said, "Keith too of course." She looked at him but he gave no reaction to the lapse. If a lapse it had been.

Pellam steered away from the domestic situation. He said, "I can't really tell you why I like it. The thing about scouting is, it's not the work itself – finding a spot that'll work for the film. I mean, that's fine, that's what they pay me for. But I like the being on the road . . ." He waved his arm. "Simmons is, what, less than a hundred miles from here? I grew up with colored leaves and Victorian houses. But I was real glad to get that call and hit the road, scout for towns like this."

He waved to Sam. It seemed his fan club had grown to a half dozen.

"One March," he continued, "I'd been sitting home for a month. I got a call from a producer who wanted me to scout for a labour union film. I got in the camper and headed right out to the steel mills in Gary, Indiana. Ugly, cold, gray. Walking through slush. That place was as close to hell as any I'd ever been. But I was so glad to get that call."

She wrinkled her nose. "I'd only go to fun places. Rio, San Francisco, Hawaii . . ."

He laughed. "You wouldn't get many jobs."

"No, but I'd have a hell of a good time on the ones I got."

"They have beer around here?"

"Probably, but don't you want some cider? They make it fresh."

"No, I want a beer. I hate apples, remember?"

"Then I guess an apple festival doesn't have a lot for you."

"I wouldn't say that."

Meg ignored the flirt and they steered toward the food concession.

As his mother and Mr Pellam were walking through the farmyard zoo Sam ran off toward a bow and arrow shoot. He thought about returning to the rifle shoot and winning something for Mr Pellam, but he remembered seeing the bow and arrow game – where you shot at paper targets of deer. One of the prizes was a small plastic football and because Mr Pellam had played in school that's what Sam decided he was going to win.

He gave the man a dollar for ten arrows and the hawker gave him a smaller bow, a straight pull, not one of the pulleyed hunting bows. Sam took it and notched an arrow, the way he'd done at camp. He went into position and pulled the string back. His muscles were quivering and his fingers let go quickly, before he'd sighted properly. He hit the deer in the rump.

"Hey," the voice called, laughing, "Got him in the ass."

Sam turned. It was one of the boys from high school. A senior, he thought. He believed his name was Ned. He was smiling but Sam followed the grade schoolers' general rule that every high school boy was a potential terrorist. They'd take your lunch away from you, tie your Keds together and swing them like gaucho's bolos over electric wires, swear and spit on you, use you for a sparring partner.

Sam swallowed and ignored him. He concentrated fiercely on the target, the way his mother had taught him when he shot – not paying attention to the bow or arrow, but to where the arrow should strike. He drew the bowstring back and fought the agony in his thin arms as he stared at his target. Finally, he released the arrow.

Thwack.

A heart shot.

"Fucking good," the boy was saying, shaking his head. Sam looked at him cautiously. Ned wasn't being sarcastic. "Thanks."

Two more heart shots, a gut shot, and then his strength started to go. The next four hit the bale of hay, but missed the deer. The last shot was another gut shot.

"Okay, you won yourself anything from the bottom shelf, son. What do you want?"

Sam hesitated. The kid was going to take his football away from him. He'd just grab it and run. He muttered, "One of those footballs."

"Okay, there you go."

Sam took the green plastic ball. He started to walk away quickly but the boy was making no moves toward him. He just said, "That was some good shooting. I wish I could shoot like that."

Sam laughed involuntarily. Here was a kid who was, like, seventeen telling Sam he couldn't shoot bow and arrow as good as him! Totally weird. "It's not hard. You've just gotta, you know, practice."

"What's your name?"

"Sam."

"I'm Ned." He stuck his hand out. No high school kid *ever* shook hands with grade school kids. Sam reached out tentatively and shook.

"Hey, you wanta see something?" Ned asked.

"Like what?" Sam didn't feel uncomfortable anymore. The boy could have grabbed the football and pushed him down any time. But no, he was just smiling and seemed to want to talk.

"Something neat?"

"I guess," Sam said, glancing toward where his mother and Mr Pellam were walking slowly, the same way his mother and father walked.

The boy walked off into a thick woods off the side of the football field. "What's here?" Sam asked.

"You'll see."

About thirty feet inside the woods was a small clearing. The boy sat down. He patted the ground next to him. Sam sat. "Let's see the ball."

Sam handed it to him.

"That's all right." He tossed it in his hand. "Feels good."

"I'm going to give it to Mr Pellam. He's the man with the movie company."

"Yeah, I heard about that. Totally excellent, making a film here." The boy handed the ball back to him. "Here you go."

There was silence for a moment.

Ned said, "I like it here. It's kind of secret."

Sam looked around and thought it looked like a clearing in a forest. "Yeah, it's okay."

"You got ten bucks?" Ned whispered.

"Naw," said Sam, who did in fact have eleven dollars and some change in his jeans pocket.

"How much you got?"

"A couple dollars. I don't know. Why?"

"You wanta buy some candy?"

"Candy? Ten bucks for candy?"

"It's special candy. You'll like it. I thought I saw you had ten bucks when you paid the guy at the arrow shoot."

Sam looked away from the older boy and squeezed the football. "Well, that, like, wasn't mine. It was my mom's."

Ned nodded. "I'll give you a sample. Then see if you don't want to buy one." He opened a yellow envelope and shook a dozen cubes of crystal candy into his hand. He held his palm out to Sam, who looked at the tiny bits cautiously. Ned laughed at his wariness and put a candy in his own mouth. "Come on, don't be a wuss."

"I don't really—"

Ned frowned. "You're not a pussy, are you?"

Sam suddenly grabbed most of the candies and slipped them into his mouth, chewing them down.

"No!" Ned shouted in horror. "You stupid shit! You weren't supposed to eat 'em all! They're ten dollars each!"

"I didn't mean . . ." Sam backed away in fear. His mouth was filled with a powerful, numbing sweetness. "I didn't know. You didn't tell me . . ." He suddenly felt warm and giddy and dizzy. In his mouth was a funny aftertaste, reminded him of the chewable vitamins he took in the morning.

Ned stepped close to him, reaching for Sam's collar; the young boy cowered away, feeling the heat and the dizziness flow over his body.

"Sam!" It was his mother's voice and from not very far away.

Then he was being lifted up. Ned had him by the shirt. "You dumb little prick! You tell anybody about this, I'll find you. I'll come get you and I'll beat the living shit out of you, you got that?"

Sam thought he should be afraid but he felt so good. He laughed.

"You hear me?"

Laughing again.

He felt himself falling into the leaves, which seemed suddenly like the ground in the Candyland game he played with his babysitter until he outgrew it. Cotton candy grass, marshmallow rocks. *Candyland.* Hey, just like the candy he'd eaten, he thought. That thought made him laugh too. He felt like laughing forever, he felt so good.

Strange thumping noises. He looked up. Ned was running, running fast, deep into the forest. Sam thought he saw the boy turn into a tree. He stared at the spot for a long time.

He tried to stand.

Laughing.

Fireworks, black sparklers, cascades, and Roman candles, pouring their fire all over him. A huge roaring hum in his ears.

Warmth and humming music.

"Sam?" His mother's voice was both magnified a thousand times and very distant, like she was trapped in an airlock on the Starship *Enterprise*.

Then the fun started to leave. He felt he was going to sleep, only it was a funny kind of sleep, like the way he felt when he'd had his tonsils out and woke up in terrible pain and so thirsty he thought he'd die. He'd been lonely when he awoke in the hospital and he cried for what seemed like forever, until he saw his mother, asleep, across the room.

That's who he wanted now. "Mommy," he called.

Sam managed to struggle to his feet. He walked forward a few steps. "Mommy, help me!"

A man's voice called, "Sam!" Mr Pellam's. And that reminded him of the football. He turned back into the black explosions, the heat, the cracking fireworks, the hum, and stumbled into the clearing, where he bent down to pick up the football. He was certain he had it but as he reached forward his hand came up with nothing more than leaves. He fell to the ground.

Then he saw nothing more; a huge wave of black filled his vision. But he kept patting the ground around him for the football. He *had* to find it.

He'd won it for Mr Pellam.

14

―•―••―•―

Her face scared him.

It wasn't just that she'd been crying, which changed
the density and texture of her skin and gave her the contours
of a battered wife; it was more the fluttering of the irises of her
eyes, unable to alight.

What Pellam saw in Meg Torrens's face was panic.

He just stood there, beside her, not knowing what to say or
whether he should touch her in a brotherly way. Thinking he
should be taking charge but with no idea of what needed to
be done.

Meg sat with her legs spread outward, boot tips pointed at
an oblique angle, her body forward, elbows resting on her
thighs, her hands washing each other absently in invisible
water. Occasionally she'd glance up and Pellam would smile
in a way that screenwriters would describe as sympathetically
concerned.

They'd waited for twenty minutes.

Keith arrived and as soon as he did, Pellam felt himself relax; he realized he'd been standing hunched forward, jaw tight. He watched the couple embrace. Keith nodded to him.

"What the hell happened?" husband asked wife.

Meg brushed aside her hair, which had come undone from the ponytail and was strewn across her face.

"We found him," she said and started sobbing again.

Pellam said, "Sam passed out and we couldn't revive him. The doctor's been in there since we got here. He hasn't said anything."

"Oh, Keith, he was so pale. It was terrible . . ."

With an anger they knew was not directed toward them Keith asked, "What happened? Did he fall? Is it a seizure?"

Meg wiped her face. "We just found him. Keith, it was so horrible. He was just lying there. It was like he didn't have any muscles. I tried to wake him up. He wouldn't wake up." She looked at Pellam with her trapped animal eyes, staring at *him* but undoubtedly seeing the horrific image of her son's pale skin against the autumn leaves. "He wouldn't wake up."

Keith looked like he wanted to hurt someone. It didn't seem to matter to him whether this'd been caused by another human being or an animal or some haywire connections in the boy's bloodstream. He wanted revenge.

Meg pressed her cheek against her husband's chest and didn't say anything. Slowly she calmed.

The doctor who resembled a vet, the one who'd tended Pellam, appeared and walked slowly down the corridor.

The man had such an expressive face that no words were necessary. There was no doubt about the boy's condition. Pellam remembered the way the man looked at him when he'd entered the room to tell him about Marty's death.

This was no tragedy.

The doctor's round jowly face zeroed in on Meg's eyes and he said, "He'll be okay."

Meg began crying again, quieter, but more desperately. "Can I see him?"

"Sure, Meg. In just a second."

Keith's anger vanished at once as if he were afraid prolonged hate might reverse the results. "What happened to him? Was it a seizure?"

"Keith, I need to ask this. Does Sam have any history of drug use?"

"Drug use?" The laugh was explosive.

Meg let go of her husband and turned to face the doctor. "He's ten years old, how could he—?"

"Drug use?" Keith repeated as if he hadn't heard correctly.

"What did—" she began.

The doctor said, "He overdosed on drugs."

With a blustery edge in her voice Meg said, "No! Not Sam."

"Oh, give me a fucking break," Keith growled. "Are you nuts?"

The doctor continued. "It's true, Keith. It looks like it was an opiate of some kind. Probably heroin."

Keith exploded. "Are you saying he was shooting up? That's the craziest, fucking thing—" Meg touched her husband's arm. He calmed. "I'm sorry. But you made a mistake."

"I'm as disturbed about this as you are . . ." The doctor lifted a small plastic envelope out of his pocket. Inside were tiny fragments of crystals. "These were in his mouth. It's extremely soluble. Which means he ingested much more than this."

All three stared at the bag.

"It's a dextrose base – sugar – but it's mixed with something else. I don't know what exactly. A synthetic heroin of some kind. Stronger than Percodan. I've never seen anything like it."

"Somebody put heroin in candy and gave it to my son?" Keith whispered. He looked at Meg and said, almost accusingly, "Who was he with? Did you see anybody, weren't you watching him?"

Pellam bristled, felt defensive for Meg. "We were both with the boy. He'd run off every once in a while but we—"

"For God's sake, Keith, we were at the Apple Festival. I wasn't letting him wander around in the South Bronx—"

He blinked. "I'm sorry, I just—"

She took his hand.

The doctor said, "I've called Tom. I had to. Whatever this is it's a controlled substance and I've got to report it."

"Fucking right you're going to report it," Keith growled. "But I don't want a story in the *Leader*. I don't want it to sound like he was doing drugs."

"I won't say anything to the paper. But this's serious, Keith. I don't know – Tom may want to bring somebody from Albany in."

In a faint voice, Meg said, "Please let me see my son."

"Come on," the doctor said. He glanced at Pellam, then down at the leg where the bruise resided. "How you doing, sir?" he asked pleasantly but without particular interest.

"Fine."

The doctor put his arm around Meg and led her down

the corridor. Keith said, "Excuse me," to Pellam and followed.

Pellam sat down in an aluminum-and-orange-naugahyde chair and looked at a month-old *People* magazine without reading a single word, or seeing a single picture.

An hour later, Sam walked unsteadily out of the room. Meg had her arm around him and Keith was trying to sound cheerful while he recited phrases like, "You're doing great, skipper" and "You're a tougher man than I." Sam would blink and look at his father as if he were speaking a foreign language.

"Hi, Mr Pellam," Sam said. His face brightened a little but there was hardly any color in it.

"How you feeling, son?"

"I got sick."

"You'll be fine in the morning."

"I don't feel too good."

"Well, get better soon. We've got to practice our football, remember?"

"Yeah."

Meg, Sam and Pellam stood together, silently, while Keith paid the bill with a check and took a prescription and instruction sheet from the doctor.

The door opened and the sheriff walked into the clinic.

"Meg, I just heard."

"Tom," she said, nodding toward him.

The sheriff looked stonily at Pellam for a long moment, then glanced down at Sam. "How you doing, young man?"

"Pretty okay, sir."

"Attaboy."

The doctor joined them, along with Keith. Meg told the sheriff about finding her son in the woods and the doctor explained about the drugs.

"What is it, you know?"

"I'm sending the sample to a lab in Poughkeepsie. I'll get you a copy of it. I think it's a heroin derivative."

The sheriff winced. "Yeah, guess I'll have to go to the NYBI."

"Second time we've had an overdose," the doctor pointed out. "That boy last year."

Tom nodded. "He was in high school. They're getting younger."

The sheriff looked down at Sam then said to Keith. "You mind if I talk to him just for a minute?"

Meg asked her son, "You mind, honey?"

"Uh-uh."

"Maybe just you, me and the boy?" Tom asked her.

Pellam and Keith took their cues and stepped outside.

The sheriff crouched next to a jaundiced potted bamboo palm, vainly reaching for a tiny, greasy window in the front door, the only source of natural light in the waiting room.

Meg was struggling to stay calm, struggling to concentrate. All she wanted to do was throw her arms around the boy.

The sheriff looked into the boy's eyes. "What happened, Sam? You remember?"

"I found this envelope. And there was some candy inside. I ate it."

"You ate it?"

"A bunch of it. I guess I shouldn't've. Mom's pretty mad at me."

Meg said, "No, I'm not, honey."

Tom said, "She's just worried about you, that's all. So you don't know where the envelope came from?"

"No, sir."

"You're sure nobody gave it to you?"

"No, sir. I mean, yeah, I'm sure nobody gave it to me."

"You just found it."

"Uh-huh."

"You know what happened to the envelope?"

"No."

"I'm going to ask you a question, Sammie, and I want you to answer it truthfully."

"Sure."

"You know Mr Pellam."

"Sure."

"Did he give you the candy?"

Meg stiffened when she heard this. This hadn't even occurred to her. She started to speak but the sheriff waved her quiet.

"You mean, that he won?"

"What?"

"He won a chocolate turkey and gave it to me."

"When was that?"

"Just before I got sick."

"It was a game," Meg said. "A booth at the fair."

The sheriff ignored her. "Did he give you the candy in the envelope?"

Sam shook his head. "No, sir."

"You found it, right?"

Sam swallowed. "Yeah, it was just lying there. I found it."

"Okay, Sammie. You go home now and get some rest."

"So he gave the boy some candy," the sheriff said.

Meg frowned, repeated, "From the turkey shoot booth. Chocolate. Not . . . that crap."

"Look, Sam claims he found the envelope but he's lying. I can see. All right, not lying exactly. He's confused. You know kids, Meg, come on. What I'm saying is I know somebody gave him those pills and *he* knows who it is."

Meg asked, "You think it was Pellam?"

"Kind of a coincidence, wouldn't you say? His friend's doing drugs and gets himself killed. Then your son overdoses." He asked, "Was Sam alone with Pellam today?"

She didn't answer at first. "No."

"Any other time they may have been together alone?"

She swallowed and shook her head. "I want to be with my son."

"Sure, Meg."

Outside, Pellam watched the two of them push out the door and head toward Keith's car. Meg hugged Sam. "Let's get you home, into bed."

"I don't feel good."

Pellam stepped forward, crouched down and took the boy by the shoulders. "When you're better, young man, you and I're going to—"

Meg took her son's hand firmly in hers and practically pushed the boy into the Cougar. Pellam stared at her. She wouldn't look back. Meg didn't say anything as she walked to her car and started it.

Keith got in the Cougar, put Sam's seat belt on him.

Both cars pulled out of the parking lot, Keith's red Mercury and Meg's gray Toyota. She didn't even look at him. Pellam stared after the import for several minutes. Finally, there was nothing left to see but a residue of haze above the asphalt in the car's wake. It was only then that he realized that while he was looking at the spot where Meg's car had disappeared the sheriff, sitting in his glossy, pristine squad car, had been staring at him.

He walked over to the man. "I drove here in Meg's car from the fairgrounds. My camper's back there. You give me a lift?"

"Sorry, sir. I'm heading the opposite direction."

"Sure," Pellam said, watching his black-and-white pull dramatically out of the parking lot, slinging gravel behind it. "Thanks anyway. Sir."

Bobby sat inside the cabin at the junkyard and read a *National Geographic*. He looked at the stain in the margin and wondered what it was. Grape jelly, maybe. Blood? Beef juice?

R&W was fat with *National Geographics*. Stacks and stacks of them, going moldy. Yellow and green. His brother didn't understand why Bobby continued to buy the old ones. Something about that magazine, people thought you shouldn't throw them out, like doing that was somehow unpatriotic. So what they did was bundle them up and take them to antique stores or tag sales or junkyards like R&W and sell them, all organized by year. Or decade. Didn't matter if they made money on them. The point was, a part of America got preserved and, besides, where else but in articles about Africa or the Amazon could a twelve-year-old boy get a look at tits and not run the chance of getting whipped?

Today, Bobby was reading about Portland, which seemed

like a great place to live. He closed the magazine and tossed it against the wall of the shack. True, they *were* starting to smell. He'd have to get out the Lysol spray.

He heard the car door slam.

Bobby knew right away, even before the door to the shack opened that there was trouble. This was something about twins, at least something about Billy and him. A telepathy thing. So now when his brother opened the door and walked through it, Bobby was staring right into his eyes, frowning with an expression that matched Billy's almost identically.

He said, "So?"

"So our ass is in deep shit," Billy muttered.

"What?"

"Torrens's kid got some of the pills. Almost OD'd."

"Fuck. That little blond kid?" Bobby glanced in a perfunctory way toward the backroom of the shack where several cartons of their special candy were stacked. "How'd he get it?" Then he knew, the message from his brother coming through loud and clear. He nodded grimly. "The pretty boy? Ned. The other day."

"Your playmate."

Bobby said, "*Our* playmate. Just 'cause I saw him first don't go blaming me. Why'd he give them away?"

"Why'd you give him so many in the first place? Damn, I'll ream that boy's ass."

Bobby gave a splinter of a smile. "You already done that."

But his brother wasn't in any mood to joke. "This isn't funny."

Bobby was nodding slowly. "The Torrens kid," he muttered. "They know it was us?"

Shallow Graves • 199

"They did, don't you think we'd've heard by now?"

"What if Ned said something to the kid? About where he got it?"

"Could be a problemo," Billy said absently. "Too bad the kid didn't take 'em all. And just, you know, die. Would've been better."

"So they've got some? Of the stuff, I mean."

"Yeah," Billy explained.

"Ouch."

"It's at the clinic. They're going to be shipping it somewhere to find out what it is."

"Fuck," Bobby said. "That's bad. Man, that's bad. What're we gonna do?"

And Billy looked at his brother as if he'd just asked the most dumb-ass question in the world. "Well, if you think real hard, maybe a couple things'll come to mind."

He didn't have to wait very long before they did.

"Hello?"

The voice of Wex Ambler's housekeeper answering the phone.

Meg didn't know the woman. She'd seen her several times since she and Ambler had begun their affair – once coming out of the brick and white-trim First Presbyterian Church on Maple Street. But Meg hadn't actually heard her voice before this moment. She sounded older than Ambler.

"Is Mr Ambler there please?" Meg, who had never typed a letter for anyone other than herself or Keith in her life, tried to sound like a Kelly Girl.

"Just a minute, please. Who shall I say's calling?"

This she'd thought about. "Dutchess County Realty."

"One minute."

"Hello?"

"Wex."

A moment later, she was listening to her lover say with a tortured formality, "Yes, Meg. How are you? I wasn't expecting to hear from you." There was a pause at the end of his sentences. She knew that Ambler liked phrases of affection and it would be natural for him to add a "darling" or "dear." Under the circumstances, of course, he'd have to watch himself carefully to avoid these.

Ambler had reluctantly agreed to Meg's demand that not a single soul in town know about their affair.

Meg asked, "Is it safe to talk?" Then she regretted the idiocy of the question.

Ambler ignored it. "What can I do for you?"

"There was an accident. Somebody gave Sam some drugs."

There was a pause. "Is he all right?"

"He'll be okay. But I can't make it today."

"Of course. I understand. What kind of drugs?"

"Heroin, it looked like."

"Are you sure?" His voice sounded flatlined. As if he hadn't even heard her.

"That's what the doctor said."

"Where did he get it?"

Meg hesitated. "I have no idea. He claims he found it."

"Will he be okay?"

"The doctor said he would."

He spoke again slowly. "I'm sorry. I wish I could have been there."

She said, "Yes, that would have been good."

Static growing on the line. She guessed he was on a cordless phone and had moved into a den, or outside. He spoke more freely. "When can I see you? I—"

Then he stopped talking and – his housekeeper undoubtedly approaching – said, "Those prices are a little high."

"I want to talk to you," she said. "There're some things we should talk about."

She was thankful Ambler wasn't alone and wasn't free to ask the questions that she didn't want to answer right now, certainly not over the phone. She heard the frustration in his voice. "I understand. It's a mutual situation. Day after tomorrow?"

"Probably."

"Have you thought any more about my proposition of the other day?"

"I don't want to talk about that now."

"I'm sorry. It's just . . . I'll look forward to seeing you day after tomorrow."

Meg found she was answering as if Keith were in the room, which he was not. "Those would be acceptable terms." She hung up.

"How you feeling, skipper?" Keith asked his son.

"Pretty good, Dad." But Sam's voice was weak and he was huddled in his bathrobe and blanket on his bed. Heartbreaking, the way he was lying, so small and fragile.

The computer's fan whirred softly; the screen was blank except for the C prompt, waiting for instructions. Keith thought about shutting it off but didn't; he figured Sam had left it on for whatever comfort the sound of the machinery might provide.

Keith sat on the edge of the bed and tucked the blankets around the boy. "How's the stomach?"

"I liked the ice cream. It didn't make me feel icky."

Keith nodded and remembered to look the boy in the eyes. Meg had once told him that he looked away from people too much. He'd explained to her that his mind wandered; he couldn't help it. She'd told him that was no excuse. When you had children, you had to give them a hundred and fifty percent of yourself.

There was a lot he wanted to say. About how he knew he wasn't as attentive as he ought to be, how he didn't like sports the way most of Sam's friends' fathers did, how he kept putting off vacations. About how if he hadn't been working today this probably wouldn't have happened. But he thought that talk like that now would just upset the boy, make him think that the incident with the drugs was worse than it was. He told himself that he simply would make it up to the boy. Not after the expansion at the factory was completed, not after the first of the year, not after the cold-season rush, but soon, very soon.

"I'm sorry about what happened, Daddy."

"We don't blame you, Sam."

"I was like pretty stupid."

"Sam," Keith leaned forward. "It is very, very important that you tell me where you got those pills."

"The candy?"

"Right. The candy. I know you didn't just find it."

Tears had started and the little boy was shaking. Keith put his hand on Sam's shoulder and squeezed it. "Don't worry. I won't let anything else happen to you."

"He said he'd beat me up."

"I won't let anyone beat you up. I promise you. Tell me."

"A kid from the high school."

"Who?"

"I don't know his last name. His first name's Ned. I think he's a senior."

"What does he look like?"

"He was like sort of tall. Like a football player . . . Oh, Daddy . . ." Sam bolted forward into Keith's arms. They hugged for a few minutes. Keith stood up. "You want me to leave the light on?"

"Uh-huh. Is it okay?"

Keith mussed Sam's hair. "I'll be up later and look in on you."

"Okay."

"Goodnight, son."

15

The fire at the clinic wasn't too bad.

Nowhere near the excitement of the Great Fire of 1912.

Only one of Cleary's trucks was needed and the men got the blaze under control with fire extinguishers, which was a big letdown because of all the hours they'd spent at hose drill. Brush fires and burning toasters – that was all they ever got. And at the clinic they didn't even get to use an axe. Like a lot of buildings in Cleary, the clinic was left open even when the all-night nurse went out for coffee, or – as in this case – to buy batteries for her Walkman.

Most of the carnage was confined to the office. A lot of patient records were destroyed as was all the outgoing mail and a number of envelopes bound for the testing lab in Albany. The gushing water had caused the most damage.

The first chief, a lean, chiseled-faced man who ran an insurance agency in town and took both jobs equally seriously, went through the office slowly. He didn't really need to, though; it didn't take any length of time, or great forensic skill, to make the discovery. He put his find into a Hefty trash bag (the Cleary Fire Department wasn't entrusted with evidence bags) and then went to his car to call the sheriff on his CB. He had trouble getting through and went back inside to call him on the phone, which was partly melted but still working.

As he stood at the charred desk and waited for Tom to come on the line he stared at what he'd found. For some reason the fire had not completely consumed the incendiary device. He knew, from the label, that the bottle at one time had held Taylor New York State sparkling wine and, from the smell, that it had more recently held gasoline.

He knew too (from research and continuing education – never having encountered a fire bomb before) that cloth was standard procedure for fuses. But this one was different. He held it up close.

The fire chief was pretty much a humorless man. But as the sheriff came on the line with a "Lo?," the chief was laughing, thinking they must be dealing with some pretty literate arsonists. Who else'd use pages from a *National Geographic* to light a Molotov cocktail?

"Mark," said Mayor Hank Moorhouse, after hearing him out, "it's no crime for the man to wander around and take pictures. If it weren't for assholes taking pictures of the leaves, we'd be a much poorer town. You know that."

It was suppertime. Succulent smells – roasts and fatty potatoes – floated through the Moorhouse's Victorian home. The sound of utensils and muffled voices came from another part of the house.

The heavyset and damn-scary young man, moving a pile of chewing tobacco around inside his cheek, said, "This guy is dangerous. You heard about Meg Torrens's kid? He got his hands on some dope."

"No! I didn't hear about that. Sam?" Moorhouse's eyes flicked down to the blond moustache then up again.

"The word is he got it from Pellam. A couple guys saw 'em together."

Mark moved the chaw around his mouth.

Moorhouse's nostrils dilated at the smell of dinner. He wanted this over with, and fast. But Mark worked for Wexell Ambler and Ambler held the first and second mortgages on Moorhouse's six-bedroom Colonial and was an assemblyman on the town council. He said, "That somvabitch." He tore off a piece of Scotch tape, wadded it up and started chewing. He'd tried to stop the habit but thought now: Better'n tobacco.

"There's more."

Mark dropped a packet of white powder down onto the desk.

"What's that?"

"What do you think it is?"

Moorhouse stared at the package as if it were from the melted core at Chernobyl.

"I saw him drop it," Mark said. "Pellam."

Moorhouse leaned forward carefully. He didn't want to touch the plastic. "We don't get much of this stuff around here. Christ, I worry about my boys –" He nodded toward the dining room. "– drinking beer. They tell me they've never tried pot and I believe 'em. But this . . . What exactly is it, Mark? Cocaine, huh?"

"Speed, I think."

"And it's illegal?"

Mark scoffed. "Illegal? A class IA controlled substance."

"What do you suppose it's worth? What's the, what do they say on the news, what's the street value?"

"You're asking me?" Mark said, his voice high with surprise. "What difference does it make?"

"Can't arrest someone just 'cause you saw him drop it." Though when Moorhouse thought about this, he wasn't so sure. Maybe you *could*. He wondered where you could look that up. Cleary had a town attorney.

Mark smiled amiably and leaned toward Moorhouse in a way that he thought of as doing what he did best. "Then we'll have to think a little harder."

Moorhouse's eyes kept circling in on the packet like a mosquito over flesh. "I don't know."

The brown envelope hit the desk with a slap. Moorhouse jumped, hesitated a moment, then picked it up. He glanced up at Mark, who said, "There's three thousand dollars in there."

Moorhouse thumbed through the bills. "Take your word for it. Where'd it come from?"

"Let's say a bunch of folk took up a collection. We don't think this guy should be here any longer. Movie ain't gonna be made here. No reason for him to hang around."

"So what's this for?" Moorhouse asked, before he realized he shouldn't be asking.

"A magistrate's fee you could call it."

His eyes darted from the money to the white packet.

He slipped the envelope in his desk and poked the powder, soft as baby talcum, with the end of his Cross pen.

He had three shots of Wild Turkey – trying to convince himself that he was celebrating – and lay back in the camper, listening to Willy Nelson sing *Crazy*.

Pellam had this theory that made for a very optimistic life. You kept considering the worst that could happen to you and then, when it didn't, whatever *did* happen wasn't so bad.

Who couldn't be cheerful with that kind of philosophy?

So, close to drunk, Pellam told himself that the worst had happened. *A*, he'd gotten fired from a job he needed and *B*, that was the one job in the world – outside of being independently wealthy – that he was temperamentally suited for. *C*, the rumor would already be burning up Sunset Boulevard that he was personally responsible for cratering a damn fine movie. *D*, he still hadn't found the man who'd killed his friend. And *E*, the woman he was spending a lot of time thinking about was mad at him for some reason he couldn't for the life of him figure out (this would be Meg, not Janine. Or . . . oh, Trudie. Too late to call her today. He would tomorrow).

He heard the car pull up.

He hoped it would be Meg though he knew it wasn't. It'd be Janine. Pellam knew what had happened: the old man was balling his current old lady under a Da-Glo Hendrix poster and somebody got stood up.

Come on, Janine, please, baby. Free love. Give peace a chance. Up against the wall . . .

Pellam was whisky giddy, almost happy. The worst had

happened. He was immune. And here was a big, horsy warm woman to bed down with.

The worst –

He swung open the door.

– had already happened.

The dirt and stones caught him square in the face before he got his hands halfway up to cover his eyes. He went blind. He inhaled a good bit of Cleary debris and started choking.

There were two of them. And one was big, a bear. He grabbed Pellam's shirt and pulled him easily out of the camper. He stumbled and, off balance, went down on his knees. Got dragged a few feet.

His eyes were burning, he was coughing loud and spitting out the bitter dirt.

"Come on, asshole, stand up," a brisk voice whispered. Arms slid under his chest. The bear tugged him up. Pellam uncoiled his legs. The top of his head collided with jaw.

"Shit, motherfucker! Cut my tongue. Shit, shit, shit!"

Pellam kicked out at the other, a smaller guy, who easily sidestepped the boot.

What he'd done – the lunging up – was just a reaction. But he knew it was a mistake. Guys like this, local tough guys, you don't play with. You just stay as clear away as you can, rolling and dodging until you get a good crack. You don't sting them; you hit them hard once or twice, really hard. Try to break their head. Make them think you're going to kill them. They'll leave, cussing you out and making it sound like you're not worth the trouble.

What happened was they'd come to have fun and Pellam had just pissed them off. Now they were mad.

The bear punched him hard on the first offered target – his shoulder, which didn't hurt much, but then he got him in a full nelson, pressed Pellam's chin down to his chest. Pellam was taller – so the bear couldn't lift him off the ground but the huge man kept him immobile. The other one came in for some low gut swings, right into the muscles, which knocked his wind out and sent blasts of nausea up through his chest. The bear said to no one, "My tongue bleeding? Shit, I think it is. God*damn*, that hurts."

Pellam opened his eyes but couldn't see a thing through the mud and tears. He gasped, "What do you want? You want money?"

The bear bent his head down further and the words got lost in a gurgle.

No, what they want is to beat the living crap out of me . . .

The smaller one came in close, aiming for Pellam's face, but couldn't get his fist in because the bear's fat elbows were in the way. "Hey, turn him loose for a second."

Which is when Pellam, gasped, shuddered and went completely limp.

"Shit, what happened?" The bear relaxed his grip. "Is he dead? Fuck. What'd you do?"

"What'd I do? I didn't do nothing. I just—"

Pellam broke free, felt his shirt rip down the back as the bear grabbed for it and swung a feint with his left fist at the smaller assailant, who dodged to the side. Right into Pellam's sweeping right fist. The snap of the man's nose cartilage was real satisfying; the howl that accompanied it was even more delightful.

Pellam turned to meet the bear but the big man was already

on top of him. He picked Pellam up, right off the ground. "So you want to play rough, huh?" he asked.

"I don't want to do anything! I want—"

The bear slammed him into the side of the camper. Something snapped but it sounded more like metal than bone. Pellam fell to the ground, gasping, then got to his knees. The bear was battering him wildly, connecting often enough so Pellam couldn't stand. The pain swirled through his body.

Finally he gave up, he lay still. Exhausted, gasping. "Enough. Okay."

In the distance was a siren. "Let's get out of here," the bear said.

"Oh, God, this hurts," his partner offered. "He broke my nose. He broke my fucking nose."

The bear whispered, "Shut up, will you?"

Pellam, trying to breathe, started to crawl under the camper. He felt the big hands reach down and grab him by the ankle. They pulled him back then reached into his pocket. Not his wallet pocket, which he would've expected, but his front shirt pocket. Why there? It was empty.

The siren wailed closer.

Pellam heard:

"Let's get the fuck outa here. *Move* it."

"My nose, man. You didn't—"

"Move it, asshole."

He heard doors slam, and the throaty, crisp sound of a motor firing up, a squeal of tires.

Pellam spit blood and tried to catch his breath. Fucking odd . . . He supposed it wasn't a robbery – they left his wallet and watch, ignored everything in the camper and only went through one pocket. If they'd been here to deliver a get-out-of-town message they'd had plenty of time to deliver it but hadn't.

He coughed and made it halfway to a sitting position, lay back down.

The cop car skidded to a stop on the other side of the camper. The siren shut off and he saw the strobe of colored lights on the trees.

His hand strayed to the pocket the bear had rummaged through. He felt the present.

Oh, Christ, no . . .

He pulled out the little glassine envelope. Coke or speed. A gram, easy. Oh, Lord. Felony possession. Pellam stared at the packet through muddy eyes.

He heard their voices. "Okay, let's find him. Search everything around the clearing."

Pellam started coughing again, deeply, as the cops rounded the camper. He recognized the two deputies even though neither was wearing their trademark sunglasses.

"Well, sir," the deputy said, "looks like you had some more of that bad luck after all."

No, don't go after the thugs. Stand there and bust my chops, why don't you? . . .

"You all right, sir?" The other one asked.

He helped Pellam to his feet. He was coughing, choking. "Water, please, some water."

"Sure, no problem." The first deputy stepped into the camper and came back with a cup of water. Pellam took it and swallowed the whole thing down. Breathing desperately, his chest heaving, like a nearly drowned man on land once again.

"Can you stand up, sir?"

Pellam was frowning, watching the other deputy going over the clearing with his flashlight, inch by inch.

"Yeah, I can."

"Good." The deputy smiled. "Because you're under arrest." He glanced at his friend. "Read him his rights. And search him."

16

"**A**nd you didn't find anything?" Moorhouse asked the sheriff.

The mayor squinted against the brilliant sunlight streaming into his office early on Sunday morning.

"Nothing. My deputies searched like you told us. But they didn't find anything."

"You're sure? No drugs? All these movie people do drugs all the time," Moorhouse said.

Which Tom knew because he and the wife read *People*. But he also knew they'd searched like a son of a bitch and found zip.

"He was out when they found him?"

"Nosir. But he was down, lying under the camper. He couldn't have thrown anything far enough so's we'd miss it. We combed the ground. And I mean combed."

Moorhouse warily asked, "Any idea who he was mixing it up with?"

"Nope. You want, I can ask around."

Moorhouse shook his head. "No. Pellam probably started the fight." He motioned with his head toward the Sheriff's Department, with its small lock-up. "Can't blame some local kid for getting tough with an asshole from the Coast thinks he owns the place. Any evidence of the, you know, the gas bomb in the clinic?"

"Nope."

"Had to've been him though."

"You'd think," the sheriff said. But uncertainly. He kept looking at Moorhouse curiously, playing with the big hammer of his chrome-plated .357.

The mayor grimaced. *Now I got an envelope of LSD or PVC or whatever the hell it is out loose somewhere in town. Where was it? What if some kid gets a hold of it? Christ.*

"What about Pellam?" he asked the sheriff. "He okay?"

"Seems to be. Brought him in last night, blood all over him. He went into the john at the station and puked his guts out. I thought maybe we oughta get him to the hospital, but—"

"The hospital that he tried to fucking burn down."

"Uh," Tom said noncommittally. "He seems okay now."

"We better have a little talk with him," Moorhouse said. "Bring him in."

Handcuffed.

Standing in front of this small-town shine, who was wearing his favorite baby-blue suit.

And handcuffed, for Christsake.

"Mr Pellam, let me say how sorry we are about what happened. Things like this you don't usually see here. Cleary's a peaceful place."

"Surprising," said the sheriff. "That it happened, I mean."

Pellam nodded to him and squinted against the cold, brutal sun that poured in through the smeared windows. The worst pain was in his right hand – the knuckles – where he'd hit bone.

"Why'd I spend the night in jail?"

"Oh." Moorhouse swivelled back in his green leatherette chair. "You were arrested for D&D. Didn't the deputy read you your rights?"

"Sure he did, Mayor," the sheriff offered.

Pellam asked, "D&D?"

"Drunk and disorderly conduct. How do you plead?"

April fool. Had to be a joke. Pellam even gave them a short laugh. "I got jumped by two assholes knocked on my door, dragged me out and beat the hell out of me. That's not D&D."

Moorhouse smiled patiently. "Guilty or not guilty."

"Not guilty. Have you found the two assholes?"

The sheriff's turn: "Seems the other perpetrators—"

"*Other* perpetrators?" Pellam laughed.

"—escaped. We searched for evidence but didn't find any." He turned to Pellam. "You weren't real helpful when it came to the description, sir."

Pellam raised his hands. The chrome bracelets jangled with a dull sound. "Somebody threw a truckload of dirt in my face before they started working on me."

Moorhouse said, "Well, under the law, of course, we don't need the others. We can prosecute the one we caught. And that's you. Now, I'm taking off my mayor's hat and putting on my magistrate's." He consulted an empty wall calendar. "I'm setting trial for one week. About bail—"

"What do you mean, one week?"

"I'm a very busy man."

"Good. Let me go. I'll be one less burden for you."

Moorhouse looked him up and down – the shirt stained with dirt and ruddy-black dots of blood, the blotched jeans, the hair upended from a night on a stiff pillow.

"To be honest with you, sir, we aren't inclined to keep you around here for any length of time ourselves."

Sir sir sir . . .

The sheriff rocked on his thick heels; a board creaked.

The light was painful as a dull razor. Pellam's eyes were watering. He waited. Moorhouse was trying to tell him something. Something he was supposed to be picking up on. Something that was not quite right for the town magistrate to be asking – even *this* town magistrate.

Pellam sniffed and blinked the tears.

"You got a cold, sir?"

"That truckload of dirt I was mentioning."

"Ah." Moorhouse looked at the sheriff. "Tom, why don't you leave us be for a minute."

"Sure, Mayor." The lean man pivoted on his heels and walked out of the room in as near to a march as a man could get without Sousa playing in the background.

"Pellam, your presence here's been, what's the word? Disruptive."

"No more disruptive than two assholes driving around town beating up people who're minding their own business."

"Ha, there you go." Moorhouse shook his head. "Did you know that the clinic near to burned down last night?"

Pellam blinked. Trying to make the connection, how this figured in his case. He asked, "What, exactly—"

"You know what was destroyed in the fire?"

Oh. Interesting. He said, "Those drugs the Torrens boy had."

"Yes, sir." Moorhouse raising an eyebrow.

"Oh, come on, you charging me with arson too? You've got no probable cause for that."

Moorhouse's other eyebrow joined the first and they seemed to be asking: *How come you're so familiar with words like "probable cause"? How come, sir?*

"Mr Pellam, you're the kind of outside influence isn't good for our community."

"Outside influence might be just the ticket," Pellam said, "you being the inside influence."

Moorhouse, smiling, sucked air in through his white teeth. "I may have to add contempt to your growing list of infractions, you aren't careful—"

Pellam put his hands, balled into fists, on the desk, and leaned forward. Light shot off the cuffs. "I want bail set and I don't care if you're busy fixing DWI tickets for the sons of your clients – I want a trial tomorrow. I'm calling my lawyer in Manhattan and getting him up here today with a habeas corpus writ and you fuck around anymore with me and I'll sue your ass for abuse of judicial process and failure to get an injured prisoner adequate medical attention—"

"Now, just let's calm down here. Let's—"

"You tell me," Pellam said between angry jaws, "how easy your town treasury'll afford a judgment of two-, three-hundred thousand?"

Moorhouse kept the false smile. His face reddened and he faked a cough to swallow. His eyes strayed to the phone. Pellam could see he was furious. Somebody'd put him in this tough position. "My, my, you are a touchy one. I'll tell you what. You just leave our town, and I'll drop all the charges."

Pellam said softly. "What's bail?"

The smile twisted and became lopsided. "Bail is set at five thousand dollars."

The door behind Pellam squealed open. A broad trapezoid of light fell into the room. He hardly heard it. He snapped, "*How* much? Where am I going to get that kind of money on Sunday?"

A woman's voice said, "From me. A check'll be okay, won't it, Hank?"

He frowned. "Morning, Meg. What're you doing here?"

She walked up to the desk. "A check?" She was already writing it out.

"You don't have to—" Pellam began. She glanced at his face, which must've been in worse shape than he'd thought since her eyes flashed wide for a second.

Moorhouse was peeling a piece of tape off the dispenser and rolling it up. He chewed on it absently. "Meg, this isn't a good idea."

She finished writing out the check. Pellam said to her, "How did you know?"

She ignored him.

"Meg," Moorhouse tried again. "It really isn't a good idea."

Meg dropped the check onto his desk. "A receipt. I'd like a receipt."

He couldn't find one and had to write one out by hand on a yellow pad.

Meg pushed through the door. Pellam, frowning, looked after her. Moorhouse spit the tape out of his mouth and said,

"Trial is set for Monday morning. I know a local lawyer, you want."

Pellam pushed his fists out toward the man's chest. "What I want is the cuffs off. They're a little disruptive."

Pellam sat in the passenger seat as Meg pushed the little car up through the gears and shot out of town.

He casually slipped the seatbelt and shoulder harness on. He noticed the knob on the manual transmission gearshift was twisted and worn from heavy use, the gear position symbol upside down. As if to show him why, she downshifted on a gentle curve and brought the speed back up to about seventy.

It was a forty zone.

Over the roar of the engine, he said, "Thanks. I—"

Meg shook her head.

He didn't know what she meant: that she didn't want him to talk or that she couldn't hear him. The tach was almost redlined.

Pellam looked around. The streets were empty. The parking lot next to a church was full of small trucks and cars. It was classic American religion – a sweeping white steeple and red brick, symmetrical, unchallenging, simple. He wondered what denomination it was, then decided it didn't really matter; religion in Cleary would be pretty much the same whatever church you happened to be in.

"Where's Sam?"

"Sunday school."

"Where's Keith?"

"Some errand then he was going to the factory."

"Oh."

They drove in silence to the house. To *her* house. In *her* car.

With *her* flinty eyes and taut mouth.

When they got there, she left four-foot skid marks in the gravel and climbed out, slamming the thin door with a crash. She walked up on the porch, leaving Pellam in the passenger seat.

She disappeared inside.

He sat.

She reappeared a minute later and said, "You coming inside or not?"

"Well, I guess I—" he said to her receding back.

The house was quiet. A funny thing, an old house like this – huge and warm with a woody-smelling heat coming up from parquet floors – being quiet. A house that ought to have a dozen kids running around in it, raising all kinds of hell, adults doing their weekend tasks. But it was still, completely still.

He followed her into the kitchen. She was setting up a Mr Coffee. She put rolls in the oven. He crossed his arms. She didn't say anything. He leaned against the counter. He unfolded his arms and sat down. He said, "I—"

She slammed the coffee can down, spun to face him. "I've only got one question."

"You got me out of jail to ask me a question?"

"Did Sam get that shit from you?"

He didn't answer.

She looked at him.

Pellam stood up. "If you think that then I'm just going to walk back to your lockup, thanks."

Meg walked over to him and stood inches away. "I want you to say it. I want you to tell me."

"I didn't give him any drugs."

She turned away.

He said, "I thought you knew me . . . I thought we knew each other better than that."

Then she was digging in her purse, pulling out sheets of paper.

He squinted. His right eye blurred. A renegade bit of dirt from the night before shifted. He wiped tears. Then he was focusing on the sheets of paper, the kind with the holes in the side. She'd printed something out of a computer.

Pellam frowned and leaned forward.

So that was it.

He cleared his throat. Even here. Cleary, New York, population 5800. Even here.

Pellam said softly, "So you know."

Meg pushed the printouts toward him. They were dirty and well read.

Honing in on his eyes, she said, "I thought I'd heard your name. When I was a model in New York I got interested in movies. I used to buy some of the film magazines, the high-brow ones. I knew your name was familiar."

He lifted several of the articles, glancing at newspaper headlines he could recite in his sleep.

Pellam's "Time Out of Mind" – L.A. Film Critics Top Pick for Independents, New Director Pellam Captures Cannes, Sundance. New York Film Festival Must: Pellam's "Sandra's Apartment."

Then the others, with words that often did come to him in his sleep: *Film Director Indicted in Drug Death of Star. Pellam Trial Revelation: Drugs "Flowed" on Set. Director, Associate Indicted in Star's OD Death. Death Movie "Central Standard Time" Shelved as Backers Drop Out.*

He dropped them on the table. He stood up. "Better be going."

—•◦•—

17

Meg stepped between him and the door. Took his arm, and held it hard.

"No, please. I don't want you to go. I was so scared about Sam. I was so hurt. I didn't think they came from you but I couldn't help but think about these." She touched the articles hesitantly.

She let go of his arm and Pellam walked to the back window, pulled aside the curtain. He said, "I never sold anything. The man who died was my friend. Tommy Bernstein."

Meg said, "He was a wonderful actor. I saw a couple of the movies he was in. They weren't yours, I don't think."

"He never worked for me. Not until that last movie. *Central Standard Time*. We were just friends. Best friends, I guess you'd say." He laughed. "God, that sounds strange. Adults saying they're best friends." He laughed hollowly. "Well, we weren't very adult."

"What happened?"

"I was directing indies – you know, independent films. Jarmusch, Seidelman. That sort of thing. I met Tommy the first week he got to Hollywood. You're right – he *was* good. But he got famous real fast, *too* fast – he never grew a thick skin. He got shook too easily and the only way he could work was high. We wrote *Central Standard* together – we went out to the desert a couple times and spent the whole day writing. Just the two of us. He was going to star. His first serious film. But the only way he could work was on coke. He wanted a lot and I gave him a lot. And more. He did too much. He had a heart attack and died. He was thirty-one."

Pellam looked at the refrigerator. A construction paper airplane was stuck to the door with magnets. Printed on it: *Love you, Mom!!!*

"It was so strange. At first nothing happened. Nothing at all. It was like the whole incident vanished. I even got up and went to work, trying to find a new star, looking at rough cuts, seeing what we could salvage. Then, everything fell apart. Me included. I couldn't work, I just didn't care. The financing backed out and I didn't have a completion bond – star insurance. So I lost my savings and my house, the equipment. I did a year for manslaughter; my assistant got suspended."

"But it wasn't your fault."

"Yes, it was. I kept supplying him. It was in the film's budget. Under 'Miscellaneous Cast-related Expenses.'"

"Was that when your wife left you?"

He smiled. "No, it was a little after."

Meg said, "That was six years ago, Pellam. You mean nobody would let you work? I don't mean this bluntly but it wasn't the end of the world."

"Well, it's funny what qualifies for the end of the world. A year in the Q – that's San Quentin. That's one way to define it. Believe me, that's *definitely* a way to define the end of the world."

"I'm sorry, John." She touched his arm. This was a different touch. Softer. Closer.

His laugh was bitter. "Hell, there were publicists in L.A.'d shake my hand and say, 'Fucking great promotion idea – you kill the star. Isn't a newspaper in the country won't do a story about you.'" He paused, listening to the mumble of the coffee machine. "Sure, I probably could have gotten it together after I got out. I'd lost a lot of contacts but that wasn't the problem. The problem was I just didn't care. I had no desire to direct any more. So I got a job scouting locations."

"I don't know what to say."

He walked away from her. "It's temporary. Things'll get better."

"You've got to watch that," she said.

"What?"

"Saying that – things are only temporary. Your life could be over before you know it." She said this knowingly.

"I like scouting," Pellam said.

"You don't think your camper's just a place you're hiding out?"

"We all have places we hide out. Mine just happens to have wheels."

"Exactly what *are* you doing here, Pellam? We aren't going to get ourselves a movie here in Cleary. You aren't real interested in colored leaves. What do you want?"

Pellam reached into his sock and pulled out the clear packet of drugs that the bear had planted on him last night.

Meg glanced at it several times, her eyes flipping back and forth between the powder and his face. "What's that?"

"A gift to me. I think from the same place Sam got that stuff he took." He explained to her about the attack the night before. "One of them planted it on me."

"No! Why?"

"So Moorhouse could throw the book at me and have more leverage to get me out of town." He saw her shocked look. "Oh, the mayor's not behind it. Someone else is."

"Who?"

"Whoever didn't want the movie made here." He looked at her. "Whoever's behind those drugs that Sam got. Whoever killed Marty. *That's* what I'm doing here. That's why I'm not leaving until I find out who it is."

"In Cleary . . ." She shook her head. "This is the town where every other car has a red ribbon on the rear-view mirror."

Pellam shook his head, frowning.

"Mothers Against Drunk Driving," Meg said. "The grocery bags at the Grand Union say, 'Say No to Drugs.'"

Pellam opened the packet, sniffed it.

She said, "Why didn't they find it?"

"I swallowed it. Then I got it back last night after they searched me, by a well-known biological process there's no need to go into on this fine morning."

"Jesus, Pellam. What if it'd broken open? You could've died."

"I couldn't really take a felony possession count." He nodded at the printouts.

"Why didn't you just flush it?"

"Sometimes, they test the water in jails."

She smiled. "I can't exactly see Tom testing the john water for drugs."

Pellam laughed. "Who knows what kind of kits he got mail order from *Small Town Cop Monthly* he's just dying to use."

He stepped to the sink, opened the packet and let the contents disappear into the garbage disposal, under the smiling observation of a cut-out wooden goose wearing a bonnet. "I know people'd cry real tears, see me do this."

Pellam dried his hands then walked up to a tall breakfront. He didn't know anything about antiques. He stood awkwardly in front of the elaborate piece. "This is really something."

The breakfast rolls came out and she set them in front of him. He ate two right away. They had a strongly yeasty flavor. Homemade.

They sipped coffee in an awkward silence for a few minutes. He was on his third roll. "The best compliment there is," she said and ate one herself. "I never gain weight. Oh, I'm not being vain. It's just a fact."

Pellam walked into the hall. Looking at the wallpaper, the furniture.

Houses.

He knew what Tommy Bernstein would have said about his little place on Beverly Glen north of Sunset Boulevard. *Shit, you got a fallee house, man. You be in trouble . . .* Houses on the top of the canyons were faller houses; at the bottom, fallee. *You gonna get squashed in the 'quake*, he'd have said. *Sell that sucker now*.

He said to Meg, "I'll bet you have nice holidays here."

"Holidays?" Meg paused. "I guess so. Quiet. Just the three of us. And friends sometimes. A house like this needs big families. It was different when I was growing up. Family all over the place." Her voice faded. Then she said, "I have a confession."

"Okay."

"The accident, when I ran into you?"

"I'm familiar."

"It wasn't an accident. Oh, I didn't want to *hit* you. But I wanted to meet you. I saw you walk up the sidewalk and I drove up there on purpose. I was going to skid the car or something. Pretend to drive off the road. So I could meet you." She was playing with her cocktail ring. Five thousand dollars of pressurized carbon spun obsessively on a beautiful, thin finger.

He asked, "Why?"

"I thought maybe I could get a part in the movie."

"That's why you came to see me in the hospital?"

"No."

He was standing right next to her. She turned, their eyes met. Outside, miles away, the cracks of shotguns rolled into silence. She said, "Well, maybe."

He leaned down and kissed her.

Just like that.

"No," she said. But that was the only resistance she offered. Her arms were around him, kissing back, and pulling him against her.

Then she stepped back.

"No," she said. And this time she was speaking to herself and, unlike him, she decided to obey the command.

She walked back to the kitchen, stood at the window, wiped the sink absently.

Pellam had long ago given up apologizing for impulse. He followed her, picked up his cup, poured more coffee.

"The thing is." Meg didn't look at him, stared out the window. "I'm having an affair."

He set the cup down.

Good job, Pellam. You can pick 'em like nobody else. Fall for a woman whose got two men in her life, while you're being chased around the ginkgo trees by a drugged-out flower child (and you, with an unblushing rail-thin Hollywood businesswoman you never call waiting at home for you).

He saw she was organizing her thoughts. Confession time. Things to get off her beautiful freckled chest. He sat down again. This might take some time. He knew that straying spouses and bad moviemakers share the same obsessive flaw: excessive explanation.

"Who is he?"

"A man here in town."

"Doesn't word get around?"

"We've been excruciatingly careful. See, Keith's a wonderful person. He's Joe solid. He loves Sam. He's never so much as raised his voice to me. He dotes. He provides. But do I feel magic? No. But *should* you feel magic?"

"I heard this line once: a relationship's like a fire. You got a few months of flame, a year of embers, then the rest smoke."

"It's comfortable."

"There's a lot to be said for comfort."

"But I want more, Pellam. Or I thought I wanted more. This thing with Sam, the drugs. It scared me bad. It shook me up. I didn't get an hour's sleep last night."

"He's okay, isn't he?"

"Oh, yeah, he'll be fine. It just made me feel so vulnerable. Here I was looking for some –" She glanced at him. "– for some flame and it almost seemed that Sam getting sick was revenge for that."

"You love him? This other guy?"

A beat of a pause. "I thought I did. But I don't think so."

"You love Keith?"

"I know I love Sam and my house. I *think* I love Keith. I'm tired of having an affair. I shouldn't be saying this to you, should I?" Her eyes were wide, and she seemed very young.

Pellam smiled. "Say whatever you want. I like listening."

"Keith's so smart. He doesn't . . . It's not like he makes me feel stupid, not intentionally, I mean. But I feel stupid."

"Why do you say that?"

"I'm just not, well, intelligent."

"What does that mean?" Pellam asked. "That you can't do calculus in your head? Or recite the periodic table of the elements?"

"Keith tries to tell me about his business, I don't follow what he's saying. I try, but—"

"Meg, he's a chemist. Why should you understand chemistry?"

"Well, politics too. And I don't read a lot. I try but it's just beyond me."

"You're talking in generalities. What's beyond you?"

There was a pop and a flash of light behind them. Meg jumped, then laughed. A bulb in one of the kitchen's wall sconces had burned out. Meg pulled the shade off, blew on the bulb to cool it and unscrewed it. "When I was a girl, I was afraid of the light. Isn't that odd? Most kids are afraid of the dark. But I hated the light. There was no door to my room and the light from the living room, that white-blue light from bare bulbs, would glare and keep me up. Even when I was older, when my mother put a sheet up for a door, that didn't keep the light out. You know why I hated it? It was that when they fought, my parents' voices seemed to come from that light. I'd hide under the blankets. Mother thought I was afraid of ghosts or something. I was afraid of the light. That's what I feel like now. Light is so hard to escape from." Meg changed the bulb. "I feel you're some kind of darkness." She laughed. "I'm sure this is coming out all wrong."

For a time, after he started scouting, Pellam had wondered why this always happened. Why people talked to him as much as they did, bared their hidden secrets and passions. Priests didn't hear the kinds of things Pellam heard. Then he realized it wasn't so much that he was a good listener; it was that he was safe. They could spill their guts and he'd be gone in a week or two. Their secrets with him.

"I knew you didn't have anything to do with Sam," she said. "I really did." The words were halting. Women are usually better apologists than men. But Meg wasn't.

"What're you going to do?" he asked.

"I'm going to stop seeing him, my lover."

"Is that what you want to do?"

"It's what I *have* to do . . ." She looked at her watch. "Pellam, can I ask a favor?"

He didn't think it was going to involve freckles on her chest or anywhere else. He'd given up on that. He said, "Sure."

"Keith's going to be working all day. But Sam'll be home in a while. Could you stay around here? Did you have any plans?"

"Nothing to speak of."

"Would you? We could all have Sunday dinner. Maybe you could do some shooting with Sam. He's got a .22 and a little .410 shotgun we gave him last year."

Pellam said, "I'd love to."

"Really?"

"Really."

Then she was smiling like a sassy schoolgirl. She looked at her watch. "We've got an hour before I pick him up. There's something we could do together – just you and me."

Where was *this* leading?

She took his hand and pulled him toward the door.

"Where're we going?" he asked.

"Raking leaves."

"Are you serious?"

She pulled him outside. "Sure, come on. It's fun."

"I haven't raked leaves for twenty years. They don't have leaves in L.A. And even if they did, I wouldn't rake them."

He resisted at first. But here she was, a beautiful woman with whom he'd shared secrets. And so he said, "I guess."

He paused on the back porch. Looked out on what must've been four or five acres of colored leaves. She tossed him a rake.

He studied it for a moment. Then said, "I don't know how it works."

The glint of light caught the deputy's eye.

He pulled the Plymouth squad car off the road and eased it into the late-morning shade of a sugar maple, scarred from past years' syrup spigots. He climbed out of the car, pulled his lavender-tinted sunglasses on and began walking through the tall grass and forsythia whips. He'd lived in and around Cleary all his life and knew the customs and routines – where people tended to be and when you could expect to see them there and when you couldn't.

And one place you didn't expect to see a car parked was in this field on Sunday morning.

He climbed over what was left of a low stone fence and walked through a row of more maples to a narrow dirt road that led into some woods and just stopped about halfway through.

The car was parked exactly in the center of this road. The deputy paused twenty yards away and looked at it. A cheap Nissan. White. New York plates and a Cleary Tigers bumper sticker. The reason he stopped wasn't because he was noting all these details. He stopped because he didn't want to see what was in the car.

Figuring he'd deduced what had happened. Two high schoolers had spent their last hours on earth making out only to doze off and die, thanks to a bum exhaust pipe. That was the only possible reason anyone would park on this road on Saturday night and the only reason anyone would still be here now.

He took a breath to calm his stuttering heart and walked forward. He found out that he was wrong. There was another reason a car was parked in the middle of this deserted road. Because the driver had been murdered.

The boy had been shot three times in the chest with a small-caliber gun. His face was serene and there was hardly any blood on the body. Which meant he'd died quickly. The boy's face was pressed against the passenger window, away from the deputy, and his hand gripped the door handle. There was no lividity – sinking of the blood to the lower extremities of the body. This meant that he'd died recently.

Damn. His heart sank. The deputy walked around to the other side of the car and looked at the face. He recognized Ned Harper. A high school boy, a football player and, he believed, a one-eighty-division wrestler. He'd remembered that he'd seen Ned's father driving the Nissan around town. He wondered why the parents hadn't phoned him in missing. Maybe when your son was an eighteen-year-old football player, you assumed he'd be out late and didn't start to worry for a day or two. The deputy's daughter was two years old and he worried about her constantly. He didn't think there'd ever come a time when he didn't.

Who'd do something like this?

Maybe the boy'd picked up a hitchhiker. Maybe an escaped prisoner from Sing-Sing down in Ossining. But then why would he leave the car? Maybe it *was* an accident. He'd been hunting with a friend, the gun went off and the other boy panicked. But, no, the deputy realized. That couldn't be it. Not with three separate wounds.

He walked in a slow circle, looking for obvious clues, but he knew the sheriff would take charge of that and call the county in too. Then he realized he was just stalling, not wanting to make the call to report it.

The sun shot off the slanted window, a dove called from deep in the moist forest. The deputy walked slowly back to the car, praying he wouldn't be the one elected to tell the boy's parents.

18

At four-thirty Pellam remembered Janine.

"Oh, hell."

Sam looked up. Probably thinking that he'd pointed the muzzle of the single-shot, break-action shotgun the wrong way or hadn't remembered one of the firearm safety rules Pellam had told him.

For the past couple hours they'd been plinking away with shotguns. Occasionally Pellam would throw a can or two into the air and Sam, sweating with the effort, would calculate the lead. Pellam noticed the determination on the boy's face. Once he overheard Sam mutter something as he fired. "Ned" was what it sounded like. Pellam had asked him what he'd said but he just shook his head and said, "Can you throw another one please?"

"Got to call it quits, son," Pellam now said. "I've got an errand back in town."

Inside the kitchen Sam said, "Mom, you should've seen me."

"I did. I was watching out the window."

"How'd I do, Mr Pellam?"

"Did good, really good," Pellam said. "You've got to clean your weapon, Sam. But I've got to run to town. We'll do it when I get back." He looked at Meg and there must have been something in his words or – goddamn it, was he blushing? He looked at her coy smile and said, "You mind dropping me in town and I'll bring the camper back?"

"Hey," Sam said, his high voice cracking into an even higher register. "Can I come?"

Meg smiled sweetly, "Oh, and can I come too?"

"Probably better if you didn't."

She let him swing for a minute then said, "Maybe you've got some other friends in town. Some people I don't know."

"Shouldn't take more than fifteen minutes."

Meg smiled innocently. "Fifteen? That's pretty fast."

He gave her an exasperated glance.

The phone rang.

Meg kept her eyes on Pellam as she made a slow turn and walked to it.

"Hi, hon . . . Aw, no. Come on. What? Problems?"

"Hi, Daddy!" Sam shrieked, jumping for the phone. "I shot a hundred cans . . ."

Meg winced and waved him down. "I'm making a roast. You can't make it?" She sighed. "Okay. All right. We'll save some for you. Love you."

"Bye, Daddy!"

To Pellam she said, "He's in a bind at the plant. He's got to work most of the night. Sunday, can you believe it? He said he'll be back at eleven . . . So we eat *a trois*."

Sam said, "What's that, Mom? Sounds yucky."

"It means there'll be three of us for dinner."

"Oh, I thought it was this weird food you were going to make." To Pellam he said, "Mom makes this totally strange stuff sometimes. All slippery—"

"Sam."

". . . and these gross colors."

"Young man, that's enough."

"And her apple butter . . ." He headed for the porch. "It starts out brownish. Then it gets kind of green."

"Sam—" Meg began good-naturedly.

Pellam asked Meg, "So, how 'bout that ride?"

"Let's go."

Pellam called to Sam, "Don't clean that gun till I get back, young man."

"Yessir. And then it goes all grayish. Yuck . . ."

Meg dropped him a block away from the camper.

She turned to him but before she could say anything he preempted her. "You don't talk about flower children, I won't talk about apple butter."

She laughed hard. "See you soon." This was a moment when he might've kissed her. But instead he just climbed stiffly out of the tiny car – his wounds still hurt – and walked quickly to the camper. Inside a light was on. He opened the door. Inside, Janine sat motionless, looking down.

She turned to him. "Bastard."

"I'm sorry I ran into some trouble last night and—"

"Bastard." What she was talking about, though, wasn't his being late but the screenplay of *To Sleep in a Shallow Grave*. The binder was open and she'd read most of it.

He closed the door.

"This character you've added. That's me, isn't it?"

He sat down slowly.

"Some of it's based on you. Some. It isn't what I feel about you, it's not the way I see you. It's fiction. A story, nothing more than that. Mostly my imagination."

She lowered her head and read, "'You're living a dream that the past can't justify . . .' 'It's the remoteness of the past that makes it such a safe place for you to live . . .' 'The Age of Aquarius was a long, long time ago . . .' *Janice*. Christ, Pellam, you could at least have done a better job changing my name."

"I didn't—"

"You!" She threw the notebook against the wall. The binding snapped. The pages cascaded to the floor. "*You're* the one living in a dream, not me. You come into people's lives – nobody invited you to Cleary – you come into town with the big fantasy, promising to put people into a movie, promising to take people away from here—"

"I never said that."

She was crying again. Her hair was pasted to her cheeks, she pulled it angrily away. "You didn't have to *say* it. What the hell did you expect people to think? Here you come, with your van and your camera, studying the town, talking to people, getting to know everyone . . . Getting to know *some* of them very well. You don't understand the power you've got. You don't understand how desperate people are. Desperate to get out of places like Cleary. And what do they do? They spill their guts to you and you betray them. Why? In the name of what? What word is sacred to you, Pellam? Art? In the name of Art? Film? Money? How do you justify taking people's lives and making a movie out of them?"

He stood up and reached out for her. She shook his arms away. "You just can't drop into someone's life, take what you want, then leave."

"I'm sorry."

She stood up. Walked to the door then stopped. Waiting for something. Neither of them knew what should come next.

"I thought . . ." Janine's voice faded and she stepped outside, closing the metal door softly behind her.

Pellam sighed. He picked up the screenplay binder then bent to the floor and gathered the pages, one by one.

Driving down Main Street, Pellam passed a grocery store and parked, bought a bottle of chardonnay and walked back outside. He looked up and down the street for Janine. No sign of her. And what would he tell her if he saw her? There was no answer for that.

He looked up the street at an approaching car, an American GT of some kind, maybe ten years old, its rear end jacked high. It came bubbling down the street. The driver parked in front of the Cedar Tap and gunned the engine into a sexy growl before he shut it off. He got out and walked into the bar. Pellam walked over to the car, looked inside.

He returned to the Winnebago, fired it up and drove slowly out of town. He rolled both windows down and felt the cool air fill the cockpit.

He is driving fast in a fast car. A Porsche. A Hun car, because in L.A. you must have a German car. It's not as easy as that, though. You also have to ignore the fact that a German car is the kind to have and it must seem as if you're the first person on the West Coast to think about owning one. Pellam's is black. He drives it hard, with the passion of someone who loves speed though not necessarily the machinery that allows the car to drive fast. Whenever anybody says, "Shit, the Germans make good cars," he always looks surprised, as if they'd just caught on to his secret.

They are going into the desert, Tommy Bernstein and him.

"Thomaso," Pellam shouts over the huge slipstream. "You're going to lose your hat."

And the man does, reaching up too late to keep the stiff, three-hundred-dollar, curly brimmed cowboy hat from sailing into the hundred-mile-an-hour slip-stream.

"Shit, Pellam, turn around."

Pellam only whoops loudly and speeds up.

Tommy doesn't seem to mind. Somehow, it would be wrong to stop the little black car. There is an urgency, a sense of mission. Tommy shouts something about the hat and illegal aliens. Pellam nods.

The sun is a plate of hot pressure above them. The wind, which makes their ears ache, is hot.

Los Angeles is behind them. Ahead is nothing but desert.

"John, give me some!" Tommy shouts. He repeats this twice before Pellam hears and four times before he chooses to answer.

"Please!" A moaning wail, a sound that the wind takes and instantly makes vanish.

Pellam tosses the salt shaker underhand. The wind plays hell with the trajectory, but Tommy catches it in desperate, fumbling grabs.

"Not funny."

"Improves your reflexes."

Tommy was trying to snort. "Too fast, I can't—"

Pellam hits the clutch and brake. The car skids and fishtails. When they slow to sixty Tommy can snort the coke. He gives the high sign. Pellam accelerates and refuses the offered shaker.

Pellam feels philosophical. He shouts, "You think the desert's minimal, right? Bullshit. It isn't. It's goddamn complex. Complex like a, you know, a crystal. Like the way colors spread under a microscope. Remember those science films in high school?"

"Yeah," Tommy shouts. "About gonads and seeds and ovum." He is grinning like the dirty little boy he likes to portray though he is clearly considering Pellam's comment. In fact he is considering it desperately. Pellam wishes he hadn't spoken.

Tommy suffers from terminally ill confidence. The actor had received one L.A. Film Critics' award and one from Cannes when he'd been courted and seduced by a big studio lot producer. The money was incredible, the movies worse than awful. His most recent, a critic wrote, could be stuffed and served at a Thanksgiving dinner for the population of the country. Tommy was trying to think of ways to redeem himself. "Don't be desperate," Pellam had told him. "This city don't love desperate men."

But Tommy snatched up even that advice like a life preserver.

Pellam drives in silence. A half hour later he notices a small road leading off the highway toward a huge rock eased out of the brush and dirty sand. He makes a fast turn and the car skids to a stop out of sight of the road.

They climb out, stretch, pee against rocks.

Tommy asks, "You bring the Geiger counter?"

"What do we need that for?"

"The fucking Army. They test atom bombs here."

"That's New Mexico."

"Fucking no," Tommy says. "Cruise missiles blasting sheep to hell and gone. I'm scared." He looks around cautiously.

Pellam says, "There're no sheep here."

"What I'm saying! They're dead. Got blasted into lambchops. We're in danger. Our kids'll glow in the dark."

"Let's go to work, hombre."

From the car they take two heavy garbage cans that ring with glass falling against itself. Pellam drags them toward the rock. There isn't much shade though there will be in an hour or two. Tommy, now pissed about his hat, rubs suntan lotion on his face and thinning scalp, then pulls a large cooler from the car. This he plants in the sand near the big rise of rock. He returns and struggles to get two lawnchairs out of what pretends to be a backseat.

"German cars, shit," Tommy says. He drives a Chevy Impala.

Pellam takes empty beer bottles out of the green bags and sets them carefully on a ridge of dirt and sand about thirty feet away from where Tommy plants the lawnchairs. He surveys his handiwork then opens a pineapple-printed beach umbrella and sticks it into the ground between the chairs.

Pellam finishes setting out the bottles. He calls, "How many pages?"

Tommy flips through a plastic-bound manuscript. "One seventeen."

"Need one more."

Tommy pulls another bottle from the cooler, pops the lid with a church key and drinks it down. He tosses it to Pellam, who plants it at the end of the row.

One hundred seventeen bottles.

They sit in the chairs, facing the bottles. Tommy takes another snort from the shaker.

He says, "Can I have the Python. Please?"

From a large, battered attaché case, Pellam takes two pistols. He keeps the Ruger .44 for himself and hands Tommy the Colt. He places yellow-and-green boxes of shells between them.

Two copies of the script appear. On the title page: "Central Standard Time. By John Pellam and Tommy Bernstein."

They begin reading aloud and rewriting the script. They correct each other, changing dialogue, argue. Pellam is quieter and grimmer. Tommy is boisterous. He'll shout, then stand and stalk around, sit again.

When they finish eleven pages – the end of the first scene – they stuff cotton into their ears, load the pistols and with fifteen shots between them take turns disintegrating the first eleven bottles. One for each page. The rules of their game.

Tommy says, spinning the cylinder of his gun, "You remember that scene, what was it from? Some old jungle movie? Stewart Granger's aiming at Deborah Kerr's head? She's scared, doesn't know what's going on. Then, blam! He wastes a boa constrictor right behind her. I always wanted to play that scene. Why don't you go sit over next to the rocks, Pellam? They got snakes in the rocks."

"Yeah, hell with snakes," Pellam says, pulling a beer from the cooler. "I always wanted to shoot me an actor."

They work until eleven that night, and blow the last three bottles apart in the headlight of the tiny German car surrounded by the sound of its bubbling exhaust. They are shivering and it takes ten rounds each to hit the last glistening bottle.

"This fucking movie's going to make us, Pellam!" Tommy shouts. "We're going right to the top!" And he empties the gun at the night sky.

The house was completely quiet.

Meg had a little time until Pellam would be back. She took her coffee and walked up the stairs. She paused, then sat on the landing for a long time, looking into the hall and those portions of the den and living room she could see. The parquet floor, the furniture. The house seemed different, a stranger's home. She didn't recognize it. There was nothing unpleasant about the sensation; it was one of those moments when you focus on a familiar object – a doorknob, a chair, your own little finger – and it seems absurd and alien to you. This was her house, the house she'd always loved. Hers and Keith's and Sam's. Only something was different.

Meg went into the bedroom, got dressed. She tied her hair in a ponytail. Her hands paused, holding the ribbon above her neck.

The doorbell rang. She bounded down the stairs like Sam on Christmas morning.

She swung the heavy door open. She'd already prepared a wry comment for Pellam about Janine and was ready to deliver it.

But she blinked in surprise.

Wexell Ambler stood there, looking shy, leaning against the

jamb. "I was driving past. Saw your car was in the drive. The Cougar was gone. I couldn't wait till tomorrow."

Meg instinctively looked back, into the house to make certain they were alone. Then she looked behind Ambler.

"Is it Mr Pellam, Mommy?" Sam called. She wondered if Ambler could hear what the boy had asked. Didn't seem he had.

"No, honey. I'll be outside for a minute," she shouted. Her hand still on the doorknob Meg said to Ambler, "Keith's at work."

"I want to talk to you. I *have* to talk to you."

"I'm expecting some company."

Ambler had no reaction to this. She was trying to decide whether to tell him who the company was if he asked. He didn't. He said, "It won't take long." Though he said it slowly, the words full of meaning, as if he wanted their conversation to last for the entire evening.

She looked behind her again, up the stairs toward Sam's room, then stepped outside and closed the door behind her. It didn't latch.

He kissed her on the cheek and she kissed him back, though he'd have to be drunk or crazy not to sense the hesitancy.

"I had to see you."

"Is everything okay?"

He looked at her in surprise. "Okay, sure. I should be asking how Sam is. You never called to tell me if he's all right."

"He's fine. He'll be fine."

"He's a wonderful boy," Ambler said.

They walked to the end of the porch and stood at the railing, looking out across the moist lawn, glistening in slight radiance from the houselights.

"What is it, Wex?"

"About what I asked. About marrying me."

She turned to him. He was such a tough man. A dangerous man too, she supposed. That bodyguard thug of his, Mark, for instance. Also, the way he liked her to be helpless, almost cowering when they made love. (Meg Torrens believed sex was a window to your soul.) She'd never actually said, No, to him before and she wondered if there was a risk to her if she did. She felt a chill, colder than the air.

What should she say?

She suddenly remembered a line from one of Pellam's movies. A character has to make a decision about turning a friend over to the police. He says to his wife, "The most important decisions are always made by our hearts."

She let her heart answer now.

"Wex . . ." She looked away, fixing her eyes on a fingernail clipping of a moon over a dark wad of trees. "I can't see you anymore."

She wondered if it would be a total surprise. If he'd nod slowly and walk away. If he'd fly into a rage. She honestly didn't know.

He didn't answer for a moment and she heard his breathing, remembered the deep sound from the times they'd lain together.

Tension filled her body, turned her to stone.

"Were you going to come to the place yesterday and tell me that?" he asked. "Or were you just going to let me figure it out on my own."

She hesitated and for the first time in their relationship lied to him. "No, I was going to come."

Meg glanced toward the house and the driveway and then took his arm. He was shaking. Anger? Sorrow? The cold?

Will he hurt me?

She continued. "I'm sorry, Wex. I loved every minute we spent together, but . . ." She was parsing carefully, but she found she had no idea of what words she could attach to her thoughts to express them right. "But it's just time for it to be over with."

"How can you say that?" he spat out.

"It's what I feel."

"What happened?"

She couldn't look into his eyes. "No. It's run its course. I was searching for something. I—"

"You're going back to Keith."

"I don't know."

"You're in love with that man, Pellam. Right?"

The hesitation must have seemed huge to him, though for Meg it lasted only a second. "No, I'm not."

Ambler stepped away from her. "It's him, isn't it?"

"No."

"I knew it," he said bitterly. "I knew from the minute you heard there was going to be a movie in town, you were going after him. What did you want? For him to sweep you away to be a star?"

"Wex, come on . . ."

"Don't you remember? We were lying in bed—"

"Shhh!" She raised her palm to silence him.

"—and it was the first day they came into town, in that damn camper of theirs and all you talked about was making a movie. How much you wanted to act."

"Maybe I did. I want to be successful at something. Why is that so hard for you to understand?"

"Meg, you can't just go start a Hollywood career. You—"

"I don't want to talk about this."

"Did he fuck you?" His voice was loud.

"Be quiet!" She whirled to face him. "You can't come to my house and talk to me that way!"

He grabbed her arm. She winced. Then he calmed, reached forward and touched her face. Her eyes focused behind him, where a fast burst of light from the opening door would warn that Sam was on his way outside. "I love you, Meg. You don't know how much. I want to be with you. I'm *going* to be with you."

"Wex, it's never been right. Not here. Cleary isn't the kind of place for this sort of thing. I see how wrong it was."

"You make it sound cheap. It wasn't that." His whisper was harsh.

"I didn't mean it that way. I don't regret anything. I just . . ."

He stared down at her for a moment then released her suddenly. Ambler turned and walked down the steps.

Meg felt the vacuum of his leaving. There was too much unresolved. Wex Ambler had been her only lover. Was this how affairs always ended? Punctuated more with question marks and ellipses than exclamation points? She leaned against the banister and watched him – without a glance toward her – get into his Cadillac.

He drove slowly away. She saw the flash of his brake lights

as he paused at the road – paused just long enough to let the Winnebago turn up her driveway. Then Ambler hit the accelerator hard and vanished into the night.

They're waiting for me to say grace, he decided.

Meg and Sam were looking at him, expectation in their faces. Pellam cleared his throat. In front of him, on the Sunday-set table, was a veal roast that would have fed enough men to rake up all six acres of leaves on the Torrens estate in half an hour. A huge bowl of beans and one of salad. Another plate was loaded with potato pancakes. He and Meg were drinking the white wine; Sam had a glass of milk.

That's what they're waiting for. Grace. What do I do now?

They'd settled in their chairs, candles were lit, and their eyes turned toward him. Then, as the seconds rolled past slowly, they looked at each other.

Pellam unrolled his sleeves and buttoned his cuffs to buy time. Meg said, "Well?"

"Last time I did this must be twenty years ago. I don't remember it too well."

She was frowning. "Twenty years?"

"Well, I don't say grace in the camper."

And Meg was laughing, her wine glass in her hand rocking, spilling the blond liquid over her fingers.

"Pellam . . . No. We're just waiting for you to carve the roast."

"Oh." He covered his face with his hands and laughed. Sam said, "I can say grace, Mr Pellam. Here goes: Over the lips and past the gums, look out stomach, here it comes! Amen."

Pellam picked up the knife and serving fork and went to work. The first couple pieces crumbled. "Can I at least pray for help in carving?"

It was an hour into the meal when the eeriness settled on him. A feeling he couldn't pin down. It happened when he was laughing at one of Sam's jokes, one that Pellam himself had told to death thirty years before, and he glanced up at Meg. Their eyes met, and for one moment, a pivotal moment, there was no movie, no studio, no camper, no Keith, just a universe centered around the three of them.

And the instant he thought how comfortable and natural it seemed, the moment ended and he became anxious.

Pellam surveyed his massive wedge of blueberry pie. Meg said to his protesting palm, "Pellam, you're too skinny."

He ate two pieces.

When they'd finished dessert Pellam helped Meg clear the table. Sam asked, "Mr Pellam, tomorrow can you teach me to shoot *your* gun?"

"What gun's that?" Meg asked.

Pellam told her about the Colt.

Meg said, "I'm not real crazy about pistols. But . . ." She looked at her son. "You listen to everything Mr Pellam tells you."

As if that needed to be said.

"Totally excellent!" the little boy squealed.

Meg said, "Next you'll be teaching him poker."

Pellam laughed.

The two of them sat in the living room for a while, sipping coffee, the unidentified feeling ebbing and flowing within Pellam. He couldn't tell whether he wanted to stay, wanted to leave. One thing he knew for sure – he definitely wanted to leave before Keith came home.

The phone rang. Meg went to answer it and returned a moment later. She didn't say who the caller was. But now she too seemed uneasy.

What the hell're you doing here? he thought to himself. She's married, she's got a lover . . . You don't need those kinds of troubles. He rose. "I better go."

"You sure?"

No. But he said, "Better. Still have a few things to do."

"Sunday night?"

He nodded. Then asked, "Got a favor."

"Sure."

"You have a bottle of whiskey I can borrow?"

"Borrow?"

"No, now you mention it, make that *have*."

"After-dinner drink?"

"Little more complicated than that."

"Sure." She smiled in curiosity. And dug down under a cabinet and emerged with a half-full bottle of Wild Turkey.

"That's the cheapest you've got?" Pellam picked up the bottle.

"'Fraid so. Say, what're you going to do, teach my little boy to shoot, gamble *and* drink?"

Pellam hefted the bottle, hugged her. "Thanks again, ma'am. You make a mean meal. See you tomorrow."

19

"Ah, it's the gunslinger's grandson," said Fred, who squinted his red, retiree's face and studied Pellam's cuts and bruises. "Hell, what happened to you?" He ordered two Buds.

"Had an accident."

"Another one?"

Pellam said, "I'm an unlucky guy sometimes. What can I say?"

"No fooling – you all right?" the old man asked with genuine concern.

"Fine, no problem."

"Weekends're rough around here. All those tourists. What'd you do, get in the way of somebody taking a picture of a leaf? Hey, how about a game?"

"Can't tonight, Fred."

"What's this shit I hear about you not making a movie here?"

"Talk to the town council about it."

"Buncha old SOBs. Shit, there goes my Hollywood career."

Pellam asked, "Where can I find Nick?"

"The kid we were playing with th'other night?" Fred's head was swiveling. "Was here a few minutes ago. Maybe he's in the backroom. That's where they got what they call the restaurant."

Pellam finished the beer. He lifted the bottle in thanks.

"Hey, Pellam, Burt Reynolds ain't available, gimme a call."

In the backroom Pellam found Nick sitting at a table with another man, skinny, long hair, a couple years his junior – maybe eighteen. Nick had a bowl of soup in front of him. He hunched over it, putting slippery noodles into his mouth.

"Hi, Nick," Pellam pulled up a chair. Nick waved then returned to the soup. It looked like Campbell's. What else at the Cedar Tap? Nick said, "This here's Rebo. This's Pellam, the guy you heard about, makes the movies."

Rebo's eyes went wide. He grinned. "Wow, movie man." They shook hands.

"How you doing?" Pellam asked.

"Wow."

Pellam turned to Nick. "Hey, Nick, why I stopped by, my studio's looking for somebody like you."

"Yeah?" The big man took some more sips of soup. "You still making that movie? I heard you weren't."

"This's another movie. I remembered you're into wheels."

"I'm like sorta into wheels."

"They need a driver, a stunt driver. But he's got to be good."

Rebo, chewing a wad of hamburger, said, "Oh, he's good.

Nick's a good driver." Rebo's T-shirt said *Mötley Crüe 1987 Tour*.

"You interested?"

A grin snuck into the fat in the boy's cheeks. "Well, I guess."

"The only thing is, you think you could show me what you can do? Like an audition?"

"I guess."

"How about now?"

"It'd be Sunday night."

"They need somebody soon. Next weekend. If I can't get anybody we'll have to bring in somebody from the Coast." Pellam tossed him a bone: "You'll get screen credit."

"A credit?"

"And the pay's great. A thousand bucks for one stunt."

Rebo's eyes were getting bigger. "Hey, man, tell him about your car."

"Well . . ."

The Mötley Crüe boy steamed ahead. "Pontiac GT. He put in a Chevy 442 all by his lonesome."

Nick's grin was back, spreading like a sunrise. "Hurst shifter," he said. "Did that myself too."

Pellam whistled. "You sure know your hardware. How 'bout it?"

Nick shrugged. "Let's go."

Rebo stood up but Pellam shook his head. "Just gotta be the two of us. Insurance problems, you understand."

Rebo nodded and dropped back into his seat as if Duane Allman himself had told him to sit.

Outside they walked to the car and Pellam looked around.

The streets of Cleary were deserted. He said, "Oh, let me get something." He disappeared into the camper for a minute and came out with the bottle of Wild Turkey. He handed it to Nick. The boy looked at it but shook his head. "Maybe afterwards, man. Not a good idea if I'm going to be doing high-speed work."

They walked to Nick's black Pontiac.

High-speed work. Like he did it everyday.

Pellam unscrewed the lid of the bottle. Nick watched him, frowning.

"You don't drink and drive?" Pellam asked. "That's funny. You were the other night. I could smell it. On top of your aftershave. That's what I recognized. Brut, right?"

The eyes were fishy and the grin came back. "The fuck're you saying?"

Pellam nodded toward the car. "Heard your car this afternoon, thought it sounded familiar. Then checked it out and smelled that same drugstore aftershave inside. Didn't your mother raise you with any class?"

"Huh?"

"How's your friend with the broken nose? I hope he's in a lot of pain."

"You fucking crazy?" He'd turned solemn as a mortician.

"I know, you're going to tell me it was nothing personal."

"What wasn't personal?" But the eyes disclosed all the facts. Nick paused then said, "You got me good." He touched his jaw. "I won't be eating solid food for a week. My tongue's sore as a whore's tit. Why didn't you tell Moorhouse?"

"What good would it've done? He'd let you go, right?"

"Yeah."

"So he was in on it, right?"

"In on what?"

"Paying you to beat the crap out of me and plant the drugs?"

"I don't know what—"

The Colt appeared in a flash, pointed straight into the boy's belly.

"Shit," he whispered. "Oh, God, mister."

"Who paid you—" Pellam paused. Suddenly he was curious. "How much was it?"

"A hundred bucks."

"That's *all*? That's crap."

"No, man, no. It's totally true. I swear."

Pellam felt insulted. "You should've charged more. Now tell me who?"

"We didn't have nothing against you. We heard—"

"Who?" Pellam whispered viciously and cocked the Colt, praying that his thumb wouldn't slip off the hammer. The gun was loaded with 130-grain, .45 caliber bullets. The boy was fat but he wouldn't even slow up a slug that size.

Both hands in front of him, palms out. "Okay. Fine. Listen, I'm going—"

"Asked you a question," Pellam growled.

"—to tell you. Just put that—"

"Who?"

"Mr Ambler. Wexell Ambler. Well, was a guy works for him – name's Mark, but I don't know his last name, I swear I don't. This guy Mark talked to Mayor Moorhouse and they wanted me and my friend to rough you up a bit."

"Where's he live? The Ambler?"

Pellam touched Nick's chest with the Colt. A good way to get directions fast. Nick became a regular Triple A guidebook. "Barlow Mountain road. Just off Route Nine, north. Past the Shell station. Go two hundred yards past then make a left. Really, mister, I didn't have nothing against you."

"Well, what's *he* got against me?"

"I don't know, swear to God. Please, mister, point that someplace else."

Pellam aimed at the ground before he eased the hammer to half-cock then slowly spun the cylinder to put an empty chamber beneath the hammer, which he then lowered all the way. He held the gun in his right hand while he handed the whiskey bottle to Nick with his left.

"Take a drink."

Nick's voice shook as he said, "I don't want to take a drink."

"We both want you to." Pellam pointed the Colt at him again.

"Oh, shit, come on—"

"Drink it down."

Nick took a swallow.

"Come on, a couple more. Drink like a man. You hit like a girl. At least drink like a man."

"Fuck you, Pellam," he wheezed.

"You tried that. It didn't work. Drink."

When he'd gotten down five, six good mouthfuls, Pellam took the bottle and threw it, open, into the GT.

"Aw, shit, what you want to do that for?"

"Well, I'll tell you. I've evened things up a bit. You're a little bigger'n me but now you're a little drunker. So we're driving out of town and I'm going to whip your ass one on one."

"You got that gun."

"I'll leave it in the car. Drive out toward the highway to the forest preserve. I'll be right behind you. Don't try to get away. I'll be aiming for the tires but I might hit your gas tank."

"You asshole," the boy muttered as he got into the car. The big Pontiac engine exploded to life and Nick pumped the accelerator.

They pulled out of downtown, the camper right behind the GT.

It turned out even better than Pellam'd thought it would be. They'd gotten two miles out of town, to the stoplight, when Nick did just what Pellam knew he was going to do: Looked for cross traffic, slipped the clutch and shot through the red light, running up through the gears with his fancy shifter, sounding like a buzzsaw.

The boy was probably in fourth when the state trooper Pellam had seen on his way into town, hidden in the bushes, a speed trap, started to pull out.

Nick came within two or three inches of taking the front end of the trooper's Chevy with him.

Pellam drove slowly past the scene of the arrest. Nick, handcuffed. The trooper, writing down Breathalyzer results.

He drove past the sign that said *Welcome to Cleary* and continued into the blackness.

Good night, officer.

Good night, sir . . .

Pellam turned the camper off Barlow Mountain Road, and eased along an overgrown side road up the hill that he supposed was Barlow Mountain. He nosed the Winnebago forward into a clump of hemlocks then killed the engine. He pulled the Colt out from under the seat and slipped it into his waistband then stepped outside. His boots made gritting taps as he walked along the asphalt toward the warm yellow house lights that glowed in the fog, a quarter mile away.

A hundred yards from the house he made his way off the road into brush and sparse woods. He smelled wet pine and ripe leaves. A hit of skunk. He saw the glistening lights reflecting on a lake to his right. A late, lone cicada made its deceptively cheerful sound and somewhere a dog barked. He moved slowly toward the house, stepping around branches.

The house was a rambling old monster, easily two hundred years old. A drab, ugly brown, Plymouth Rock chic. He heard water lapping and saw the lake clearly; it came right to the edge of the property. The dog barked again, the sound rolling across the lake. There was no other noise or motion, not even wind. The house was still and the lights were dim; Pellam wondered if they'd been left on while the residents were out to discourage the potential intruders that Pellam now understood Ambler would have good reason to worry about – the state police, for instance.

He thought of the drugs that had been planted on Marty – and on him – and the odd heroin Sam had taken. He recalled that Meg or someone told him about other overdoses and murders in the area. Ambler was probably responsible for it all.

He knelt in the grass and felt the cold dew through his denim. After five minutes, during which he saw no motion, he ran in a crouch to the separate garage, a two-story saltbox, and looked in the window. Only one car inside, a Cadillac. And there was an oil stain on the concrete, about ten feet to the left of the Caddie, which told him that Ambler had two cars.

A family out to dinner on Sunday night? Probably. But even when he walked to the house Pellam stayed in the shadows and edged up to the first-floor windows slowly. He bobbed his head up and looked in one quickly, seeing small rooms, decorated with rough, painted furniture, wreaths of dried flowers, primitive Colonial paintings of spooky children and black-clad wives – everything stiff and spindly and uncomfortable.

He saw no movement at all.

The windows, he noticed, were mostly unlocked.

The third room was the one he wanted.

It was dark paneled and inside were two large gun cabinets, glass faced, set against the wall. Several trophies were mounted near the low ceiling – a couple of antelope and a good-pointed buck. But they were on one wall only, as if the hunter had gotten tired of displaying his kills. Pellam, squinting, saw a number of rifles in the cases. Several looked like they were .30 caliber and at least two of them had telescopic sights.

Pellam lifted his hands up to the window and tested it. Unlocked. He stood completely still for a moment, his face millimeters away from the smooth, expensive paint job. Then he eased up the window, which moved slowly. He opened it about two feet. A hard climb, though, he thought – considering his bruised thigh, his damaged joints.

It was then that he glanced inside and noticed something odd.

What's wrong with this picture?

The second gun cabinet. The third space from the left.

Empty.

Thinking: If a man was as organized as Ambler seemed to be, and he *didn't* have enough guns to fill a cabinet, he'd probably keep the ones he did have centered in the rack. Which meant—

"Don't move," the man said.

The jump was involuntary, though the cold touch of the shotgun barrel at his head brought the movement under control real fast.

The voice was that of a middle-aged man. He asked, "You have a gun?"

"Yes."

"Hand it to me."

If he was impressed with the Colt, the man didn't say so. He slipped it into his pocket and, leaving the Remington over-under at Pellam's neck like a nesting kitten, said, "Let's go inside."

20

Pellam moved back and forth slowly in the bentwood rocker he'd been politely invited toward by the blunt 12-gauge trap gun. (Pellam hated shotguns. Shotguns were really loud.)

The man – he *was* Wex Ambler, according to his muttered introduction – studied Pellam carefully. Pellam gazed back. It was an odd contrast – hateful dark eyes and an L.L. Bean Sunday gardener's outfit, complete with bright green Izod shirt.

"What were you doing?" Ambler asked.

"Thinking of shooting a movie here. I was—"

"You know I could shoot you now. Blow your head clean off and all the sheriff'd do is tell me how sorry he was I lost a window and bloodied my floor."

Pellam saw the stillness in Ambler's eyes and knew this was a man who could easily kill.

He said, "I wanted to see if you were really the man who was trying to send me to Attica for ten years."

Ambler said, "I didn't want you to go to prison. I wanted you to leave town. Get the hell out and not come back."

"You could've asked."

"You *were* asked. Several times."

Goodbye . . .

Ambler's eyes flashed. "You people . . . We have a decent town and you think you can come here from Hollywood, and make your movies, but you're laughing at us. Behind our backs you're laughing. I hate you people."

Pellam *was* laughing. "Bullshit. I came to town to rent a few houses and stores for a couple of weeks. That's all we wanted. My friend gets killed and I get beat up and somebody plants drugs on me . . ."

Ambler shook his head, whipping Pellam's words off like they were gnats.

Pellam's eyes measured distances, noticing that the shotgun's safety was on, that Ambler's finger was outside the trigger guard, that the muzzle was aimed sixty or seventy degrees away from him. Noticing a carving set on the counter, antler handled, a burnished, well-honed blade on the knife. Even the serving fork looked vicious.

"Sin city," Ambler said.

Pellam rocked forward. His legs tensed, thinking he could probably make it. He wondered what it was like to stab someone. "It's just a business," Pellam said.

Ambler didn't hear him. "People here go to church, they have children, they teach them Christian values, they work hard, they—"

Pellam thought: *Make millions selling smack.*

"—don't need your kind of influence."

Outside influence. So it was a script. Moorhouse and Ambler and the sheriff all had the same script and the lines were terrible. They'd all be in on it, of course. This man with a million-dollar house was probably the ringleader. He'd arranged to bring the drugs in from someplace out of the country. Then he'd distribute them in small towns like this. An untapped market. Moorhouse, Tom the sheriff and the pastel-sunglassed deputies were his enforcers.

Ambler was lecturing. Sin, providence, promises unkept.

The words didn't quite harmonize with the fact the man had killed Marty. Or was seeding God-fearing Dutchess County with exotic drugs. (But Pellam recalled a former acquaintance – E Block, West Wing, San Quentin, California – who went to church every day.)

Ambler kept talking like a crazy person on the street, furious. Flecks of spittle in the corner of his mouth. The muzzle of the gun rose and fell like surf.

But Pellam wasn't paying much attention to Ambler's mania or the moral purity of Dutchess County.

He was thinking about the carving knife.

His feet rested themselves under the sensually curved chair.

Pressing the balls of his feet against the tile. The knife, the knife, the knife.

He felt the tension, like blued spring steel, building in his calves.

The knife . . .

He kept his eyes calm, staring right into Ambler's. That was the give-away in a fight. You could always tell when a man was about to swing or go for a weapon – his eyes. He'd learned that from another acquaintance (D Block, North Wing). Pellam looked at Ambler and kept his eyes very still.

He rocked forward. The chair swung back and then forward, his weight moved with it.

The knife.

On your mark.

Goddamn, shotguns were loud.

Get set.

Blood on the tiles? No, sir, there'd be blood on the ceiling, the walls, the fancy granite countertop . . .

Go.

Ambler's harsh voice asked, "What did you tell her?"

Pellam froze, stopped rocking. "Who?"

Ambler's feverish eyes danced out the window for a moment, as a car drove past. It continued on.

Pellam rocked back. His quaking legs relaxed. Shotguns didn't so much shoot you as obliterate you.

Ambler continued. "That you'd make her a star?"

"What are you talking about?"

Ambler said, "She told you she'd been a model, didn't she? And you promised to get her jobs. Promised to take her out to California. 'Leave this backwater little town. Leave your son'? And then you seduced her, didn't you? You promised her a job and you fucked her."

"I don't—"

"She's just fodder for you, isn't she?"

"I don't know who you're talking about."

His first thought was: Janine. But then he asked cautiously, "Meg?"

Ambler nodded.

Him? He's the one?

Meg, come on . . . *This* guy?

Ambler muttered sarcastically, "Oh, she'd be in good hands with you . . . Jesus. You gave Sam that fucking heroin or whatever it was and practically killed him . . ."

The surprise in Pellam's eyes must have seemed genuine. Ambler stopped talking.

"I didn't give Sam that stuff."

Ambler frowned. Finally he said, "You seduced her, didn't you?"

"Nothing happened between us. We talked. We had dinner."

Ambler looked at him for a moment, a lover's examination of a possible rival. How they hang on every flutter of eyelash, every syllable.

Pellam said, "She's a captivating person."

Ambler said, "Too good for you."

"That's probably true."

Ambler said, "I love her."

"That's why you did it?" Pellam asked. "Why you had me set up? Because you thought I was taking her away from you?"

"Yes! And here you come to threaten me. To tell me to stop seeing her—"

Pellam said, "I didn't even know you *were* seeing her."

"Then what're you doing here tonight?"

Pellam looked at Ambler's face carefully, judging. Tommy Bernstein had said there were times when a man has to make a leap. He meant it philosophically, muttering something about a leap of faith, though when he said it he was drunk and poised to leap off the second story of his Beverly Hills house into the swimming pool that Liberace had supposedly done something scandalous in.

Pellam said, "I'm going to show you something."

"What?"

"I'm going to reach into my pocket, okay? I just want to show you something."

Pellam's hand disappeared into his pocket and it returned with the two shell casings.

"What are those?"

"These were the shells from the shots that killed my partner. Whoever did that is the same person who's been selling the drugs that Sam got. I assumed it was the same person who had me beat up."

"And you thought it was me?" Ambler's face was horrified. Pellam slowly rocked forward, off the balls of his feet. He'd forgotten about the knife. Ambler said, "I'm a Christian."

Pellam laughed. "Well, you vandalized our camper, right? You planted the drugs in the car and you called the sheriff and said Marty was selling stuff, right?"

Ambler didn't answer for a moment. "The day you and your friend came to town I was with Meg. She was so excited. I've never seen her that way. She was obsessed with the idea of being in a movie. That's all she talked about. If you made a movie here, I was afraid I'd lose her. She'd try to get a part, she'd go off to Hollywood. I *did* have somebody plant something in the car. And then, yes, he called the police. But I didn't have Marty killed. I'd never do that."

"You were the one who ordered the parking lot plowed over?"

"When the accident happened – when the car blew up – I was terrified that I'd be accused of it. I told Moorhouse to have it dozed to hide any evidence."

"And Sillman? The rental place."

"I had my man talk to Sillman. We arranged to offer Marty's family some money. A lot of money. It looked like an insurance settlement."

"And you had those two locals pay me a visit? Beat me up?"

Ambler nodded. "I wanted you gone so badly. All she did was talk about you. Talk about movies. I was losing her. I was desperate." He looked down at his hands, studied his long fingers. Ambler broke open the shotgun and put it on the counter. He picked up the bullet casings. "Winchester .300's. But there's something different about them."

"Magnums," Pellam said.

"I don't have a gun that'll take these." He looked up. "You want to check?"

Pellam glanced at the shotgun, which Ambler could still grab, close and loudly obliterate Pellam with before he was halfway to the knife. He said, "I believe you."

Ambler handed the cartridges back. "Those're unusual rounds."

"Used for real long distance shooting."

"What kind of weapon would that be?" Ambler asked.

"You can get a Beretta bolt-action chambered for them. SIG-Sauer has a .300 Magnum and—"

"Beretta, you say?"

Pellam said, "You know somebody who's got one?"

"I do, but I don't think—"

"Who?"

"You don't know them. A couple brothers."

Something flashed through Pellam's mind.

Pellam said, "They wouldn't be twins, by any chance?"

"Yeah, as a matter of fact, they are."

* * *

"You aren't gonna like it," the deputy said to the sheriff.

"I don't like a lot of what's been happening around here lately," Tom said.

They were in the police station, Sunday night, though one thing about Cleary: the Sabbath wasn't any quieter than any other day. The only difference now was that all three of them were working – two in the office, and the other deputy in the field – and they were expecting a visit from a detective and another deputy from the County Sheriff's office, who were going to be assisting in the investigation of Ned's murder.

"I was talking to people who had seen him in the past twenty-four hours. Who'd seen Ned, I mean."

The sheriff knew this, since he'd sent the deputy to do just that. "And?"

"A coupla folks saw him with Sam Torrens. At the festival."

"So?" Tom was exhausted. A blown-up car, drugs, arson, fights. And now a high school boy murdered. Life in small-town America. Crap.

"It was just before the kid got sick."

"Kid? *Which* kid? Explain it to me, will you?"

The deputy said, "I'm saying that it looks like Ned was the one who gave the drugs to Sam Torrens. That heroin shit."

"Oh." The sheriff closed his eyes and rubbed them with his knuckles. "What aren't I going to like? You said before I wasn't going to like something."

The deputy continued. "Keith Torrens got his boy a .22 for Christmas last year. I seen him buying shells."

"When?"

"I don't mean recent. I just mean I know he's got a .22 in the house. And had some shells."

"Come on, Randy. Everybody in town's got a .22. They practically come with the house when you buy one."

"I'm just saying."

"And we don't know for certain it was a .22 killed Ned. Could've been a .25 or a .222."

"Maybe. But you'd think there'd've been more damage—"

"We. Don't. Know."

The deputy nodded. Finally he said, "Closest thing to justifiable I've ever seen."

The sheriff wondered where the hell that was coming from. The deputy had worked on exactly one murder in his four years on the force and that had been when Barnie Slater's wife used a deer slug in his sleep to keep him from taking the lamp cord to her anymore. She had fresh coffee for the deputies when they'd arrived. The sheriff said, "Justifiable's the prosecutor's decision, not ours."

After a moment Tom asked, "When was the time of death?"

"About ten this morning."

"Church time. Meg was here bailing out that movie guy – now *that's* a fact I don't want to think too much on. What about Keith? He do church?"

"I don't know," the deputy answered. "We can call. They're in First Presbyterian."

"Who's that? The Minister?"

"Jim Gitting. Good man. Gives a good sermon."

Tom didn't care whether he was the devil's own brother. "Call him. Find out it Torrens was there today."

The deputy picked up the phone. "Reverend Gitting please . . .

Hey, Reverend, how you doing? Look, I'm real sorry to be—"

Tom took the phone from his hand. "Reverend, this is the sheriff. Was Keith Torrens in church this morning?"

"Uhm, no, Sheriff." The voice was whiny. Didn't sound like he'd give a good sermon at all. "Can I ask why?"

"Just looking into some things. He usually attend services?"

"Hardly ever. He was working this morning – like usual."

"Wait. You said he wasn't there. How'd you know where he was."

"He wasn't *in* church. He just dropped off Sam for Sunday school. Is this about that thing with Sam this morning? It wasn't a big thing. Just gave the teachers a little fright is all."

"What 'thing' with Sam?"

"Well, the boy disappearing. Is that what you're calling about?"

"What happened?"

"The boys had a study group outside, the weather was so nice. About a half hour later the teachers noticed Sam was gone. We called Meg but she wasn't home—"

Bailing out that asshole from the movie company.

"—and we called Keith."

"At his office?"

"Right. He was about to leave but then Sam came back. He was upset about something but wouldn't say what. Mrs Ernhelt had a talk with him about going away without saying anything and he seemed okay. It really wasn't anything."

"What time was this, Reverend?"

"I don't know for sure. About nine forty-five or ten."

Brother . . .

"All right, sir, thank you."

"Can you tell me what this is all about?"

"Nothing important. 'Night."

The deputy finally said what he'd apparently been eager to say for some time. "Tom, if somebody gave my kid drugs like that I'da done something to him too. Maybe not killed him. But I'da done something. You can't hardly blame Keith."

"The minister called Keith when Sam disappeared. He was in his office." Before the deputy could nod in relief Tom said, "But his boy wasn't accounted for."

"Sam? Come on, you're not thinking . . ." But the man's voice faded.

Trash.

The mystery of what lay behind the stockade fence at R&W was solved: not surplus, not salvage. Forget about antiques. Not even good junk.

Robert and William owned a trashyard and nothing but.

Pellam had circled far around the back of R&W and was slowly moving through the woods. Unlike the pristine woods surrounding Ambler's house, the air here was raw, pungent, ripe. He smelled garbage and methane, which filled his throat and made him gag. Several times he had to swallow down nausea. Under the dim moonlight, halved by mist, he felt he was plodding through a dead animal's viscera. The ground under his boots was slick and pasty.

He came to the foothills of the junkyard: A doorless refrigerator on its side then ten yards further along, amputated pieces of laminated furniture, plush toys, books, tangles of wire, hunks of iron losing shape to oxidation.

Twenty yards more and he came to the boundary of R&W. He'd brought a small bolt cutter and though he saw now at one time there had been a cheap chain link enclosing a portion of the yard it had long ago sagged or been pulled down by vandals or gravity. Pellam stuffed the cutter into his back pocket and hopped over an indented portion of the fence.

He paused and listened for dogs.

Nothing. No voices either. Just the sour smell and a tangle of vague moonlight reflecting off a thousand varied surfaces. Pellam walked forward slowly toward the shack that must have been the office of the place, looking for footholds through the maze of scabby, broken trash.

Pellam pressed his back against the shack. He looked quickly in the window then ducked below the sill. Empty. He looked again.

A filthy place. Fast food cartons, empty beer cans, more magazines (he expected *Penthouses* but all he could see were *National Geographics*, *Cosmopolitans* and *Readers' Digests*), moldy and stained clothes. Books, dishes, newspapers, slips of paper, boxes.

He also saw two leather guncases in the corner.

He looked around, then tried the window. It was locked. Pellam took the bolt cutter and whacked out a pane of glass, reached up and undid the latch. He lifted the window and after a struggle to boost himself up, the pain shooting from his thigh to his ribs to his jaw, he half-fell and half-climbed over the windowsill.

He listened for a moment. And heard nothing but the rustle of a car moving by. He walked quickly to the corner, and hefted one of the gun cases. Inside was a Colt AR15, the civilian version of the Army M16.

The other case held the .300 magnum Beretta.

A simple-looking gun, a bolt-action. Walnut stock, dark blued metal, a black shoulder guard, a high-riding telescopic sight. There were no iron sights; it was a sniper's gun. The shells Sam had found fit it perfectly.

Cinderella's slipper.

Was it proof enough? Pellam didn't know. His only bout with the law had been on the other side (and from there it looked pretty damn easy to get yourself arrested and convicted). Pellam replaced the gun then began looking through desk drawers, the closet, the battered olive-drab rucksacks stacked on the back wall.

Which is where they had the drugs hidden.

Thousands of little tubes like the kind crack came in. Must've been five, six thousand of them. And inside each one was a little crystal like the doctor had showed them, the crystals someone had given Sam. A little piece of rock candy.

That solved the probable cause problem. If the gun didn't do it then this ought to.

A car went by. It seemed to slow and he quickly shoved the bags back into place, drew his pistol. Then after a moment, when the car was past, Pellam knelt and opened the rucksack again.

———◆◆◆———

21

"Nekkid," Bobby said.
His brother nodded.

They were in the Cleary Inn, eating prime rib. It was a pretty ritzy place for Dutchess County. Not as damn countryish as most places, the inn was filled with chrome and mirrors and plastic all shoved together and cemented down with plenty of money. The twins sat at a table with red linen tablecloths; in their laps were thick napkins that left whitecaps of lint on their matching dark slacks.

They may have owned a junkyard but these boys loved to eat and didn't mind pampering themselves. A goodly part of the money they made – from the drugs, of course, since they'd had a loss on the junkyard every year they'd operated it – a goodly part of that income went into their mouths. Disposable income. ("We own a junkyard – all our income's disposable! Ha, ha, ha.")

Tonight their fingernails were perfectly clean and under the aroma of coal tar shampoo they smelled sweet as the perfume aisle of a CVS Pharmacy.

Bobby said, "So there I was, nekkid as a jaybird." He paused, wondering what a jaybird was exactly. "And the shades were up. She couldn't've been more than fifteen feet away. In the backyard."

"Fifteen feet."

"In a white bra. Like torpedo tits."

"This's a dumb shit story."

"No, no, no," Bobby said. "It gets better."

Billy said, "It ain't got good yet. How can it get better?"

Bobby paused to eat his Yorkshire pudding, which was new on the menu. He'd never had it before. Well, pudding it wasn't. It was like a pancake that got out of hand. Bobby thought he could show the cook here a thing or two about making pancakes.

Billy ate some more Caesar salad.

Bobby continued, "Then she kind of waves. Only it was, she didn't want to come right out and wave. You know, that kind of wave."

Billy chewed.

"And the next thing, I'm turning around to face her full and she was looking at my ding-dong, smiling."

Billy said, "You talk more about that thang than you use it."

"I sure did use it that night," Bobby said. Then, after another triangle of Yorkshire pudding disappeared into his mouth: "How long is he going to be there?"

He didn't explain that he was talking about Pellam being at the Torrens place (they'd seen the camper on their way to the Inn) but Billy knew that's what his brother was talking about.

"I don't know. How would I know?"

Bobby said, "So, we're just going to do it? It'll look kind of obvious, won't it? First his friend in the car. Then him."

"Uhm," Billy muttered and didn't say anything more. Not

because he was chewing salad but because he was thinking.

Bobby looked at a twelve-point mounted above a smoky-glass fireplace. It was weird to have a trophy in a restaurant that looked like it ought to be on Fort Hamilton Parkway in Brooklyn or someplace in Paramus, New Jersey. He studied the animal's dead eyes and slick fur and he began salivating, imagining that he could smell fresh morning air and feel November stub grass under his boots, the heft of a good rifle in his hands.

He said, "I can't picture that, you know. Traveling around the country. I'd get kind of, you know . . ."

"Disoriented," Billy said. Billy often supplied the words that Bobby couldn't think of.

"Yeah. I'd like to travel, though. There's a lot of the world to see. I just mean I wouldn't want to travel all the time."

"Uhn."

"You're not talking a lot tonight." He tapped a crispy part of the pudding with his fork. The thing that was odd was that you were supposed to put gravy on it. Bobby thought they ought to give you Log Cabin and was close to asking for some.

Pancake pudding with gravy on it. Brits were fucking crazy.

Billy said, "There's one thing that still bothers me. The Torrens kid."

"What about him?"

"Ned gave him the candy, right? So they must've spent some time together. What's a like logical question for the kid to ask?"

Bobby couldn't figure it out. "Tell me."

"He's going to ask where Ned got the stuff, and Ned is – was – just dumb enough to tell him."

"The kid's nine or ten. What's he going to know?"

"Sometimes," Billy said, "you just don't think."

That was not exactly true. Bobby thought a lot. It was just that usually his thoughts weren't helpful; they didn't go anywhere. So he was happy to mix up batter and flip flapjacks like bones that sailed through the air in space movies and drill a deer's shoulder from three hundred yards with a shot aimed through his Zeis-Daiwar 'scope and keep the roadsides of Dutchess county free from any trash that had the slightest use and a lot of things that didn't. Beyond that, okay, he left a lot of the thinking to Billy. Who couldn't shoot and who couldn't cook. And who, fuck him, didn't like *National Geographic*.

Billy said, "He could know a lot. Just 'cause he's a kid doesn't mean *he's* stupid."

Bobby, wondering if he'd been insulted. "So, what are you saying?"

But Billy answered by asking, "What do you think of the Missus?"

Torrens. Meg Torrens. Had to be.

"I dunno," Bobby said. "You going to eat your pudding?"

"Huh?"

"Your pudding?"

"I thought it was like a potato or something. Yeah, I'm gonna eat it." Billy added, "Whatcha think about her?"

"I dunno."

"She's no hausfrau."

"Hausfrau? What's that? Like a Nazi?" Bobby pronounced it Nat-see.

"You think she has big tits?" Billy mused.

"I dunno. What're you—?"

Billy asked, "What do you think about Torrens? I mean, *really* think?"

"Think about him?" Bobby often repeated his brother's questions in a tone that made it sound like it was a dumb thing to ask – usually so he could buy time to figure out an answer.

Billy continued, "You think he's smart?"

"Smart enough."

Billy looked at his brother, then laughed. "What does that mean, 'smart enough'? That's like saying his dick is long enough."

"Okay," Bobby said, "he's smart enough not to put his dick where it don't belong. Which it sounds to me is what *you're* considering doing."

There, dude, how's *that* for thinking?

"How much you think Torrens's worth? How much you think he makes?"

"Man, you're asking for—"

"Compared to what, let's say, we, for instance, make?"

"—fucking trouble."

Billy ate his pudding, every last bit. Bobby watched this with disappointment. He thought that thirteen ninety five, which bought you a good-sized slab of wet, red prime rib, ought to buy you a little more in the Brit pudding department.

"They got themselves a real nice house," Billy said, continuing this line of thought that Bobby didn't quite get but knew he didn't like."

"It's okay."

Billy stared at his brother as if he'd just turned down playoff tickets. Bobby said, "Okay, it's fucking wonderful. Happy?"

"Let's just . . ." Billy began.

"I think you're nuts is what I think."

". . . consider a possibility."

———◆◆◆———

22

S he was wondering where Pellam was. What he was up to. Taking the whiskey, disappearing mysteriously like that.

Meg Torrens felt a brief splinter of jealousy, wondering if he'd gone off to see Janine. Then she forced that thought away. Said to herself: You got yourself a pretty full plate at the moment, babe.

Still . . .

That damn sound again. From the day they'd met in Pellam's hospital room. The Polaroid. *Bzzzt.*

For your information I've lived here five years . . .

She thought about him kissing her, about how she wanted to kiss him back.

Enough . . .

She tucked Sam into bed and went down to the kitchen, poured herself another glass of wine and was returning to the living room, turning the lights down. She'd had them up high while Pellam was here, despite her hatred of bright lights.

Didn't know why she'd done that . . . Okay, yes, she did. Less romantic. Less of a message. She—

A knock on the door.

She hoped it was Pellam but was afraid Ambler had returned. She recalled that he must have seen Pellam leave and wondered if Ambler had parked up the road and been spying on them, waiting for him to leave. To return and try his proposal yet again. How could such a strong man be so desperate?

I'm just not in the mood for this . . .

But when she opened the door she found the sheriff standing on the front porch.

"Tom."

"Evening, Meg."

She felt a jolt. "Is Keith okay?"

"Oh, I'm not here about him."

"Pellam?"

"Not him either. Mind if I come in?"

He was grave but then he was always grave. She nodded him in, setting the wine on a nearby break-front. He walked inside, pulling off his hat the instant his boot touched the threshold.

"Coffee or anything?"

He shook his head. Sat down on the couch.

"What is it?"

"Just wanted to ask you a thing'r two about Sam. You know he left Sunday School for a while this morning."

What was this?

"I didn't know that was a crime," she said stiffly.

"Meg, I think we both know it isn't. And I think you know there's more to me asking than that."

"Which is what?"

"Did you know about Sam? Would you tell me please?"

She opted for the truth but it was a close election. "Yes. Keith told me. They tried to call me here but I was out. They called him at the factory. Sam came back after a few minutes."

"After forty-five minutes."

"What is this all about, Tom?"

"And you talked to Sam about it?"

"Of course." The sheriff said nothing more and Meg felt compelled to continue. "He was upset about what happened. With those pills. He said he didn't feel well. It was a nice day. He went for a walk." She was rambling and stopped. "I want to know what you're asking."

Tom nodded. "Meg, not long after he left the church Ned Harper was killed. It was a mile away – that's a bit of a hike but he could've made it in the time he was gone."

"Ned? What does Sam have to do with Ned?"

"We think Ned was the one gave him those pills. And we think Sam might've killed him."

"No," she said firmly.

"We don't know for sure. But it'd make sense for Ned to've threatened the boy. You saw how scared he was. And it'd make sense for Sam to want to get even."

"Sam wouldn't hurt anybody."

"Ned was killed with a small-caliber. Might be a .22. We haven't got the slugs yet. Randy Gottschalk, my deputy, he was telling me that Keith got Sam a .22 last Christmas."

Her eyes strayed to the den – where the small Winchester usually resided. Her heart jumped when she noticed it was gone. But then she remembered that Sam and Pellam had been shooting that afternoon. Had they been using the .22? Or the little shotgun? Maybe they were on the back porch, awaiting cleaning. Or the basement. The only gun in the cabinet was the antique Springfield – the only surviving bequest from her parents, other than the intense dislike of bright lights.

"Tom, you've known Sam since he was born. You think he's capable of killing somebody?"

"I don't, no. But I'm not the only one going to be asking. We've already had more'n our share of trouble in Cleary – those deaths last year, a couple of other overdoses. The state police're going to be handling this one. And they're going to want to talk to Sam and check out his gun. Run some ballistics."

"What that'll prove is that he's not the one." But even as she said these words a terrible doubt was forming. No, her son was incapable of killing anyone.

Yet she remembered his face today – when he was shooting with Pellam. It looked so determined. So adult. Scarey, at times.

"Can I talk to him?"

"He's asleep."

Tom smiled, looked past her. "Doesn't seem to be."

Sam was standing in the hallway, in his pajamas, staring at the sheriff uneasily.

"I heard a noise, I got scared."

"Hi, Sam. How you doing?"

"Hi, Sheriff."

"You feeling better?"

"Yessir, I am."

"You must've heard me. Sorry I woke you up."

"I wasn't asleep. I heard you come in. This was a different noise. Outside my window."

Meg was looking at his round, sleepy face. She thought: No, he'd never kill anyone. Yet . . . His eyes seemed so cold. He seemed so different. She struggled to smile. "Honey, it's probably that owl. Remember."

"Wasn't the owl."

Meg was thinking: Where is that .22? But, no, he *couldn't* have done it.

Tom stood. "How 'bout I take a look?"

"I guess," Sam said.

"Tom—" Meg began.

In a whisper the sheriff said, "Okay, Meg, tell you what. I'll come by tomorrow. You and Keith'll be here and you can have a lawyer too, you want. Okay?"

She nodded.

Tom put his hand on the boy's shoulder and they started up the stairs. "Now let's check out that noise."

"I'll be there in a minute to tuck you in," Meg called.

Where was that gun? She had to find it.

She was halfway to the back porch when the gunshot, from upstairs, shook the house.

A scream burst from her lips. She ran to the stairs and leapt out of the way just as Tom stumbled down them, a terrible wound in his chest.

"I . . ." He glanced at her with unfocused eyes, crawled toward the front door. He got three or four feet. Then dropped to the floor, lay still. Blood soaked the carpet.

"Jesus . . . Sam!" She started up the stairs again.

For a terrible moment she believed that her son had done it all – killed Ned and then lured the sheriff up to the second floor to kill him. And felt too that it was all her fault – for her infidelity, for her not being grateful for the wonderful life Keith had given her.

But then the boy appeared on the stairs, running in panic, tears streaming down his face.

"There was a man! He hurt Sheriff Tom. He shot him!"

"Where is he?"

"I don't know. He was at the window. I'm scared . . ."

Then she heard the noise.

Coming from the basement, the sound reminded her of the time she'd pulled apart an old lettuce crate for the wood, using a claw hammer to pry the nails. The loud squeal from the rusty friction.

Then a snap and the tinkle of glass on stone.

The basement window.

"Mommy! It's him. He's there. He's in the—"

"Shhh."

Meg ran to the basement door. She locked a small brass latch and grabbed the telephone. The line was dead. She tapped the button.

Silence.

She glanced at Tom but the pistol was no longer in his holster. He must have dropped it somewhere or the intruder had stolen it.

"Sam, where are those guns you and Mr Pellam were shooting?"

"I don't—"

"Sam, it's okay, honey. It's going to be fine. Where are the guns?"

He gasped in fear. "I put them in the basement. We were going to clean them. He said he didn't want me to by myself."

"All right, baby."

She led him to the first-floor guest room, which was windowless. She put him inside. "You lock the door when I close it. And don't open it for anybody but Daddy or me."

"I'm scared."

Hugging him hard. So hard it seemed that she'd never be able to let go. "You'll be all right. I promise."

She closed the door and heard it lock.

Meg sprinted into the den, tore open the gun cabinet door. The carbine, smelling of oil and sulfur, was in her hand. The hundred-year-old Springfield (*breechloader, not muzzleloader* . . . Oh, Pellam where are you?). The saddle ring jingled as she blew dust off the brown metal barrel.

She found a dozen of the long, heavy shells, put one in the chamber and the rest in her sweater pocket. She closed the breech with a snap and ran into the hall.

On the first floor she checked the front and back doors. They were locked. The windows on the ground floor? She usually kept them locked but had she aired the house recently? She couldn't remember and she wasn't going to check now.

She paused, heard delicate scraping sounds. Metal and wood being adjusted. She walked to the kitchen. Slow, determined. Okay, asshole, she thought. With both hands pulled the hammer to half-cock.

Footsteps were coming up the stairs.

Meg clicked out the kitchen light. She took a deep breath, reached forward, undid the latch and swung the door open wide. She stepped back so fast she almost tripped.

The man was three-quarters up the stairs. She couldn't see his face. He stopped. There was a laugh of surprise. He held a flashlight in his hand. His high, playful voice – vaguely familiar – said, "Meter reader."

Meg said, "I've got a gun. One more step and you're dead."

The light beam started to sweep toward her.

"Shine that light in my eyes and you're dead."

"Risky place, this house."

"What do you want?" She tried to keep her voice from quivering.

"Just passing Go. Looking for my two hundred. But seriously, folks . . . Tell you what, just let me wander out and I won't report you."

"I want you to lie facedown on the floor."

He laughed. "Uh, nothing personal but it's not real clean. And there might be spiders. I don't like spiders."

"Now!" With one thumb she managed to put the gun on full cock. The click reverberated through the kitchen.

He took a step down the stairs. He was debating. Then he said, "Don't think so. Thanks for the offer but I believe what I'll do is leave. Keep the jewelry, the silver. Wasn't my pattern anyway. Hey, just want to say . . ."

She held the gun up to her shoulder, started to squeeze the trigger.

He took another two slow steps into the darkness. ". . . dinner smells great, lady. Sorry I couldn't stay. Maybe some other time."

Now! Do it!

Her finger was frozen on the trigger. *Shoot, shoot, shoot . . .*

The man disappeared.

"Shit."

She slammed the door, slipped the latch, and heard him

running through the basement. She sprinted to the front of the house. She peered out through the lace curtains beside the door. She couldn't see anyone.

Hell, hell, hell. Where is he? Where'd he go?

Pellam, she thought, please come home . . .

Keith . . .

She started toward Sam's room.

Which is when the other man stepped into the hall from the living room and got his arm around her chest, saying in the same sort of sick voice that his partner had been speaking in, "Whoa my! Big gun for a little girl."

My God, she recognized him! It was one of the twins. The ones who owned that disgusting junkyard outside of town. Billy, or Bobby, had his hand over her face and groping for the stock of the gun, trying to pull it out of her strong, desperate grip.

She felt painful pressure on her breast as he fondled her with his other hand. "Hmmmm," he said with approval. She smelled his cheap musky aftershave and coal tar.

He was very strong but so was she. Neither could wrest the gun from the other's grip.

So she pointed the gun into the kitchen and pulled the trigger.

The explosion filled the hall with sulfur-stinking smoke. The Sanyo microwave blew into a dozen pieces. The recoil slammed Meg backwards into the twin. Through the ringing in her ears she heard him inhale in surprise. With a resounding crack his head hit the front doorknob.

"Ow, damn! Shit, that hurts." He let go and grabbed his head with both of his hands.

Meg dropped to her knees, tore open the breech of the

gun. The spent cartridge, hot and smokey, popped out, and she reloaded the rifle.

The twin blinked, squeezing the back of his head, spun around, undoing latches and locks on the front door. Blood stained the white enamel door and spattered the carpet.

Chain off, one latch, deadbolt.

Meg slammed the breech closed.

The door swung open.

Cocking the gun . . .

"Fucking cannon," he called to his brother, who must've been outside. "She's got a fucking cannon!"

Then a scream behind her.

"Mommy!" Sam had left the guest room and was running down the corridor toward her.

Meg turned toward him. "No, Sam, no!"

She spun back. But it was too late. The twin jumped toward her. Meg couldn't get the gun on full-cock in time and she swung it like a club. He caught it easily and jabbed his fist into her jaw.

"Mommy," Sam cried again as she dropped to her knees.

The brother stepped forward and, furious, hit her again, harder. A burst of electric pain just under her ears. Her vision went black and grainy around the edges. She slid down against the cornflower-blue wall. Tried to get up. Billy ripped the gun from her hands. Her head sagged against the wall.

Sam reached her, put his arms around her head. He screamed, "Go away, go away, you!"

The twin opened the door and shouted. "Yo, Bobby. It's under control. Come on in."

Bobby walked inside. Sniffed the air. "Stinks. Brimstone.

Lookit that thing." He nodded at the Springfield in admiration. Then he saw the sheriff's body. "You have to do that?"

"He seen me coming through the window," Billy said, massaging his head where he'd struck it on the doorknob. "The fuck you think I should've done? Said 'Howdy-do'?"

Bobby closed the door, looked over at Sam. "Hey, young fella. Don't worry. You'll be okay."

His brother muttered, "Son of a bitch, I'm bleeding." He looked with satisfaction at Meg, whose head lolled back and forth against the wallpaper. Her face was white. He asked, "Where's Keith?"

Meg didn't answer. He slapped her hard. Still silence. She was only half conscious.

"No!" the boy cried.

"Where's your father?"

He hesitated then said, "He's at the office but he's coming home any minute and he's going to kill you."

"Any minute," Billy repeated, looking at his brother.

But Bobby was looking over at the little boy. "How 'bout you and me go watch TV or something. In the living room there? While we wait for him."

"No."

"You don't want me to hit your mommy again, do you?"

Sam didn't say anything, just shook his head, wiped tears.

Bobby smiled. "Come on. Let's you and me go in there."

Billy said, "We don't have time for that now."

Feeling good that he'd thought of something his brother hadn't, Bobby said, "We gotta wait anyway, don't we? May as well enjoy ourselves."

23

T he roadside signs gave him messages.

The scientist within Keith Torrens would see a yellow warning sign with a curve and a side road painted on it and he'd think of a sigma bond. And his mind would shift into thoughts about electron sharing and the unequal charge distribution in a chloride-bromine molecule.

Or he'd see a yield sign and think, *delta*, and, bang, there it would be in his thoughts: the Gibbs free-energy exchange formula.

Wandering, his mind. Going down those odd paths, just like it did when he was a pudgy kid with a slide rule. The Magic Moments happened then too, didn't they?

Another sign – this one on an old, abandoned White Castle hamburger stand. Castle . . . He saw the faded paint of the parapets as he sped past.

Castle. Medieval castles. Alchemists.

He thought about the location scout.

Pellam . . .

He was tired. It was nearly eleven and he'd put in a full fourteen hours at the plant. Another Sunday gone. Pushing the Cougar along the deserted, dark road, listening to the damn front-end squeak. A scientist. I'm a scientist and I can't fix a noisy hunk of metal.

But none of that mattered: the fatigue, the squeak, the headache. He didn't care. What was there to bitch about? He'd buy a new goddamn Cougar, a Cadillac, a Mercedes.

He was riding on a Magic Moment.

The answer had come all at once. At two that afternoon in a crisp unfolding of thoughts that he fought to put into numbers, Greek letters and scientific symbols. He had run from the factory into his office, closing the door, shutting off the telephone, and wrote furiously – frantic, terrified that he'd miss something. Keith had felt the shock of fear rise up to his scalp, like the first and only time he took speed – in college, struggling to get his master's degree project in on time. That warm clarity, everything focused, sweeping forward.

A Magic Moment.

That the problem solved – a new stabilizer for one of his company's cough syrups – wasn't exactly earth-shattering or in proportion to his euphoria didn't occur to him. And if it had, the excitement wouldn't be the least dampened.

The magic worked. He'd packed a problem into his brain, let it bake and out came a solution. He was high, he was alive. Those moments validated everything – all the business bullshit he put up with, all the long hours, the risks, the ulcers he was sure he was developing. All the time away from Meg and Sam.

All of that was paid for in one moment. A Magic Moment.

Thinking about Meg . . .

And he regretted for the tenth time that day, as every day, that she couldn't really be a part of what he'd done, his business. She'd benefit, of course. She'd be a millionaire too. But she couldn't be a partner.

That was Keith Torrens's greatest regret.

Castles, medieval alchemists.

Alchemy, turning gold into brighter gold.

Rings of gold. Wedding rings. Meg.

He remembered a line from some country-western station – one that she listened to all the time.

If we tell a lie while we're lying together, then that's nothing more than a port in bad weather . . .

He wondered again whether she was seeing anyone. He didn't think so. But Keith Torrens (who'd never cheated on his wife) believed that while men and women both had an equal capacity for deception, women were better equipped to cover their tracks. Keith (empirical, rational Cartesian – a *scientist*) had decided this was because as mothers, with broods to attend to, and possessing less physical strength than men they had honed their skills in guile for protection.

A tertiary basic nitrogen . . .

So, he'd found no circumstantial evidence. Nothing in her eyes. No Amex receipts (he could imagine what bastards those little blue tissue clues must be). Couldn't recall any times she was supposed to be at home when she wasn't (though how would he know? He was at the plant twelve hours a day). Sam had never referred to an uncle who'd come to help mommy with the yard, the gutters, the shopping.

. . . a quaternary carbon . . .

Who could be more devoted than he was? A better father? He never took long business trips, like some of the men who worked for the big companies by the Hudson. He didn't uproot Meg and Sam and drag them around the country. He wasn't like the fellow he'd met at the golf course one Sunday, a friend of a friend, who worked for IBM (I've Been Moved) down in Westchester. Four houses in six years.

. . . *an ethylene chain and a ketone* . . . *Put them in the oven, and let them bake. Bang, a Magic Moment, and out comes something new.*

No, she was faithful. Though questions of fidelity were the type you ask yourself in a certain way – fast, distracted – so as to avoid the possibility of a real answer. A scientist is not equipped to ask questions like that. Scientists aren't happy until they find the truth and he wasn't sure he wanted the truth.

Keith Torrens drove toward his home. He'd make it up to her. Make up for what?

He wasn't sure.

How?

He didn't know.

Pellam pulled the camper into the driveway.

He saw the beige car parked in the road just past the drive and thought: Oh, hell. No . . . He recognized the car. Knew who the visitors were.

Thinking about Big Mountain Studio's promise to put mobile phones in all the campers. None of Lefkowitz's minions had ever gotten around to it. And here the nearest house was several miles up the road. No time to get there.

No time for anything.

He doused the lights, parked on the grass, opened the camper door and climbed out.

No one inside seemed to have noticed him.

Everything seemed slowed up, the way they shoot karate fights in those charmingly bad Hong Kong karate flicks, or the way Sam Peckinpah shot his violent scenes. Pellam stepped out of the camper, breathing deeply. He started toward the house, avoiding the gravel.

At least he had surprise on his side.

Man, no question it was fall. That smell of the air's dry coldness, the sweet scent of oak or cherry fires.

Pellam was thinking how seasonless the big cities are. New York, L.A. And it was odd how returning to the country during a blatant time of year – the first deep snow, the week of the most colorful leaves – is more than anything a return to youth. Painful nostalgia, a rearrangement of priorities and possibilities.

Blatant seasons.

Pellam figured that was a pretty good observation and he wondered if he'd live long enough to use it in a film.

The sky was almost completely clear now, swept clean by the cold front. He glanced up, seeing the stars in the black vacuum that domed over him from one horizon of trees to another.

A perfect fall night in Cleary, New York. Home of the perfect cemetery.

That's how they'd ended up in Cleary in the first place, looking for the ideal, A-number-one cemetery.

A perfect fall night.

As he moved over the lawn. He saw shadows inside. The flicker of a TV screen. Keith's car was gone. So the twins were in there alone with Meg and Sam.

He hurried toward the house. He slipped the gun in his waistband. There was an open window to the right of the door, opening into a dark room. He could go up a rose trellis and through the window. Come around from behind.

Two of them, both armed, probably.

At least he had surprise on his—

A car pulled into the driveway, catching Pellam in its beams. It gave a long blare on the horn.

From the house, fifty feet away, security lights clicked on, blinding him.

"What's going on?" Keith called from the driveway. He'd parked and gotten out of the car. Pellam called, "Stay there. Stay back."

He turned back to the house. The front door opened and one of the twins stepped out, holding a pistol at Pellam's chest.

So much, Pellam thought, for surprise.

24

Pellam supposed that he'd known all along it would come to this.

He walked to the right, out of the glare, onto the driveway, gravel scrunching beneath the worn sole of his Nokonas. He stopped and felt an odd sensation – growing into the drive, like roots going down, solid as the granite slabs the gravel used to be. "Hey, mister. Hey, Mr Torrens."

"What the hell—"

"Quiet," Pellam ordered Keith. The man froze.

This was definitely the ending of a film – not like one of his, though, in which viewers felt all that tension, then nothing happening, the principals moving vaguely off into the credits (boy, he took flak for those endings. *Resolve it, John, resolve it*. How the world hates the truth of ambiguity).

But here it was. Pretty damn clear to him. A man slouching out onto the porch, holding in his hand an automatic pistol. Meg said she didn't like handguns. They're man-killing guns, she'd have been thinking, no other purpose for them.

The man slouching.

"You interrupted me," the twin said. "Was just about to sit down and watch some TV with a little friend in there."

And where's the other one, Pellam wondered, his brother?

Behind him?

Behind me?

Inside, with Sam?

"Where's Meg?" Pellam asked.

"Whatcha doin' here, mister?"

"Which one're you?"

"Bobby. Hey, don't you move there, Mr Torrens. You do, I'll have to kill you too."

Pellam asked, "You the one who did it?"

"Did what?"

"Killed my friend."

"S'pose you know if I tell you I'll have to make sure that fact doesn't go any further."

"That's pretty much on the agenda anyway, isn't it?" Pellam asked.

"Heh."

"I just want to know if it was you killed Marty."

"Was a hell of a shot, I do say so myself." Not smirking. Just mentioning the fact.

"Whatcha got there?" Bobby asked. "In your belt?"

"It'd be a Colt Peacemaker."

"No kidding. Smokeless powder? Reproduction?"

"Nope. It's the real thing."

"No kidding. Forty-four?"

"Forty-five."

"Heh."

"Where's your brother?"

"Maybe he's behind you."

"So you'll die first," Pellam said.

"Heh."

"Please . . ." Keith was begging. "Where's my son?"

They both ignored him.

There was no motion. Pellam stood on the wet gravel, his feet, in scuffed black boots, slightly apart.

There was no noise.

There was nothing else in the world except a man standing in front of him with a gun in his hand. A tall Victorian house. With a woman and boy inside, her husband nearby. Under a canopy of a dry, clear fall night.

Pellam had shot ducks and geese and a number of Gila monsters and rattlesnakes and hundreds of Heineken bottles.

He'd never shot a man.

The security lights poured into his eyes, making Bobby a silhouette. (Pellam recalled that, on various target ranges, he'd shot as many silhouette targets as Gila monsters and rattlesnakes combined.)

No face, no motion, no sound.

In the stillness, in this dense peace, a thought came to him. Something he remembered from researching a script about the Indians of the Great Plains. The Sioux, he believed. Waking up on a beautiful day, they wouldn't think how good it was to be alive. What they'd say was, "It's a good day to die."

Good, Pellam. Good thought.

Well, Wild Bill himself hadn't lived to see forty.

Then, finally, motion intruded on the scene. It was a cliché – one that Pellam, if he were directing a Western, wouldn't have allowed the writer to use: He pulled his blue jean jacket open slightly wider to fully expose the grip of his pistol.

The way Bobby saw it (Bobby who *had* shot a man – several of them, in fact – but only in the backs of their heads after being paid ten thousand dollars each to do it) these were good odds. Pellam had glare in his eyes and he had a single-action gun so he'd have to draw and cock it before he could shoot. It was a six-shot gun and it would take probably three minutes to reload. If he had extra ammo on him. Which he probably didn't.

Also, he figured Pellam hadn't shot anybody in the back of the head or anyplace else for any money.

Bobby, on the other hand, was already holding a cocked Browning automatic .380 with twelve rounds in it. Which all you had to do was aim and pull the trigger. The light was behind him. He could reload the Browning in two seconds.

Torrens was in the yard, true, but he wasn't going to do diddly except stand there like a scared rabbit.

He hoped Billy was watching him. He never missed a chance to impress his smarter brother.

What he'd do is let the guy go for the gun then shoot him in his leg. Watch him fall. Then let him crawl a little. Shoot again.

Maybe he'd aim for Pellam's boots. They were a good contrast, black on the white gravel. But so were the man's eyes, which glinted two reflections from the yellow porch light. And his white shirt under the dark jacket.

But then he decided there was something about the way the man had opened his jacket that made Bobby uneasy. Don't play games. Do Pellam, do Torrens. Go back to the boy. Or the mother. Or both.

Go for a chest shot.

Without really deciding, or thinking, Bobby dropped into a crouch.

He swept the gun upward in an arc, keeping his arm straight the way he knew to do and practiced every week. None of this two-hand combat shooting that nobody who knows guns really ever does. Squinting, but leaving both eyes open, as the blade sight rose right toward the white slash of Pellam's shirt. He started to pull the trigger.

Thunk.

A shovel.

Bobby thought: Goddamn . . . who did that?

Somebody'd snuck up and hit him in the chest with a shovel. Or . . . Damn, it hurt. He coughed. Or maybe it was an ax handle. Bobby dropped his unfired gun. He looked down. Where'd it go? He looked behind him. There was nobody. He looked at his chest again and saw the blood. Oh, that hurts. He was getting dizzy. Then he saw Pellam holding the Colt at his hip, surrounded by a cloud of smoke. Bobby reached for his gun. He fell to the porch. He looked for the shovel.

He asked, "Who? . . ."

He died.

Pellam spun around, looked behind him, into the fields to the side of the house.

No Billy.

He whispered to Keith, "Get down. Don't move." And started forward. But he didn't get very far. The door crashed open and Billy, staggering out, dropped to his knees over Bobby, shrieking. He lifted his own gun and fired sloppily at Pellam.

Ragged blue flashes appeared in the man's hand, the huge crack of the shots filling the night. A bullet popped the sound barrier inches from his left ear with the noise of a huge snapping finger.

All Pellam had time for was one shot, from his hip. He felt the kick, smelled the sulfur from the black powder. He saw the slug dig out a chunk of the porch. Billy fired fast and Pellam dove to the ground. He hit hard, landed on his right elbow. There was a loud snap, followed by breath-taking pain. His vision went black and dusty from the dislocation. He rolled onto his back. His shoulder joint popped back into alignment. He fainted for a second. Sweat shot from his forehead and he felt nausea in a bristling wave.

He lifted the Colt. It fell from his hand. His right arm was useless.

"Bobby, oh, Bobby . . ." Billy was moaning.

More shots from the automatic. Bullets dug into the camper and the ground near him.

Six shots, seven, eight.

"Sonabitchsonabitch! Son . . . of . . . a . . . bitch!"

Pellam lifted the Colt again. But it was a replay – the gun did a double gainer to the ground.

Christ, how many shots in that clip?

Ten, eleven, twelve . . .

Click, click, click.

Empty. He was out. Thank you . . . Pellam raised his head and watched Billy reload.

Pellam felt the cold wet touch of the gravel, smelled the sour earthy-oily scent of the stone. He saw Billy coming closer. He lowered his head and heard the crunch of the gravel under the man's loafers.

Pellam grabbed for the Colt. He hit the butt with his fingers and knocked it out of reach.

He heard the man's breathing. Pellam looked up, opened his eyes. He saw the bore of the gun in the man's hand, six feet away.

Billy stopped.

A good day to die . . .

Billy stopped.

He looked behind him as if he'd heard something.

Then he was flying through the air.

Sailing, the way stunt men did, off springboards mounted on either side of black powder charges in the war movies.

Billy sprawled on top of Pellam, knocking the wind out of him with a high, love-making grunt. The twin rolled over, uttered, "Bobby," then studied the gravel an inch away from his face. "Son of a bitch." He closed his eyes. "Son of a bitch." He shuddered once and was still.

Pellam pushed himself up, fainted for a few seconds. He came to then sat up again.

In front of him, on the porch, Meg was crying, clutching the smoking Springfield. She dug frantically into her pockets – for more ammunition, he guessed.

"Meg!" he called. "It's okay. They're gone. They're both gone."

But she paid no attention, dropped to her knees and slid a new shell into the gun, cocked it with both hands. She stood once more, wiped tears and scanned the yard like a sentry then returned to the house, calling to her son.

———◦✦◦———

25

"You all right?" Keith asked. Pellam nodded, gasping at the pain. And Keith continued into the house, following Meg.

Pellam made sure that Billy was dead then staggered inside.

He found them in the living room, Keith's arm around Meg, standing over Tom, the sheriff. He was dead.

Meg looked toward the front door, at Pellam, with eyes wide in terror.

Keith was on his knees, hugging Sam. Who glanced at Pellam but said nothing. He was crying. "Did they hurt you?" Keith asked.

The boy shook his head.

Meg, crying too, gasped. "He was going to . . . He took him in there. . . ." She nodded toward the living room. "But then they heard the horn and he went outside to see who it was."

"Oh, honey . . ."

Keith stood and Meg lowered her head to Keith's shoulder.

"What happened?" Keith muttered

"Honey, your phone, in the car. We've got to call the police."

"My phone?"

"In the car. They cut the line here. The phone doesn't work."

"I left it at the factory," he said. He seemed numb, unable to say any more than a few words at a time.

"Then drive to the Burkes, use theirs!"

"What happened? I don't . . . ." He looked around the house. "I don't understand."

"It was so terrible . . ."

"Why was Tom here?" Keith asked.

Meg glanced at Sam and whispered something to her husband. He frowned. She nodded. "Then one of them shot Tom. They got in somehow. I don't know why. I have no idea why."

Keith said nothing for a moment, just stared at the sheriff's body. He glanced at Sam. "I'm going to take you up to bed. Your mother and I have to talk."

"Keith . . ." Meg started after him. But Pellam, wincing at the pain in his shoulder, stepped forward, touched her arm. "Meg, wait."

Father and son disappeared up the stairs.

She turned. "You're hurt . . ."

"Sit down."

Meg hesitated. "I have to talk to you. I have to tell you why I came back tonight . . ."

She was staring at Tom. "Keith has to call. He has to go to the Burkes."

"Meg . . . Listen to me. Tonight I went to see your friend."

She stiffened and her attention on the body in her living room vanished. "My friend?" she asked.

"Ambler."

She considered this, then asked, "How did you know he was my friend?"

"We had a talk." Pellam paused, looking at the stairs. But Keith was still with Sam. He added, "He likes you. He likes you a lot."

She wasn't sure what to do with this information. She found an afghan, placed it over the sheriff's head and chest. Pellam wanted to put his arm around her but he would probably have fainted; any motion was pure pain in his shoulder.

"Why did you go to see him?" Meg asked.

"I thought he might've been the one who had Marty killed."

"What?"

Pellam shook his head. "He didn't. But he did plant the drugs and he had me beat up."

"Wex wouldn't do . . ." But her voice faded and she obviously concluded that, yeah, he could very easily do that.

"The reason he did it was that he was afraid I was going to take you away with me."

"He did?"

She looked troubled but he wondered if he wasn't seeing a little pride in her face too. There probably isn't a woman in the world who isn't thrilled by a man who goes to those kind of lengths to keep her for himself.

"We decided it was probably the twins who were behind the shooting. I went to their junkyard. That shack of theirs. I found the gun they killed Marty with. Some other things too. I found—"

Footsteps nearby. Keith walked slowly down the stairs. He caught Pellam's eyes and paused. Then continued. "Sam's okay. I gave him something. He's sleeping."

Meg ignored him. Said to Pellam, "Why are you telling me this?"

But Keith preempted her. He'd overheard Pellam and he asked, "What else did you find in the shack?"

Pellam said to Meg, "I found some of that stuff, the drugs Sam got."

"So they're the ones?" she blurted. "They're the ones behind it . . . But why would they come here? Because Sam was a witness?"

"They weren't after Sam."

Keith had stopped walking. He sat down. Pellam said to him, "They had five or six thousand vials there. All packaged and ready to go . . . So, Keith, tell me: Were they distributing? Or were they skimming from you?"

Keith's eyes swam around the room. "Both, apparently."

Meg stared at her husband. "What do you mean?"

"Your partners came here to kill you," Pellam said. "And your family."

"Partners?" Meg gasped.

Pellam said to Keith, "Would they have enough information to make the drugs themselves? Could they do it without your factory?"

Keith didn't say anything.

Both, apparently.

Keith looked at the wall beyond which two of his employees lay. "I paid them enough."

"There's never enough."

"How'd you find out?"

Pellam said, "In one of the bags in their shack were notes from you. Some of your letterhead. Some cash." He nodded. "I came here to tell Meg."

She turned to Pellam. Wanted to say something, it seemed, but couldn't.

Keith said, "They were just punks but they had contacts in New York, New Jersey, Brooklyn. I needed them."

Pellam asked, "What is it exactly? The drug."

Keith explained. "It's an oral synthetic narcotic."

To her husband Meg whispered, "No. This isn't happening."

Keith took a breath and Pellam could see he was running through the inventory of lies he might choose from. A boy in front of a broken window. He looked at both Pellam and Meg and said, "It's not what you think."

"No, no, no . . ." She shook her head.

"Meg, it's just a product. I—"

"Product!" Meg said. "This shit is poison and you call it a *product?*"

"You don't understand, Meg," he snapped. "It's not like that."

"What *is* it like, then?"

"It's a fantastic discovery! It took me two years to perfect it."

"Discovery?"

Pellam said wryly, "State of the art. Normally, heroin you have to shoot up to get the best rush. This stuff, all you do is chew it."

Keith said, "What I developed was a new vasodilator. It's brilliant. The narcotic goes into the blood cells under the tongue in milliseconds."

Pellam continued. "A new Yuppie drug of choice. No need to shoot up. No needles. No AIDS risk . . ."

Keith said, "I was going to license it. I mean I am going to license it for legitimate medical purposes. We just needed a little more capital . . . We were going to distribute samples to medical research companies – you don't need FDA approval for that. But Dale started selling underground to get some cash flow. By the time I found out we were in too deep."

"Liar."

"No, Meg, really—"

She stepped toward him. "Tell me how my poor baby got in too deep! You and Dale had cash from day one. You bought out your contract . . . Oh, you had somebody bankrolling you and knew exactly who you were going to sell this shit to from the day you opened your factory."

"Stop it!"

"Tell me how someone put a gun to your head and forced you to—" She stopped speaking, frowned. "Wait." More horror in her eyes. "And what happened to him, to Dale?"

"He . . ." Keith looked away.

"They killed him. Those twins . . . Why? Was he getting too greedy?"

"It all got out of hand," Keith said furiously. "It wasn't my fault."

She was continuing, "And those other men, the ones from New York . . . And the boy who overdosed last year . . . And Ned! This morning. They killed him too! And Tom thought Sam had done it! Oh, Jesus Christ."

"And Marty," Pellam said.

It took Keith a moment to realize who Marty was. He said,

"That was an accident. I swear to God. Bobby and Billy were trying to scare the two of you out of here. That's all. We didn't want strangers in town. We couldn't risk any publicity."

Pellam said, "Accident? You killed your partner and who knows who else – and you expect me to believe that you just wanted to scare Marty?"

Meg, incredulous. Shaking her head slowly, her ponytail lolling. "And you almost killed our son?"

"I told them –" Nodding in the direction of the front yard. "– never to sell to anybody around here. But they didn't listen to me. It wasn't my fault. I—"

"Not your fault? You made it and now you're selling it. How do you mean it's not your fault? Explain that to me, Keith."

Keith couldn't hold her eyes any longer and looked down.

She simply shook her head. Her rage was too great.

Pellam could see that he'd fallen into a particular persona – one that must have suckered Meg all along: Keith the boy with the thick hair, the round face. Imploring, needing love. The pudgy boy.

"We have nothing to talk about. Nothing at all."

"Please, let me explain."

She turned to look at him as he slouched in the doorway, pressing against the jamb with his shoulder as if he needed the house itself to hold him upright.

Meg said, "You've lied to me all along."

"I didn't want to tell you. For your own protection."

Meg said bitterly, "How did you figure that?"

"If anything were to happen I didn't want you to be involved."

She laughed in astonishment. "How *wouldn't* I be involved?

My husband's making drugs! How *wouldn't* Sam and I be sucked right into the middle of it? I mean, look what happened the other day with Sam. He could've died."

"That won't happen again."

She was crying now. "Oh, God, Keith . . . You sound like you're not going to stop. Tom's dead! There're two bodies in my front yard. It's over with. We're calling the police."

"No, Meg. What I've come up with, it's magic." His eyes gleamed. "Nobody's ever made anything like this before. Nobody else can."

She spat out, "You sound proud of it."

He shouted, "I am proud! You really don't know who I am. You've never made the least effort to see me. I'm not the same as everybody else. My mind doesn't walk, it runs. I was born that way. I'm not like you. Or him." He glanced at Pellam. "Or anybody."

"But we loved each other," Meg cried.

"What does that have to do with anything? Don't sound so self-righteous. I did it for you. And for Sam. Why do you think? You were always harping about a nice house, having money, your fucking jewelry! How was I supposed to do that on a chemist's salary?" He pointed to her ring. "You think I could afford that if I was still at Sandberg?"

"Are you seriously trying to blame me? You should blame whatever's in you that makes you think you've got a different set of rules than everybody else. And, what? We're just supposed to forget everything that's happened? Well, I'm not forgetting. Sam and I are leaving."

"You're going with *him*?" Keith glanced at Pellam. His voice was filled with disbelief.

"I'm just leaving. That's the only explanation I owe you. Sam and I, we're both leaving."

"You can't just desert me."

"Desert you?" Meg laughed.

The tension in the room was like energy itself.

"I'm not going to let that happen!" Keith's voice jarred in the room, a sound to match the glare of light. "You're my wife. You're staying with me. In six months, I'll have the patent and I'll stop selling on the street. We'll get a license from Pfizer or Merck. We'll tell the state police the twins tried to break in and rape you. Tom was here about Sam and they killed him. We can say—"

"No more." Her eyes closed and her head moved back and forth slowly. "No more." She stood up. "We're not staying here tonight."

"Meg, no." He wasn't a boy any longer. He was mean, dark, brooding.

Their words swirled around Pellam. As they talked, husband and wife, he heard what they said and he observed their expressions but it was from a distance.

Here you come, with your van and your camera, studying the town, talking to people, getting to know everyone . . . Getting to know some of them very well. You don't understand the power you've got.

But no, he thought, I have no power. Nothing he could say or do could teach them about happiness and lift them out of the ruts they'd fallen into. He made movies. He helped people escape from their lives, sure, but only for two hours and only in that one special place: a darkened movie theater. "I'm leaving now."

Keith focused on Pellam, said to him, "You mention this to

anyone, I guess you can figure out what'll happen to them." He nodded toward Meg.

"What are you saying, Keith?" she asked.

Pellam said, "He's saying that if I go to the police, even if he beats the murder charges, there'll be a RICO case against him. The U.S. attorney'll close up the factory and take the house and your savings."

Keith nodded. "That'll be on your conscience."

Pellam laughed, said nothing. He looked at Meg. "You want a ride someplace? Family or friends nearby?"

Keith said, "She's not coming with you."

"That's not your decision."

Meg said to Pellam, "Let me get Sam."

Keith said, "Meg, you're my wife! You—"

"Stop it!" she screamed. Keith the boy, Keith the man stopped speaking. "You don't own me. I'm leaving!"

Pellam sensed it then. In an intuitive flash, he knew.

A combination of things told him – the peripheral sight of Keith reaching for his waistband, his gasping breath, the click of spring metal.

The sound of a gun cocking – Bobby's, of course, which Pellam had forgotten about, left lying under the twin's body on the front porch. Keith had retrieved it on his way inside the house.

The click that was almost hidden by a rising shout, a single word.

One word – his own name – filling the night, as Keith shoved the gun toward him and wailed in primitive rage, "Pellam!"

"No, Keith!" Meg cried.

Pellam's left hand shot forward in a futile, automatic gesture to ward off the scalding bullet.

A ringing explosion. The muzzle blast struck him in the face and hand.

Meg screamed, "John!"

They froze, like children playing the game of statue. Three of them.

There was an endless moment of silence, the sweet piquancy of smoke filling the room.

The gun fell from Keith's hand to the floor and with a wail of anguish he dropped to his knees.

Pellam, waiting for the pain, the blackness, the crawl of blood, stood completely still.

Nothing. He was unhurt.

The man had missed. From fifteen feet away Keith had missed.

He whispered to Meg, "It's all right, I'm okay."

She was shaking her head. "What'm I going to do about this?"

"What?" Pellam asked.

Meg didn't answer. Her head was lowered in concentration, frowning as she studied the diamonds on her finger. "Look at this ring. Look at it. What a mess."

Meg held up her hand, covered with the blood that spread from the front of her blouse. "Can you help me? I'll never get it clean." Her smile faded. Her eyes fluttered closed. "Can you help me," she whispered as she spiraled slowly to the floor. "Can you?"

———◦•◦———

26

Trudie, tanned and dark-haired and model-thin (the best calves of any women he'd ever known but, alas, no freckles anywhere on her body), drove east on Santa Monica, moving slowly in the morning traffic toward the expressway.

John Pellam sat on the passenger side of her white Mercedes 450 SL.

He sat silently, with his suitcase (purchased on Main Street, Cleary, not Rodeo Drive) on his lap. Trudie was animated. She was preoccupied with a teleplay Lorimar was kicking around. She had a fifty-two percent interest in the property. He thought that's what she'd told him. The radio was loud and she nodded in time to the beat, smiling broadly, though Pellam knew that what she hummed was the tune of business, not a Top 40 hit.

Pellam thought she was a wonderful woman. He'd enjoyed going out with her. He'd enjoyed staying with her, lying in a huge bed, sipping sweet liquor drinks on a cement patio high above a junglish canyon (Trudie had a fall-*er* house).

They passed the park in Beverly Hills where one morning – must have been five a.m. – he'd found Tommy Bernstein, in a tuxedo, passed out. Pellam himself had been wasted. Tommy had said to him, "Fuck, it's the U.S. Cavalry. Get me home. Am I in bed? I don't think so, no, I don't. Get me home!"

After much time and effort Pellam had.

At Tommy's funeral the minister had been a hired gun, which wasn't too surprising, since Tommy hadn't been inside a church in thirty years. The somber man said a lot of innocuous things. Generic-brand sentiments. Not to put that down, of course. Pellam thought the doughy old guy with the stiff white collar had done a good job, under the circumstances. "The lively spirit that Thomas had, the spirit that touched us all with the love for the characters he played . . ." Well, Tommy'd have said, "Barf on that," and howled. But that was hardly the minister's fault. The funeral had been near the intersection they were passing through just then. Avenue of the Stars.

"I talked to that exec producer."

Trudie liked that, shortening words and slinging them around. *Exec, photog, res*, as in *Make a res at a restaurant*.

"Yeah?" he asked brightly.

"He was like beside himself."

"Yeah?" Pellam couldn't remember exactly which exec she was talking about, or why he was, or should be, beside himself. They drove in silence, through that brilliant light, California light, that seems to bring out some essential radiation from the grass and trees. It gets right in your face, like a beautiful, obnoxious teenage girl. From behind his sunglasses Pellam watched the scenery. And the cars – a thousand German cars, it seemed – moving opposite, toward Hollywood.

"Won't be back for a while, huh?"

"Probably not."

Trudie didn't answer, just squeezed his knee. She turned the radio up. They were in Beverly Hills; sentiment didn't exist.

"So," she said. "You sure you want to do this?"

"Yep," he said and didn't add anything else.

Ten silent minutes later she dropped him at the airport. He didn't want or expect her to get out. They kissed like siblings and the only clues to the deepest moments of their on-again, off-again year together was a shallow shaking of her head and the sad, mystified smile she lapsed into from time to time.

"Call me sometime," she said.

Pellam promised that he would.

He handed his suitcase to the curbside check-in attendant, and when he turned back, Trudie was gone.

John Pellam sat on a hundred-year-old gravestone, looking out over this upstate New York valley, filled with trees gone to vibrant yellow red. The sun had just disappeared under a row of clouds and the beautiful scenery had taken on an ominous nature.

Adding to which was the young man moving stealthily toward Pellam. He was dressed in a dark shirt and jeans. When he was twenty feet away the man paused and closed his eyes, as if finding strength from somewhere, then drew a black pistol from his back pocket.

He started forward once more.

Pellam rose from the cold stone and squinted at the furtive approach.

Suddenly motion on the ground nearby. The man reared back

in surprise and stumbled over a low tombstone. "Jesus Christ," he called, dropping the pistol.

"What?" Came a booming voice from a loudspeaker.

"It attacked me!" the man called, standing up and brushing grass from his slacks.

The electronic voice of God yelled, "Cut it, cut! What the hell happened?"

The field filled with people. The crew walked around from behind the Panaflex camera, makeup went to work on the actor's face. He called, "A squirrel . . . he attacked me!"

A stuntman grabbed his jacket and leapt into the graveyard, crying, "*Toro, toro!*"

"Hilarious," the director called sarcastically through the loud-speaker.

Pellam walked away from the gravestone and sat down in an old green-plaid lawn chair next to his Winnebago. He said, "You cold? You want to go inside?"

Meg squeezed his hand and said, "No, I wouldn't miss this for anything."

"I want a continuous shot," the director sighed and walked back to the camera. Somebody from Wardrobe was rolling up the actor's cuffs so they wouldn't get dark from the moisture on the grass. The continuity girl began making notes of his position when the wild animal had attacked and the location of all the cameras and backgrounds.

"What's the take?"

"That'll be eight," someone called.

"Jesus. And we'll lose the light in ten minutes. What's the weather supposed to be tomorrow?"

"Rain."

"Jesus."

Pellam and Meg watched the crew in the field. He said, "That's the movies for you. Do it over and over then you wait for a while and do it again."

But Sam at least was enjoying himself, even if he would have preferred a space wars flick or something with machine-gunning robots over some stupid love story called *To Sleep in a Shallow Grave*. Mostly, it was the huge, complicated camera that he loved.

"Wow," he'd say to Pellam. "It's like a spaceship." And Pellam got the okay from the director of photography to put him in the operator's seat for a few minutes.

Alan Lefkowitz ducked out of his honey wagon and trooped toward the director. He was wearing his play clothes, his on-set clothes – chinos and a red-and-white striped shirt (Pellam told Meg, "That's what the refs would wear if Hollywood had its own hockey team"). The producer said, "Hey, Johnny." To Pellam he lifted his hand, which held an invisible glass of a very expensive single-malt scotch, and raised his eyebrows.

Pellam said, "Can't. I've got plans."

"Around *here*?" Lefkowitz joked, gazing longingly at Meg's jeans-clad butt, and began waving papers at the director again.

"So," Pellam said, "what's happening in Cleary?"

She laughed and didn't answer. "Let's go for a walk. That'd be okay?"

"They've got the telephoto on. We walk that way, toward the forest, we won't be in view. You feeling okay?"

"Hell, yes."

She took the cane and got up without his help. They walked past the crowd of locals, which had grown by the dozens with each day of shooting; small-town life had skidded to a stop for the duration of the principal photography. The spectators were enthralled with everything – even the squirrel attack – and they stood silent and frozen as if their fidgeting motion might knock the magic camera to the ground.

Meg and Pellam walked a short distance down the road, Meg glancing back every few minutes to keep Sam in view. She said, "The doctor told me if I'd see a physical therapist and get some exercise the limp would go away in a month."

"And?"

"I see all these young professional gals on TV, running and doing aerobics and lifting weights . . . it all looks so silly. I'll wait till it goes away by itself."

"How's the brokerage business?"

"Sold a house last week. Got a couple of maybe-but-let-me-ask-my-wife. Nobody said it's easy."

"How's he doing?" Pellam's head swivelled back toward Sam.

"We keep talking about it. I don't want to, but I think it's for the best. That's what the therapist says. Get it out, get everything out. Maybe it's best for me too. Sam'll say, 'Tell me again about Daddy.' And we have our talk and he understands or he says he does. I don't, of course."

"What do you hear from him? Keith?"

"Trial's next month."

Pellam nodded. "They're going after your house?"

"It's a possibility. My lawyer says there's a chance we'll lose it. But that also means there's a chance we won't."

He felt her eyes turn toward him. A pause then she said, "I'm seeing my friend again."

"Ambler?"

"He was real good after I got hurt."

"He seems like a nice guy."

For a neo-Bircher, rampant capitalist bigot.

"I didn't really want to at first. I mean—"

"You don't have to explain," Pellam said.

She looked at the horizon. "I know I don't." She smiled. "Pellam, you think . . ." Her voice faded.

He had. A great deal.

And concluded that the answer was pretty clear and they both knew it. He didn't answer or look at her and she didn't repeat the question.

They came to a sign on the edge of the road, facing away from the shooting.

> *Welcome to Simmons.*
> *In the Beautiful Catskills.*
> *Population 6300.*

"What was it when you grew up here?" Meg asked. "The population, I mean."

"Oh, I don't remember. I think maybe the same as Cleary."

"How come they're shooting here?"

"It's a dirty little town. That's what I needed for the story."

"They liked your screenplay after all, huh?"

"Most of it. Of course, the director's ignoring my camera directions."

"Why don't you tell him?"

"Writers don't tell directors where to put the camera. Except euphemistically and only after they get paid."

"Why didn't you set the movie in Cleary?"

"We've got a better cemetery here." He nodded back toward the actor. "For the shooting scene. And the funeral later. When Janice confronts Shep."

"Better cemetery than Cleary's? I'm insulted."

Pellam looked at her hair, now cut short (revealing a good dusting of freckles on the back of her neck), the country-girl jeans, a blue Saks work shirt, brown suede boots.

"Tonight," he said, "Let's have dinner at the inn, okay? Just the two of us?"

"She won't mind?" Meg nodded up the road, toward Pellam's childhood home, three miles away. Meaning Pellam's mother.

"She's seen more of me in the past week than she has in the past five years. She'll be glad to get rid of me. She doesn't cotton to men who drink whiskey. We'll loan her Sam for the evening."

A film crew assistant, a young woman in jeans and a brushed-denim jacket, a fringe of curly hair crowning her forehead, patrolled the road like an Israeli soldier. A huge walkie-talkie bounced on her hip.

He asked Meg, "When are you going back to Cleary?"

"Tomorrow. We can only stay the night. I don't want to keep Sam away from home too long. It's better, I think."

Meg was looking down at the long grass. In the coming dusk the day was taking on a sepia atmosphere. Very still. Quiet.

He motioned her to follow and walked slowly into the graveyard. He pointed to a grave, ten years old.

Meg looked at it. "Your father's name was Benjamin?"

"After Benjamin Franklin, he said."

Meg said, "I'm surprised he didn't name you William."

"William?"

"After Wild Bill, your ancestor."

Pellam gave an exaggerated sigh. "His name was James, not William. James Butler Hickok."

"Oh, right. You told me."

They heard the assistant director call through the bullhorn, "Quiet, everybody, quiet down!"

Pellam and Meg paused and watched the scene begin again. The actor stalking slowly through the tombstones, ready to murder.

Meg said, "So you're a writer now?"

"Nope. Still unemployed. Lefkowitz's gotta give me a writer's credit but that's only because of the Guild. I'm just here in case they need to doctor it. I'm still canned. I'm guilty of the worst crime in Hollywood. Aggravating a producer's ulcer."

"So write more scripts."

Pellam laughed and looked at his watch. "When the mood takes me. I've got a free-lance scouting job in Utah."

They heard the rise and fall of the actors' voices.

Then the director's staticky shout in the bullhorn. "Cut, cut! Somebody . . . you, yes *you!* Get that effing squirrel out of here. I don't believe it, I do not *believe* it."

They returned to the camper and sat down in the lawn chairs – slowly. Meg, because of the gunshot. Pellam, because of the popped shoulder.

"Any chance you'd get back east?"

"Lots of movies to be made."

Meg said, "If you do, why don't you come upstate for a visit? Sam'd like it."

Pellam stretched his legs out in front of him, the sharp tips of his stained Nokonas pointed up toward the gray sky.

"Suppose it's a possibility," he said, and they watched the crew fan out into the cemetery to adjust the grass, pluck up leaves, fix makeup, straighten cuffs, chase a squirrel toward the trees. Everyone serious, everyone rushed, trying to get one more take in the can before the November darkness fell.

AUTHOR'S NOTE

———

John Pellam's comment about fire, embers, and smoke comes from one of his favorite authors, Reynolds Price, whom he was not, under the circumstances, inclined to attribute.

ABOUT THE AUTHOR

Jeffery Deaver is an internationally best-selling author of thirteen suspense novels. He's been nominated for four Edgar Awards from the Mystery Writers of America and is a two-time recipient of the Ellery Queen Reader's Award for Best Short Story of the Year. His book *A Maiden's Grave* was made into an HBO movie starring James Garner and Marlee Matlin, and his novel *The Bone Collector* is a feature release from Universal Pictures, starring Denzel Washington. His most recent novels are *Speaking in Tongues*, *The Empty Chair*, and *The Devil's Teardrop*. He lives in Virginia and California. Readers can visit his Web site at www.jefferydeaver.com